THE SECOND YEAR OF
CLARKESWORLD MAGAZINE

OTHER WORKS EDITED
BY MAMATAS AND WALLACE

———

Realms: The First Year of Clarkesworld Magazine

NICK MAMATAS
Phantom 0
The Urban Bizarre

SEAN WALLACE
Bandersnatch, with Paul Tremblay
Best New Fantasy
Fantasy, with Paul Tremblay
Fantasy Magazine
Horror: The Best of the Year, 2006 Edition, with John Betancourt
Jabberwocky 1
Jabberwocky 2
Jabberwocky 3
Jabberwocky 4, with Erzebet YellowBoy
Japanese Dreams
Phantom, with Paul Tremblay
Weird Tales: The 21st-Century, with Stephen H. Segal

THE SECOND YEAR OF
CLARKESWORLD MAGAZINE

Edited by
Nick Mamatas and Sean Wallace

REALMS 2: THE SECOND YEAR OF CLARKESWORLD MAGAZINE

———

Interior design and typesetting by
Linduna [www.linduna.com]

Wyrm Publishing
www.wyrmpublishing.com

For more information, contact Wyrm.

ISBN: 978-1-890464-10-3 (paperback)
ISBN: 978-1-890464-09-7 (hardcover)

Visit us at:

www.clarkesworldmagazine.com

TABLE OF CONTENTS

TABLE OF CONTENTS

INTRODUCTION: TOMORROW CAN WAIT

Sean Wallace

Change is a constant in our lives, and it also plays an important role with the internet, which continues to grow and evolve at an awesome rate. (Surely the Singularity is right around the corner . . .) Mind you, the accelerating and approaching future can be dizzying, confusing, scary yet exciting, and online magazines such as **Clarkesworld Magazine** are trying to move with the times, looking forward always, but with the occasional backwards glance.

This introduction is your backwards glance, covering all the changes with our online incarnation, giving you a peek at what's been going on, covering October 2007 all the way through September 2008. A lot can happen in twelve months, and it has.

But where to begin?

Well, starting with the October issue, a nonfiction department was introduced, covering a wide range of material, usually running two pieces, sometimes three times, a month. And when I say wide, I mean wide, with articles focused on the introduction of science fiction and fantasy literature to Hispanic audiences; discussions about mainstream/genre readerships, with recommended top ten lists for both; explorations of the fantasy world of professional wrestling; the impact of baby-rearing on one's writing; diving into modern fantasists and the influence of role-playing games; and much more.

And that wasn't all, as **Clarkesworld** also ran interviews every month, either with an author, an artist, or editors, with Daniel

Abraham, Kage Baker, Laird Barron, KJ Bishop, Steven Erickson, Margo Lanagan, Richard Morgan, John Picacio, Steph Swainston, Catherynne M. Valente, Sean Williams, Vernon Vinge, Gene Wolfe, and more.

That's a lot to take in, but in June **Clarkesworld** also started presenting audio fiction, beginning with "Clockwork Chickadee" by Mary Robinette Kowal, and narrated by Kowal. We try, whenever possible, to have the author do their own story, though this doesn't always work out!

This is a lot of change, of course, and a lot of firsts, at least for **Clarkesworld Magazine**, but it's also been nice to be recognized, with stories appearing for the first time ever in several anthologies, including:

The Year's Best Science Fiction: Twenty-Sixth Annual Collection, Gardner Dozois, ed., with "The Sky that Wraps the World Round, Past the Blue into the Black" by Jay Lake

Unplugged: The Year's Best Online Fiction, Rich Horton, ed., with "A Buyer's Guide to Maps of Antarctica" by Catherynne M. Valente

Year's Best Fantasy 9, David G. Hartwell and Kathryn Cramer, ed., with "A Buyer's Guide to Maps of Antarctica" by Catherynne M. Valente

Best Horror of the Year, Volume 1, Ellen Datlow, ed., with "When the Gentlemen Go By" by Margaret Ronald

Stories also appeared on the 2008 *Locus* Recommended Reading List, along with tons of honorable mentions in various year's best anthologies, but to top that all off, **Clarkesworld Magazine** was nominated for the 2009 Hugo Award for Best Semiprozine, and then moninated for a World Fantasy Award.

All of this points out simply that the future (and change) is always charging forward, and we are slaves to it, but surely you can take a moment out of your day, and read these stories, now, today, and kick back.

Because tomorrow can wait.

SUMMER IN PARIS, LIGHT FROM THE SKY

Ken Scholes

Life is marked by intersections and measured by the choices we make at each pause in our journey. I am fortunate to have made a good choice at the right time but more than that, many before me did the same and so the stones were set in the path long before the day of my birth. Will you not come after me and walk the stones so many before you have helped to put in place?

Adolf Hitler
Commencement Address,
Yale University School of Human Rights and Social Justice,
1969

Adolf Hitler came to Paris in June 1941 feeling the weight of his years in his legs and the taste of a dying dream in his mouth. He spent most of that first day walking up and down the Champs Elysées, working the stiffness out of his bones and muscles while he looked at the shops and the people. Some of the dull ache was from the wooden benches on the train from Hamburg; most of it was age. And beneath the discomfort of his body, his soul ached too.

He'd never been here before, he thought as the Parisians slipped past in the noon-time sun. He snorted at the revelation. A fine painter you are, he told himself.

Of course, it was only for the summer. Then Paris . . . and painting, he imagined, would slip quietly to the back row of his memory. He

13

would return to Berlin and take a job for the government buying supplies he would never see for people that he would never know. In the end, he realized, he would become his father's son and live out the rest of his days as a quiet civil servant.

Alois Hitler had been a hard man, even a cruel man, before the accident. But death up close can change the hardest heart and after nearly a month in the hospital, he returned to his family with a deep faith and a sense of compassion for all humankind . . . especially his children. He listened. He prayed. He studied St. Francis, St. John of the Cross, Meister Eckhard and even Buddha. He became gentle and warm toward his wife and their five children. Until the very end, he encouraged Adolf's dreams. And when he died, still working as a customs official for Napoleon IV's puppet chancellor, he left behind a small but sufficient inheritance to finance his son's art.

By living frugally and occasionally taking odd jobs, Adolf stretched it as far as he could. He'd even set aside a bit for his old age. But come September, he'd decided, it was time to put away the canvas and brush. Time, at fifty-two, to put away childish things.

Adolf sighed.

And then something happened. He stood in the shadow of the Arc de Triomphe, dwarfed by that first Napoleon's grandiose gesture of complete victory, dwarfed by the size of his own dreams in the shadow of over thirty years of failure. He stood, feeling his breath catch in the back of his throat and his eyes turning to water. And suddenly, he was no longer alone.

A girl—a pretty girl, a dark girl dressed in ragged clothing— separated from a crowd of passing students. She walked up to him without a word and kissed him hard on the mouth, pressing her body against him while she fastened a flower into the button-hole of his Prussian great coat. After the kiss, she vanished back into the crowd.

Adolf licked his lips, tasting the apples from her mouth. He took in a great breath, smelling the rose water from her skin and the sunshine from her hair. He listened to the sound of his racing heart and the drumbeat it played. He felt the warmth of her where it had touched him.

It was his first impression of Paris.

His second impression was the perpetually drunk American, Ernie Hemingway.

After a day of wandering aimlessly, as the sun dropped behind the horizon and the sky grew deep purple, Adolf found de Gaulle's and went inside because he heard American music.

Americans had always fascinated him. He'd met a few—not many because they tended to have little use for Europe. America was an entire continent without kings or emperors or royalty of any kind. A place where they selected their own President every four years and where any one of the ninety states from Brazil to Newfoundland was a thriving nation in and of itself united by democracy, progress and freedom.

A middle aged man stood on the bar leading the room in a bawdy tune. He worked the song like a conductor, waving a pistol instead of a baton, and scattered drinkers around the room joined in the song. A man in a ratty suit crouched over the piano, mashing the keys with his fingers with a rag-time flair. Adolf watched and smiled. The man sang too fast and slurred too much for the lyrics to make much sense but the gestures and pelvic thrusts conveyed the gist of it.

When the song was done, the man dropped lightly to the floor amid cheers and brushed past Adolf on his way to a table at the back of the room. Adolf found an empty table near the American and sat down. The pianist launched into another song, this time in French—a language Adolf grasped better—and he blushed. Looking around, he was the only one who did.

"Are you a priest, then?" the American shouted across at him in English.

Adolf looked up. "I beg pardon?"

The American grinned. "You're blushing. I thought you might be a priest."

He shook his head. "No. Not a priest."

"Well then, are you a homosexual?"

The word escaped him at first, then registered. He blushed even more, looking around for a different table to sit at. He had heard that Americans were quite forward but until now had never experienced it. "I'm sorry, sir," he said. "I'm not liking men, though I am very flattered by your . . . " He struggled to find the right word, couldn't find it, then said the closest one he *did* find. "By your . . . love."

For a moment, he thought the American might hit him. But suddenly, the American started to laugh. The laugh started low and built fast, spilling over like an over-filled bathtub. Adolf wasn't sure what to do so he offered a weak, tight smile. The American leaped up with his beer in his hand, staggered a few steps and sat heavily in the empty chair at Adolf's table.

He leaned in and Adolf could smell days of alcohol rising from his skin. "Deutsche?"

Adolf nodded. "Ja."

The American stuck out his hand. "Ernie Hemingway."

He took the hand, squeezed it firmly and pumped it once. "Adolf Hitler."

Ernie waved to the bar. "Hey, de Gaulle!"

A slim man looked up. "Oui, Monsieur Hemingway?"

"A beer for my new friend Adolf Hitler."

The bartender nodded. "Un moment, s'il vous plaît."

Then Hemingway leaned in again, his voice low. "You got any money?"

Adolf nodded. The man's fast speech and unpredictable movements made him nervous. He found himself blinking involuntarily.

"That'll save us both a bit of embarrassment."

He nodded again, not quite understanding. The bartender arrived with two pints of light, foamy beer and Hemingway raised the glass. "To life, liberty and the pursuit of happiness," he said.

"To your health," Adolf said.

"I'm afraid it's far too late for that," another voice said. The pianist—finished with his tune—pulled up a chair, flipping it around backwards and straddling it. He was a short man, wiry with curly hair gone gray, blue eyes and a brief but contagious smile. "We just have to hold out hope that somehow he'll manage to pickle himself before he begins to decompose."

Adolf didn't understand but said nothing.

"Adolf Hitler," Hemingway said, "Old Mother England's wittiest bastard child, Chuck Chaplin."

They shook hands.

"Fresh from the train?" Chuck asked in perfect German.

Adolf nodded. "Yes. This morning."

"Looking for work here? It'll be hard. You're not Jewish are you?"

"No, not Jewish. I'm a painter."

Chuck nodded. "Are you any good?"

Hitler smiled. "My English is better than my painting."

The pianist returned the smile. "And your English is atrocious."

"Your German is quite good."

Chuck grinned. "Benefit of an English education."

Ernie looked perplexed, trying to follow the rush of German in his drunken state. "What are you two going on about?"

Chuck turned to Ernie. "Drink your beer, you silly sod." Then, back to Adolf in German: "Do you have a place to stay yet?"

Adolf shook his head. "I was going to ask after a boarding house or hotel."

"Nonsense," Chuck said, switching to English. "You can stay with us. At least until you find something more suitable."

Adolf looked around again, suddenly unsure what to do. He lowered his voice. "I'm not a homosexual," he said in a quiet voice, nodding towards Ernie. "Tell him for me? In English?"

"What's he saying?" Ernie asked.

"That he admires your mustache and the light in your eyes," Chuck answered. "Particularly the way you dimple when you smile."

"Bloody British fairy," Hemingway muttered into his beer.

"That's not," Chuck said slowly and deadpan, "what your mother said to me last night."

Perhaps, Adolf thought, Paris was a mistake after all.

17

Very little is known of his life before the Revolution. The records and recollections of those who might have known were lost in the heavy fire-bombings during the final days of the War for Democratic Change. And the man himself rarely offered up a personal detail, despite having given over five thousand documented speeches over the span of his life. In an early American lecture, he casually mentioned coming to Paris to be a painter. In a spontaneous speech at his son's wedding, he fondly recalled a kiss in the shadow of the Arc de Triomphe. We may never know more than these scattered references. But would knowing matter? Or would it merely add to the legend of this great but humble man?

Nicholas Freeman, Editor
Preface, A Kiss in the Shadow: Essays on The Pre-1942 Life
of Adolf Hitler,
Harbor Light Press, Seattle, 1986

By day Hitler wandered the city with his easel and stool and pallet and canvas. At night, he sang and drank with his new friends down at de Gaulle's. He never did move out. He slept on a cot in the corner of their large loft and tapped into what little remained of his inheritance to help with expenses. Ernie and Chuck took him under their wing, showing him around the city and helping him with his English.

The economy was struggling as a massive influx of Jewish refugees fled the Russian Civil War. The Empire was already stretched thin with footholds in Africa and Indonesia. There were quiet rumors that Napoleon IV was gradually losing his grip on sanity as he entered his eighties and even quieter rumors that his military advisors and generals had plans of their own.

Still, the summer was hot and bright and one afternoon in July, Adolf looked up from painting the Arc de Triomphe and locked eyes with the girl who had kissed him there over a month earlier. She was staring at him, a slight smile pulling at her mouth.

He licked his brush and tried to resume work, suddenly uncomfortable with her wide, dark eyes. She took a step closer.

"You're no good at it," she said to him in heavily accented French. "You've gotten the colors all wrong."

He shrugged, feeling a stab of annoyance though her voice was playful. "It's how I see it."

"Perhaps you need spectacles," she said, taking another step closer.

Adolf chuckled. "And this from a girl who kisses men old enough to be her grandfather?"

"You don't look so old," she said.

"Perhaps you are the one who needs spectacles?" He looked at her. She was tall, slender, with long arms and legs. Her breasts were small but high on her chest.

"How old are you?" she asked. When he didn't answer right away, she grinned. "I'm nineteen."

"I'm . . . old." He set down his brush.

She laughed; it sounded like gypsy music to him. Then she repeated herself. "You don't look so old."

He nodded.

She stretched out her hand. "I'm Tesia."

He took it, uncertain what to do with it. Finally, he raised it to his mouth and kissed it lightly. "Adolf."

"German?"

"Yes. You?"

"Polish."

"We're neighbors then," he said, not knowing what else to say.

She smiled. Her teeth were straight and white. "Yes." She pointed at the bench near his stool. "May I sit and watch?"

"May I paint you?"

She laughed again. "I couldn't let you. You'd get the colors all wrong and I'd be cross with you." She caught her breath. "I wouldn't want to be cross with you."

He snorted and went back to work. She was right, he realized. He could never paint her.

He painted quietly and she watched in silence. When it grew dark, he asked her if she wanted to have dinner with him and she said yes. He packed up his supplies and tossed his canvas into a nearby waste-bin.

"Why do you do that?" she asked.

"Like you said: I'm no good." He shrugged. "Sometimes I use them to keep me warm at night. They burn well."

"Ridiculous." She dug the unfinished painting from the garbage. "I like it." She tucked it under her arm.

They walked to a small cafe that overlooked the Seine. He went in first as she paused at the door. From inside, the smell of roasted rabbit, baking bread and fresh sliced onions drifted out. The waiter frowned when he saw them.

"No," he said.

"Pardon?"

He pointed to a newly painted sign near the door. "No Jews."

Adolf felt a stab of anger. It passed quickly. "Monsieur," he said in careful French, "I'm not Jewish."

"Not you," the waiter said, pointing at the girl. "Her."

Adolf looked. She blanched, her eyes a bit wide and her nostrils flaring. She clenched her jaw. He saw the band on her arm now. He hadn't noticed it before but why would he? He'd heard about the new laws but they had seemed far away to him. He shook his head in disbelief. "You are making a mistake."

The waiter said something under his breath that Adolf couldn't quite understand. He opened his mouth to protest but felt a firm hand on his arm.

"We'll go somewhere else," Tesia said.

They had a quiet dinner by moonlight. She stole two apples from a cart. He bought bread and cheese. After eating, she kissed him again, this time more slowly.

He pulled away. "I'm too old."

"Nonsense," she said and kissed him again.

Afterwards, he asked her, "Why did you kiss me that day when you first saw me?"

"Because," she said, "you were beautiful and you stood alone."

He walked her home. Twice, as blue-coat soldiers passed them on the street, she pressed herself closer to him, concealing the band on her arm.

"Why don't you take it off?" he asked her.

"I don't know," she said, standing on the doorstep of a run-down hotel. Inside, he could hear loud voices conversing in Polish and Yiddish and Russian. "It's against the law, I suppose."

"It's a silly law."

"Most laws are." She smiled, kissed him quickly and fled inside.

Whistling a love song he dimly remembered from his youth, Adolf made his way back to de Gaulle's and his waiting friends.

When he looked for her the next day and the next, she was nowhere to be found. When he returned to the old hotel, he found it somber and empty.

July slipped into August.

My father never talked about the events leading up to the war. He simply smiled, waved his hand and said it was unimportant. After he died, I found a photograph in his belongings. He and two other men sitting at a table in some nameless bar raising their glasses to the camera. He was gaunt, bearded and hollow-eyed, dressed in a tattered Prussian coat. The back of the photograph reads Summer in Paris, Light from the Sky, *scrawled in his pinched, careful German script and it seems to have been taken at night, possibly in 1941, the year he met my mother. His companions, their connection to my father and their present whereabouts are unknown.*

Jacob Ernest Hitler
Memories of My Father: An Introduction to the 50th Anniversary Edition of Unser Kampf, Penguin Books, New York, 1992

The explosion was all anyone could talk about.

On August twelfth a blast ripped through Notre Dame Cathedral as Napoleon IV knelt to receive Mass from his archbishop. Fourteen people were killed, including the Emperor and his young wife. Photographs of the bombers, arrested later that night, filled the newspapers. Four frightened Jewish youth. Hanging them, the generals now in command claimed, would not even scratch the surface of the conspiracy that threatened the Empire. Still, they hanged them quickly.

Hemingway threw down the newspaper in disgust. "Those sons of bitches," he muttered.

Chuck and Adolf looked up at him.

Ernie kicked the paper. "Do you believe this?"

He'd been drinking most of the day. At least once, they'd taken his pistol away as he waved it about. There were more soldiers in the streets these days and though the patrons of de Gaulle's little tavern thought their American mascot eccentric, the blue-coats might not be so inclined.

Chuck shrugged. "Name of the game, my friend."

"It's a goddamn travesty," Ernie went on. "They killed their own goddamn Emperor and then they blamed the Jews."

"It's just four," Adolf said.

Ernie pulled back one fist, reaching for his pistol with the other. "Four? It's not just four. Don't you see it coming? There will be more laws. It's a shell game, Adolf. They will whip up the people and keep them focused on their chosen scapegoat. They will move the Jews now to a separate place for their own good, to protect them from the angry mobs that they themselves have created. When the dust settles, there will be a lot of dead Jews and a new Emperor who is *not* a Bonaparte." He pointed to the picture of a French general in the newspaper. "Behold your new Emperor."

People were listening. They looked uncomfortable. Chuck lowered his voice. "That's enough, Ernie. You're making a scene."

Ernie jumped up, his chair tumbling backwards. "Someone sure as Christ needs to. What you people need is a revolution."

Adolf caught his sleeve. "Sit down, my friend."

Ernie looked around as if suddenly coming to his senses. He sat.

Chuck laughed. "You and your revolutions."

"It worked for us, didn't it?"

"If it worked so well," Chuck said, "why are you here?"

Ernie stole Adolf's beer. "Because I'm an American. I'm free to come and go as I please."

Adolf remembered stories about the American Revolution. He'd studied it in school, though his textbooks said little. No one really believed that the young nation of upstarts would live beyond its cradle. But Lincoln averted civil war over slavery and assisted the Canadians in gaining their own independence. Naturally, the grateful northerners joined the Union. And shortly after, the Spanish-American conflict left the United States with an entire continent under its sway.

"A revolution would never work here," he told Ernie.

Chuck agreed. "He's right. The army's far too strong."

"Ah, but words are stronger," Hemingway said.

Adolf leaned forward. "Words? Against rifles?"

Ernie waved for another round. Suddenly, his eyes glinted with an almost savage intelligence. "Listen," he said. "I'll tell you just how I'd do it." The beer arrived, de Gaulle looking pained when Ernie waved the ticket away. "Later, mon ami. That's a promise." He looked around to make sure no one was listening. "First," he said, "I'd write a book."

Chuck laughed. "But you're a terrible writer. Your words stumble about on the page like drunken soldiers in women's shoes." He paused for dramatic effect. "And those were just your grocery lists."

Ernie pointed, eyebrows narrowed in a mock scowl. "You're quite the bloody comedian."

Adolf chuckled at his friends. "So you'd write a book?"

Ernie nodded. "Yes. A book about all of the horse-shit here. A book so passionate, so full of raw rage and sorrow that people'd sit up and take notice."

"And that would bring about a revolution?"

"In time it would. Yes."

"Nonsense," Chuck said. "Who'd read it? The Jews? The gypsies? The Marxist refugees? They don't have pots to piss in or blankets to sleep in. It'd do them more good on the fire, keeping them warm."

"Not the Jews," Ernie said. "The *Americans*."

Adolf sat up. "The Americans?"

"Naturally. You'd have to get them involved. First, with the book. Then with speeches. Maybe even a traveling troupe of the persecuted and oppressed. They'd eat it up for breakfast, lunch and dinner. And they've got the resources. Strong army. Strong navy. Airships."

Adolf swallowed. "Why ever would they be interested in a Frankish Revolution?"

"Two reasons," Ernie said, holding up two fingers. "One: A democratic foothold in Europe. Two: The liberation of the Jews."

"The Jews?" Adolf asked.

"Freedom for every race, color, creed," Chuck said in German. "You saw what they did with their emancipated Africans. Liberia's doing quite well; shining that blessed light of liberty for all of Africa to see."

Adolf leaned in. "But most Americans are Christian, aren't they?"

"They are indeed," Ernie said with a grin.

"And?" Chuck asked.

"Jesus Christ was Jewish," Ernie said. "It's all a matter of perspective." He raised his glass. "To democracy," he said.

They raised their glasses, too. A boy who sold photographs to tourists pointed his camera at them and raised his eyebrows. Ernie winked at him.

A bulb flashed. A shutter snapped.

The next night, Adolf gladly handed over a handful of coins for the photograph and tacked it up on the dressing mirror in their loft.

He never considered himself to be a great man but an adequate man. He never considered himself to have made history but rather to have been in the right place and the right time to do his small part. Well-spoken but shy, intelligent but unassuming, he caught the public off guard with his dry wit, his careful words and his passionate commitment to human rights. For this reason, it is said that only Hitler could go to America.

Dr. John F. Kennedy
Out of the Ashes: A History of Modern Thought from the French Revolution for Democratic Change to the Re-Birth of the Nation of Israel, 1941 - 1952, Harvard University Press, Boston, 1971.

Throughout August, he kept an eye open for Tesia but Adolf was convinced he'd never see her again. She was a smart girl, he told himself. Smart enough to see the stirred pot start to boil. As badly as he wished to see her, he hoped he would not because that would mean she hadn't left this dangerous place.

There were more soldiers now and more laws. More signs in shop windows. Rumors flew of outlying rural churches desecrated by Jews. The local synagogue was burned to the ground by angry citizens while the police and soldiers stood by.

"It's heartbreaking," Adolf told Chuck one afternoon as they walked to de Gaulle's. They spoke in exclusively in English now; Adolf had gotten quite good at it.

Chuck kicked an empty can. "It is. Man's inhumanity to man, I think they call it."

Adolf stopped. "I think Ernie was right."

Chuck laughed and stopped, too. "About the book?"

"Maybe. About the Revolution. About the Americans."

"Perhaps," Chuck said, resuming his brisk pace. "But I don't think it will happen."

"Why not?"

He clapped Adolf on the shoulder. "Who's going to do it? Are you going to do it?"

"Of course not."

"Why not?"

Adolf opened his mouth. He started to say *because I'm not a Jew* and the realization of it twisted his heart in his chest. "It's not my line of work."

"Exactly," Chuck said. "This sort of work requires more than just a willing body."

"More?"

Chuck's hands moved as he talked. "Joan of Arc, King Arthur, Moses. What did they have?"

Adolf thought about it for a moment. "I don't know."

"God," Chuck said. "They had the voice of God, the vision of the grail, a light from Heaven. A power they could point to over their shoulder."

"A light from Heaven?"

Chuck pointed up. "Licht vom Himmel."

Adolf nodded. They stood outside de Gaulle's now, waiting to go in. He smiled at his friend. "And when they have that?"

"One spark to start the fire," Chuck said.

They walked in. Ernie waved them to their table. He was remarkably sober for the time of day. He grinned. "You're becoming popular, Adolf."

Adolf raised his eyebrows. "Yes?"

Ernie nodded towards the bar. "De Gaulle said a girl was in looking for you earlier. Said she'd be back later."

He coughed as a shudder passed over him. "Did he mention her name?"

"Foreign girl. Dark." He lowered his voice. "He thought she was Jewish; I assured him she was not."

Adolf took the meaning from his words and nodded. "Thank you."

He shrugged. "She's more trouble than you need, friend. These are bad times for love."

"I don't love her," Adolf said. "I hardly know her. And she's just a girl."

Ernie patted his hand. "That's what they all say." He opened his mouth to continue but the sudden opening and closing of the front door stopped him. A young man stood panting in the doorway and the room went quiet.

"They're relocating the Jews tonight," he said. "Outside of the city. For their own protection, they said."

"*Who* said?" de Gaulle asked.

"I heard it from a soldier. They're lined up along the Champs Elysées. Blue-coats for block upon block. They've even called up the reserves."

Ernie looked at Adolf. "For their own protection," he said quietly.

Outside, the shouting started. Whistles blowing, sirens wailing. Adolf hung his head. "They'll go, *won't* they? They won't fight back."

"They might," Chuck said. "But after a few of them are killed, they'll stop. They'll go like sheep and hope the butcher is a shepherd."

Adolf rubbed his eyes, disbelief gnawing at his stomach. "What do we do?"

Ernie looked up, his face pale. "We wait here for it to be done. Then we leave Paris."

The bartender dimmed the lights. He passed around shot glasses and bottles. The handful of men drank themselves drunk and fell asleep at their tables.

In a whisky fog, Hitler dreamed of another life, another time. A dark time, a time when a caricature of himself strutted about in uniform, barking out orders and gazing with pride upon a broken cross. And other men in uniform, men who saw the light from the sky spreading out behind Adolf like a halo, raised their hands to him and cried "Heil." And on the hands that they raised, blood shone out in that awful light. Blood of the martyrs, blood of the ages, and Adolf looked down at his own hands and saw that they were bloody, too, and he reached back to find some of his father's faith and compassion but found that in *that* life, in *that* world, there was nothing but rage and hatred to reach for.

Hitler wept.

He woke to screaming and leaped to his feet.

Ernie mumbled; Chuck stirred.

He heard the screaming again, distant from the alley behind the tavern. Either the others were too drunk to notice or too drunk to care. He moved quickly to the back door and stepped out into the night.

"Hello?"

The screaming stopped. Instead, he heard muffled, muted sound. He followed it.

Behind a pile of crates he saw two large forms crouched on the ground over a smaller bundle that bucked and twisted. As he drew closer, he realized they were two soldiers and a girl. One blue-coat held the girl down, a razor at her throat and a hand over her mouth. The other had pried her legs apart, his own trousers pushed down to his knees as he raped her.

"Wasn't enough to kill our Lord," one of the soldiers hissed. "You had to kill our Emperor, too, Jew-bitch."

Adolf stopped. His heart fell into a hole somewhere inside him. His stomach followed after. His eyes locked with the girl's and suddenly she stopped struggling.

She's waiting for me to save her, Adolf thought. He couldn't move. He stood transfixed while powerlessness and shame washed over him. Tesia lay still and the soldier thrust twice more before looking up.

"You there," he said. "You this girl's father?"

Adolf cleared his voice. "No."

"Then mind your business. You can come back for your turn later."

Something snapped like a guitar string in his spine. Adolf turned and fled for de Gaulle's, his feet pounding the cobblestones. Behind him, he heard Tesia struggling again, trying to scream but unable to do more than moan. He ran into the tavern, kicking over chairs and tables as he went, until he reached his own. He stood panting, sobbing over his friends, then bent over Ernie to frisk him.

Ernie stirred. "What the hell—"

Adolf found the revolver, yanked it from the pocket, and wordlessly stalked out of the tavern. Each step steady, deliberate, until he saw the soldiers. Until he saw Tesia beneath them. Then he stopped and looked down at them.

A blue-coat looked up. "I thought I told you—"

The pistol didn't roar or buck like at the cinema. It popped and shimmied just a bit and he thumbed the hammer and pulled the trigger again to be sure it had really worked though the soldier was already falling sideways, his mouth working like a landed trout.

The other soldier let go of Tesia and scrambled backwards on his heels and hands, fear white on his face. The revolver popped again once and he thrashed away, popped twice and he rolled over with a sigh.

Adolf, still clutching the pistol, dropped heavily to his knees. Tesia lay still, her dress and blouse ripped, her eyes closed. He reached for her, pulled her to himself and she fought him, kicking and flailing and growling low in her throat. He released her for a moment, then tried again. This time, she let him pull her in and he cradled her, rocking back and forth. He had no idea what to say so he said nothing and let that silence sweep him aside like a giant hand. After a few minutes, shouts from over rooftops brought him back from that quiet place he'd gone to.

He shook her gently. "Tesia, we have to go."

He stood, pulling her up and keeping her close. The revolver dangled in his hand and he looked again at his handiwork. The two soldiers were dead now or soon would be. They lay sprawled like cast away dolls. The realization of what he'd done struck him. Blood on his hands.

Hanging on to her, he bent as far away as he could and threw up on the ground. When he ran the back of his hand over his mouth he smelled whisky and cordite.

He heard a quiet cough and looked up. Ernie, Chuck and a few others from the tavern stood there watching him.

Chuck looked at the bodies and then the girl. "Adolf, what have you done?"

Ernie stepped forward, snatching the pistol from his hand. He tucked it into his waistband. "I think he did the right thing, Chuck. This is where it starts."

One spark, Adolf thought.

Were he alive today, he would say himself that this monument is not about one man's struggle but about the struggle of many.

29

Our *struggle, as he put it so well. From 1942 to 1952—when the charter was finally signed—he struggled alongside us, raising support and awareness for our cause, never asking for anything for himself. With his wife and his children often by his side, he went from city to city speaking in any venue that would listen. And though originally published in his native German, his book was a shot heard 'round the world, translated into over forty languages within its first five years in print. I heard him speak shortly before his death: "Well-aimed words will always be more powerful than rifles," he said. And his words roused a slumbering giant, turning its head towards cruelty and oppression, towards a cry for freedom in a far away land.*

Rabbi Benjamin Levin
Dedication Speech, Hitler Memorial, Jerusalem, Israel,
1992.

They told Adolf to take her to the loft and wait for morning. De Gaulle had a nephew who was driving to Calais the next day; they'd hide Hitler and the girl in the back of the truck and hope for the best. He ripped off Tesia's armband and tossed it away.

"Listen to me," he told her. "You are not Jewish. You are my daughter, Klara, and you are ill. We are looking for the hospital. We left your papers at home by mistake. Do you understand me?"

She nodded. Her eyes were red and she limped now, but she stood on her own.

"Good." They set out at a brisk walk. More shouting and sirens punctuated the night, suddenly joined now by occasional gunshots.

Along the way they saw soldiers running. They saw groups of men and women, some now fighting back. People called news to one another from their opened windows. Two soldiers had been killed raping a girl, someone cried. A band of drunks was storming the police station looking for guns, another shouted. Adolf heard it as if it were far away and kept pushing them towards safety, towards home.

He locked them inside. He took down half a bottle of schnapps from the cupboard and poured two drinks with shaking hands. Tesia did not speak and did not meet his eyes. He knew she was still in shock, the color drained away from her skin and her face slack. He tucked her into his cot, wrapping his great coat over her and when he pulled away, she clutched at him and mumbled something.

He bent in closer and heard the words. "You were beautiful," she said, "and you stood alone."

He held her as sobs racked his body. The world had never seemed so grim and despairing and he wondered if it had always been that way, if he'd just never seen it before. He felt the broken girl in his arms, felt her breath against his neck and smelled the sweat and dirt on her. Behind him, in the window, something like Heaven's light grew beyond his wildest imaginings, filling that cavity in the world's soul. His tears subsided; Tesia slept.

After an hour of holding her, he left her side to pack his things. He'd leave his paints, his pallet, his brushes. He knew he'd never use them again. But he did pack his suitcase with clothing, bedding and canned food. He also checked his papers and counted his money. Somewhere, he could buy her the papers she would need.

On a scrap of paper, Ernie had hastily scribbled a name and an address—a friend of a friend at the U.S. Embassy in London. Ernie had pressed it into his hand before leaving with Chuck and the others to storm the police station and start their Revolution for Democratic Change.

"Viva la France," they had said as they went racing down the cobblestones.

Adolf took down their photograph from the mirror. He looked at it and smiled at his friends.

If I'm to be a writer, he thought, I should write something about this place, this time. Something so I will never forget.

He found a pen, turned the photo over, and after a moment's thought, wrote on the back of it in his pinched, careful, German script: *Summer in Paris, Light from Heaven.*

Hitler weighed the pen carefully in his hand and wondered if one man could make a difference. He weighed his destiny carefully in his heart and wondered if the Americans would listen.

TETRIS DOOMS HERSELF

Meghan McCarron

Andy kidnaps me at 11:12 PM. I see the time on my microwave. He clamps a hand over my mouth while I'm making a pot of coffee, and I scatter the grounds all over the floor. It's late, and I have work to do, but that doesn't matter now. "I have a gun," he says in a movie-villain voice. He forces a blindfold over my eyes. I giggle.

When I go to see Catherine, she cuts off my hands. She likes to take off the left one first because it's more useful to me. She uses a hunting knife that she's never sharpened, and when she saws into my wrist she hisses, "*Sinister! Sinister!*"

When I first came home with a bloody stump, my roommates shrieked, *What did she do to you?* Now they roll their eyes and go back to playing Scrabble. They like Andy better. *It takes a lot of effort to kidnap someone,* they say.

Usually Andy kidnaps me at some bright sunny hour when his wife is at work. But tonight she is sick, "from stress, mostly," he says. Also from the flu. "She looked so sad tonight," he says. "So sick and sad." He tells me this as he tightens my blindfold, and then waves his hands in front of my face to make sure I can't see. Air fans my cheeks.

He takes my hand, then changes his mind and takes my wrist instead. He pauses at the door, checking for roommates; the apartment is silent, though sometimes roommates are just hiding. He leads me out the door and down my creaking stairs to a car. It's not his car; it smells new, or fake-new, a smell achieved only through the relentless application of cleaning products. The seat fabric feels cheap to the touch and the anemic motor sputters and kicks. A rental. Economy size, if I had to guess.

He buckles me in and says, "Now you're mine," but in Andy-voice, not movie-villain voice, leaving me unsure how to take the line.

Once my roommate Marcia came home with a hunting trap clamped on her leg. We heard her coming all the way up the stairs, step *CLANK* step *CLANK* step *CLANK*. She said she and her boyfriend were playing cops and robbers in the woods, and she stepped in the wrong place. No one asked why her boyfriend didn't help her home. Other roommates whispered that he must have been the robber. I was not convinced. At the very least, he must have caught her cheating.

Andy and I drive for a long time, probably in circles, since Andy barely leaves this neighborhood. Not that I blame him—things get weird further out. There's downtown and mountains and a desert, somewhere. While we drive, he tells me about his latest career developments. He has an agent now, or is it a manager? I don't understand the music business. I thought it was better than the writer and his prizes, or the lawyer and her golf tournaments, but now they all sound the same.

I ask Andy about his music, instead. To him it's a color or a smell or even a different kind of sound, like bees or sandpaper. I love when Andy talks like this. His voice is the color of mahogany. I forget I can't see where we're going.

The car rolls to a stop on what sounds like gravel. My calm breaks, and I clutch my hands on my knees. Why am I nervous? Andy gets out without a word and opens my door. The night air is sharp; it smells like forest fires.

Every time Catherine cuts off my hands, they come back smaller, so when Andy takes my hand in his, I feel engulfed. I smell rust, and something chemical, in addition to the faint tang of burning wood. It's the smell of the river. I wish I could take off my blindfold, because

I love staring at the river's concrete expanse, but I'm pretty sure the blindfold is a rule.

Andy pulls me toward him and kisses me, hard; if someone could hit someone else with their mouth, it would feel like this. He shoves me away and takes off at a run. His footsteps fade, *PAT PAT Pat Pat pat pat patpat* . . . and I'm out in the open, alone.

"Bet you can't find me!" Andy calls.

"Andy, is this blind man's bluff?" I say. "That's so lame."

He shoots his gun off, which until now I didn't believe he had, and I realize it's something a little different.

Once, Catherine and I tried to have sex. She bit my nipple so hard I yelped; it took me days to find her clit. There were snippets that approached loveliness, and I could maybe see why people fumbled towards the good parts. But I could still taste her in my mouth when she turned to me and said, "Let's never do that again."

Andy and I have fucked on any number of occasions, but we always set rules ahead of time.

Andy is shouting and shooting at the same time, which is half annoying and half terrifying. I thought he said, "Take off your shoes," but when I did he just started shooting again. I throw myself on the ground until he figures out what he wants from this game.

The shooting stops.

"Goddamnit! Get up!" Andy shouts.

"I can't—understand—you!" I shout back.

"Oh," Andy says. Then he gets gruff again. "Take off your shirt!"

I half-heartedly throw my shirt off and hold my arms against my cold, naked skin. Andy likes strip games. I don't. I thought he had a better idea than this.

I'm still on my knees, half-naked, when one of the bullets hits me in the shoulder. The pain explodes outward from the point of impact, I am cold with it, then nothing, then hot hot hot.

I pop the bullet out of my wound—they were cheater bullets, thank god—and hurl it at Andy. It clatters on the gravel. "Fuck you!" I cry. There is a moment of silence as I double over, panting with pain. Just my breath, my heaving chest, pant pant pant. It is gorgeous, this silence. It is such a relief.

"Fuck *you*," Andy says, and starts shooting again.

The first time Catherine cut off my hands, it was to free me from handcuffs. I was chained to her refrigerator and we wanted beer. We could have picked the lock, or dislocated my thumbs, but those methods seemed too obvious. Which is funny, because cutting off my hands is really obvious.

The hunting knife was sharp then, left over from a knife-throwing game with one of Catherine's exes. When it cut into my skin, pain welled like pleasure. The sensation built as Catherine sliced through muscle and tendon, cracked through bone. When my hand dropped to the ground, I saw white light. I screamed.

Now the pain is ragged, the relief the barest break. I grunt. I've begged her to sharpen the knife, or to get a new one, but she insists that the knife is a rule. My forsaking pleasure is a rule, too. Someday, if she gets her way, it's just going to hurt.

When all my clothes are gone, I throw myself on the ground again, by the car. The gravel is gritty against my bare skin. The little pebbles against my nipples are strange and uncomfortable, but uncomfortable like lace panties, not like splinters, or the cuts on my feet. Despite this, I don't feel remotely turned on.

The tall, dead grass rustles.

"Aw, baby, look at you," Andy says. "Stand up."

I pull myself up, and the cool air shocks my bare skin. I hear the wind again. I touch the wound on my shoulder and clean away the gravel, though I let the stones stick to the rest of me. I feel covered, that way.

Andy takes a few steps towards me, and I can feel the edges of his heat, his halo. His breath washes over my forehead, and his clothing whispers as he takes his gun out of his pocket.

"You're all dirty," he says, like I'm a little girl, brushing the gravel off my breasts. His fingers are light and loving. They flick the gravel off with ease.

I imagine what we must look like, a naked, blindfolded woman and a clothed man standing in the dead grass. I try to imagine his wife standing here instead of me and almost laugh. I wish I understood why I'm the one who can be blindfolded, stripped, and shot, and then gently cleaned—gently kissed. The standard answer is that wives are boring, but I don't buy that. Wives will kick your ass if you give them the chance.

But if you shoot your wife, you have to listen to her toss and turn because her shoulder aches. Or you have to wonder if she'll pull a gun on you at breakfast. Andy can walk away from me. So maybe the real question is—what about me makes it so easy to walk away?

He puts the gun against my back and prods me. "Let's go," he whispers in my ear. His voice is warm and, again, I'm not sure how to take the line.

Everyone plays the same game. I'm not just talking about the trends that go around—cartwheel contests, speed eating, naked relay races. Those games are sham games, fakes for people with nothing better to do. But when you find a naked roommate giggling to herself outside your building for the fourth time in a month, and she's not even running with a baton, or running at all, it's more like a jog, you get suspicious. If you can play a sham game wrong and it still gets called a *game*, what the hell kind of system is this?

I march barefoot towards the sounds of whirring generators and rustling trees. I step on metal, on glass. My feet must be a bloody mess.

"I didn't do too good at this game," I said. "Did I?" It's a canned line. One he likes. I want to please him, suddenly.

"No, you didn't," Andy says. The gun is getting warm from being pushed against my skin. The sound of rustling is actually water rushing.

Where is the water coming from? It builds as we walk towards it, until I lose the sound of my footsteps, of Andy's footsteps, of anything but this impossible sound.

He puts a hand on my shoulder and pulls me to a stop. The sound roars below me. It has to be the wind, whistling through the concrete. I can smell the forest fires again.

"What now?" I say.

"Take off your blindfold."

I'm standing on the edge of the concrete wall, where I expected to see ancient graffiti, cracked concrete, slow, dirty water. Instead, a river rushes below me, dark except for where the moon is reflected in a distorted circle. The river is deeper than the channel ever was, like the concrete was ripped up to expose a secret below. It smells like acid rain.

"Jump in," Andy says.

I look over my shoulder so fast I almost fall. "What?" I say.

Andy softens his tone and puts a hand on my ass, cupping it like it's his favorite thing in the world. "Come on, baby. Jump in."

"That's not even supposed to *be* here," I said.

"I found it last night. A friend sent me photos." He gazed at it, the midnight-dark water, the splotches of electric light.

"You're not jumping in?" I say.

"Baby," he says, patting my ass. "You lost the game."

The river can't be real, and yet it looks more solid, more dangerous, than anything that is. The second-to-last thing I'm doing is wasting the river on Andy, and the last is getting shot in the gut for refusing to jump in.

I turn around and snatch the gun from Andy's hand.

I have always known I could do this, but from the look on Andy's face he hasn't. He gapes at the gun like I pulled it out of thin air.

"You jump in," I say.

"Me?" he says.

"You're the loser now."

Andy's face collapses, then hardens into a glower. "You cheated."

I have cheated. If he walks away, I'll let him.

"I changed the game," I say.

He looks down at his shoes, screwing up his face like this is a huge problem, one that takes mighty effort to solve. He shifts back and forth on his feet and screws up his face. I keep the gun pointed at him. I'm still cold.

He bends down and unties his shoes. He removes his pants, shirt, shocks. He climbs up on the wall next to me and looks out on the river with his hands on his hips, like it's his newly conquered domain. Like I'm not even there. The gun is close enough for him to snatch back, but he doesn't even look at it. He just stands there, staring at the water.

I thought snatching the gun would make it like one of those childhood games, where I grant myself invisibility so he gives himself invisibility goggles, I call lightening so he turns himself to metal— perpetual one-upmanship until one of us runs out of ideas. Andy stares down the river, naked and silent. Every so often he shuffles his feet, or peers down farther, as if readying to jump that never comes. My hand aches from holding the gun, and the cuts on my feet burn. Andy ignores me, frozen between fear of the river and fear of not finishing the game. Is he out of ideas?

I keep telling myself *a little longer, just stay a little longer,* but finally I give in. I hunt and gather my clothes from the scrubby field; Andy is still standing on the ledge when I finish. I dress behind him, shaking the dirt off my underwear, easing my shirt over my bloody shoulder. Andy twitches once or twice, but otherwise does not move. I force my bloody feet into their shoes.

I pick up Andy's pants from the pile of clothes and fish out the car keys. I jingle them, to see if that catches his attention. He peers down into the rushing water again. I think about climbing up on the ledge with him to see what he's looking at, even bending my knees, diving in. But I called bullshit on the game, and it felt wrong to step back in.

I looked back at him, once, on my way to the car. He raised a hand. At first, I thought he was waving me back, and I stopped in my tracks. He was waving goodbye.

I take the rental car back to Andy's house on the east side of town. He lives in an ancient craftsman bungalow with a long low porch and two giant palm trees in the front yard. I walk in the screen door and find his wife playing Tetris, crumpled tissues surrounding her in white clumps. I try to introduce myself, but when I open my mouth, she rolls her eyes and thrusts the other controller in my direction. I sit down next to her on the couch and play at manipulating shapes, finding a place for everything. Andy's wife kicks my ass at this, but that's kind of the point.

Around three AM, Andy comes in. He's sopping wet and, weirdly, drunk.

"I got cold," he says, as if this was an explanation.

He shuffles into the kitchen before I can even open my mouth. His wife doesn't look away from Tetris, as if her husband shows up soaked and wasted on a regular basis. He comes back with three beers and hands them out. I have ignored my side of the game, and bricks are choking the top of my screen.

Andy looks as if he's undergone a religious conversion. Perhaps it's just the wetness, my mind adding in a false baptismal glow. Did he really go in? My whole conception of Andy changes, struggling to imagine him diving into the river, fighting the current, pulling himself ashore. But he had been naked, standing on that edge. I try to imagine him stepping down, putting clothes on, and getting back up. Maybe he was afraid of losing them?

No, Andy is still just Andy.

He plops down on the easy chair by the couch and, without a word, flips the TV off. My disaster Tetris, and his wife's high score, disappear. We sit in silence. Not-new Andy, his sniffly wife, and me.

"How was the water?" I say to him.

Andy takes a sip of beer. "Excuse me?" he says, as if I was some rude stranger.

"How was the river?" I repeat, trying to sound casual.

Andy takes a swig of his beer and looks at the blank television. He takes on an expression he imagines is deep. "Real," he says.

"Oh really?" I said. "How'd you get back here, then?"

"Wouldn't you like to know," Andy says.

"A real river would chew you up and spit you out—"

Andy looks away, as if ignoring me will make me disappear.

"Do you know why he's like this?" I say to his wife. She's blowing her nose, and looks at me from behind her tissue. I take off my shoes, my socks, and show her my filthy, scabbing feet. I pull back my shirt, where the blood on my shoulder was starting to soak through. "He did this and then tried to get me to jump in this . . . river. Now he's pretending like he went in, lying to us—"

"I'm not lying!" Andy says.

"Why in the hell are you clothes wet?"

"I took them with me," Andy says.

His wife stares at her husband. "What is she even doing here?" she says, guesturing at me with her controller.

"Returning your car," I say.

"She stole it," Andy says, as if this trumps anything I might say.

"What did you do, rent one of the public showers?" I say. "Jump in the ocean? You kinda smell fishy—"

His wife groans and drops her controller. "I'm going up to bed," she says, standing up. She leaves her pile of tissues on the couch.

Andy's head snaps up. "So am I," he says, and gets up a little too fast. She looks at him like he's crazy, but doesn't say anything to deter him. He pretends to ignore the look. His wife walks a step ahead of him towards the stairs so she can't see him following her. Their feet move in perfect unison up the stairs, *step. step. step.* Andy's footsteps squelch. Neither of look down at me, once.

This was my cue to leave, but I stay on the couch. I turn the TV back on and watch Tetris bricks pile up on both our sides. I find it comforting to watch it play itself. When both sides clog up, I hit the controller with my least-cut toe to start another round.

Plunk. Plunk. Plunk. Plunkplunk plunkplunkplunkplunk plunk. GAME OVER. Click.

Andy and his wife start snoring upstairs; Tetris keeps dooming itself. I feel like an asshole. Why do I even care, if Andy lies? Why waste my time, barge in on his wife?

I wonder if the river's still there. I wonder if I could make myself jump. Would I float out somewhere, wet but still me, still here? Would I drown? Or would I dive for the dark, rushing water, and hit a dirty puddle on concrete?

BLUE INK

Yoon Ha Lee

It's harder than you thought, walking from the battle at the end of time and down a street that reeks of entropy and fire and spilled lives. Your eyes aren't dry. Neither is the alien sky. Your shoulders ache and your stomach hurts. *Blue woman, blue woman,* the chant runs through your head as you limp toward a portal's bright mouth. You're leaving, but you intend to return. You have allies yet.

Blue stands for many things at the end of time: for the forgotten, blazing blue stars of aeons past; the antithesis of redshift; the color of uncut veins beneath your skin.

This story is written in blue ink, although you do not know that yet.

Blue is more than a fortunate accident. Jenny Chang usually writes in black ink or pencil. She's been snowed in at her mom's house since yesterday and is dawdling over physics homework. Now she's out of lead. The only working pen in the house is blue.

"We'll go shopping the instant the roads are clear," her mom says.

Jenny mumbles something about how she hates homework over winter break. Actually, she isn't displeased. There's something neatly alien about all those equations copied out in blue ink, problems and their page numbers. It's as if blue equations come from a different universe than the ones printed in the textbook.

While her mom sprawls on the couch watching TV, Jenny pads upstairs to the guest room and curls up in bed next to the window.

Fingers of frost cover the glass. With her index finger, Jenny writes a list of numbers: pi, H_0 for Hubble's constant, her dad's cellphone number, her school's zip code. Then she wipes the window clear of mist, and shivers. Everything outside is almost blue-rimmed in the twilight.

Jenny resumes her homework, biting her nails between copying out answers to two significant figures and doodling spaceships in the margins. There's a draft from the window, but that's all right. Winter's child that she is—February 16, to be exact—Jenny thinks better with a breath of cold.

Except, for a moment, the draft is hot like a foretaste of hell. Jenny stops still. All the frost has melted and is running in rivulets down the glass. And there's a face at the window.

The sensible thing to do would be to scream. But the face is familiar, the way equations in blue are familiar. It could be Jenny's own, five ragged years in the future. The woman's eyes are dark and bleak, asking for help without expecting it.

"Hold on," Jenny says. She goes to the closet to grab her coat. From downstairs, she hears her mom laughing at some TV witticism.

Then Jenny opens the window, and the world falls out. This doesn't surprise her as much as it should. The wind shrieks and the cold hits her like a fist. It's too bad she didn't put on her scarf and gloves while she was at it.

The woman offers a hand. She isn't wearing gloves. Nor is she shivering. Maybe extremes of temperature don't mean the same thing in blue universes. Maybe it's normal to have blue-tinted lips, there. Jenny doesn't even wear make-up.

The woman's touch warms Jenny, as though they've stepped into a bubble of purloined heat. Above them, stars shine in constellations that Jenny recognizes from the ceiling of her father's house, the ones Mom and Dad helped her put up when she was in third grade. Constellations with names like Fire Truck and Ladybug Come Home, constellations that you won't find in any astronomer's catalogue.

Jenny looks at her double and raises an eyebrow, because any words she could think of would emerge frozen, like the world around them. She wonders where that hell-wind came from and if it has a name.

"The end of the world is coming," the blue woman says. Each syllable is crisp and certain.

I don't believe in the end of the world, Jenny wants to say, except she's read her physics textbook. She's read the sidebar about things like the sun swelling into a red giant and the universe's heat-death. She looks up again, and maybe she's imagining it, but these stars are all the wrong colors, and they're either too bright or not bright enough. Instead, Jenny asks, "Are my mom and dad going to be okay?"

"As okay as anyone else," the blue woman says.

"What can I do?" She can no more doubt the blue woman than she can doubt the shape of the sun.

This earns her a moment's smile. "There's a fight," the blue woman says, "and everyone fell. Everyone fell." She says it the second time as though things might change, as though there's a magic charm for reversing the course of events. "I'm the only one left, because I can walk through possibilities. Now there's you."

They set off together. A touch at her elbow tells Jenny to turn left. There's a bright flash at the corner of her eyes. Between one blink and the next, they're standing in a devastated city, crisscrossed by skewed bridges made of something brighter than steel, more brilliant than glass.

"Where are we?" Jenny asks.

"We're at humanity's last outpost," the blue woman says. "Tell me what you see."

"Rats with red eyes and metal hands," Jenny says just as one pauses to stare at her. It stands up on its hind feet and makes a circle-sign at her with one of its hands, as if it's telling her things will be all right. Then it scurries into the darkness. "Buildings that go so high up I can't see their tops, and bridges between them. Flying cars." They come in every color, these faraway cars, every color but blue. Jenny begins to stammer under the weight of detail: "Skeletons wrapped in silver wires"—out of the corner of her eye, she thinks she sees one twitch, and decides she'd rather not know—"and glowing red clocks on the walls that say it's midnight even though there's light in the sky, and silhouettes far away, like people, except their joints are all wrong."

And the smells, too, mostly smoke and ozone, as though everything has been burned away by fire and lightning, leaving behind the ghost-essence of a city, nothing solid.

"What you see isn't actually there," the blue woman says. She taps Jenny's shoulder again.

They resume walking. The only reason Jenny doesn't halt dead in her tracks is that she's afraid that the street will crumble into pebbles, the pebbles into dust, and leave her falling through eternity the moment she stops.

The blue woman smiles a little. "Not like that. Things are very different at the end of time. Your mind is seeing a translation of everything into more familiar terms."

"What are we doing here?" Jenny asks. "I—I don't know how to fight. If it's that kind of battle." She draws mini-comics in the margins of her notes sometimes, when the teachers think she's paying attention. Sometimes, in the comics, she wields two mismatched swords, and sometimes a gun; sometimes she has taloned wings, and sometimes she rides in a starship sized perfectly for one. She fights storm-dragons and equations turned into sideways alien creatures. (If pressed, she will admit the influence of *Calvin and Hobbes*.) But unless she's supposed to brain someone with the flute she didn't think to bring (she plays in the school band), she's not going to be any use in a fight, at least not the kind of fight that happens at the end of time. Jenny's mom made her take a self-defense class two years ago, before the divorce, and mostly what Jenny remembers is the floppy-haired instructor saying, *If someone pulls a gun on you and asks for your wallet, give him your wallet. You are not an action hero.*

The blue woman says, "I know. I wanted a veteran of the final battles"—she says it without disapproval—"but they all died, too."

This time Jenny does stop. "You brought them here to die."

The woman lifts her chin. "I wouldn't have done that. I showed them the final battle, the very last one, and they chose to fight. We're going there now, so you can decide."

Jenny read the stories where you travel back in time and shoot someone's grandfather or step on some protozoan, and the act unravels the present stitch by stitch until all that's left is a skein of history gone wrong. "Is that such a good idea?" she asks.

"They won't see us. We won't be able to affect anything."

"I don't even have a weapon," Jenny says, thinking of the girl in the mini-comics with her two swords, her gun. Jenny is tolerably good at arm-wrestling her girl friends at high school, but she doesn't think that's going to help.

The woman says, "That can be changed."

Not *fixed*, as though Jenny were something wrong, but *changed*. The word choice is what makes her decide to keep going. "Let's go to the battle," Jenny says.

The light in the sky changes as they walk, as though all of winter were compressed into a single day of silver and grey and scudding darkness. Once or twice, Jenny could almost swear that she sees a flying car change shape, growing wings like that of a delta kite and swooping out of sight. There's soot in the air, subtle and unpleasant, and Jenny wishes for sunglasses, even though it's not all that bright, any sort of protection. Lightning runs along the streets like a living thing, writing jagged blue-white equations. It keeps its distance, however.

"It's just curious," the blue woman says when Jenny asks about it. She doesn't elaborate.

The first sign of the battle, although Jenny doesn't realize it for a while, is the rain. "Is the rain real?" Jenny says, wondering what future oddity would translate into inclement weather.

"Everything's an expression of some reality."

That probably means *no*. Especially since the rain is touching everything in the world except them.

The second sign is all the corpses, and this she does recognize. The stench hits her first. It's not the smell of meat, or formaldehyde from 9th grade biology (she knows a fresh corpse shouldn't smell like formaldehyde, but that's the association her brain makes), but asphalt and rust and fire. She would have expected to hear something first, like the deafening chatter of guns. Maybe fights in the future are silent.

Then she sees the fallen. Bone-deep, she knows which are *ours* and which are *theirs*. *Ours* are the rats with the clever metal hands, their fingers twisted beyond salvage; the sleek bicycles (bicycles!) with broken spokes, reflectors flashing crazily in the lightning; the men and women in coats the color of winter rain, red washing away from their wounds. The blue woman's breath hitches as though she's seeing this for the first time, as though each body belongs to an old friend. Jenny can't take in all the raw death. The rats grieve her the most, maybe because one of them greeted her in this place of unrelenting strangeness.

Theirs are all manner of things, including steel serpents, their scales etched with letters from an alphabet of despair; stilt-legged robots with guns for arms; more men and women, in uniforms of all stripes, for at the evening of the world there will be people fighting for entropy as well as against it. Some of them are still standing, and written in their faces—even the ones who don't *have* faces—is their triumph.

Jenny looks at the blue woman. The blue woman continues walking, so Jenny keeps pace with her. They stop before one of the fallen, a dark-skinned man. Jenny swallows and eyes one of the serpents, which is swaying next to her, but it takes no notice of her.

"He was so determined that we should fight, whatever the cost," the blue woman says. "And now he's gone."

There's a gun not far from the fallen man's hand. Jenny reaches for it, then hesitates, waiting for permission. The blue woman doesn't say yes, doesn't say no, so Jenny touches it anyway. The metal is utterly cold. Jenny pulls her fingers away with a bitten-off yelp.

"It's empty," the blue woman says. "Everything's empty."

"I'm sorry," Jenny says. She doesn't know this man, but it's not about her.

The blue woman watches as Jenny straightens, leaving the gun on the ground.

"If I say no," Jenny says slowly, "is there anyone else?"

The blue woman's eyes close for a moment. "No. You're the last. I would have spared you the choice if I could have."

"How many of me were there?"

"I lost count after a thousand or so," the blue woman says. "Most of them were more like me. Some of them were more like you."

A thousand Jenny Changs, a thousand blue women. More. Gone, one by one, like a scatterfall of rain. "Did all of them say yes?" Jenny asks.

The blue woman shakes her head.

"And none of the ones who said yes survived."

"None of them."

"If that's the case," Jenny says, "what makes you special?"

"I'm living on borrowed possibilities," she says. "When the battle ends, I'll be gone too, no matter which way it ends."

Jenny looks around her, then squeezes her eyes shut, thinking. *Two significant figures,* she thinks inanely. "Who started the fight?" She's appalled that she sounds like her mom.

"There's always an armageddon around the corner," the blue woman says. "This happens to be the one that *he* found."

The dark-skinned man. Who was he, that he could persuade people to take a last stand like this? Maybe it's not so difficult when a last stand is the only thing left. That solution displeases her, though.

Her heart is hammering. "I won't do it," Jenny says. "Take me home."

The blue woman's eyes narrow. "You are the last," she says quietly. "I thought you would understand."

Everything hinges on one thing: is the blue woman different enough from Jenny that Jenny can lie to her, and be believed?

"I'm sorry," Jenny says.

"Very well," the blue woman says.

Jenny strains to keep her eyes open at the crucial moment. When the blue woman reaches for her hand, Jenny sees the portal, a shimmer of blue light. She grabs the blue woman and shoves her through. The last thing Jenny hears from the blue woman is a muffled protest.

Whatever protection the blue woman's touch afforded her is gone. The rain drenches her shirt and runs in cold rivulets through her hair, into her eyes, down her back. Jenny reaches again for the fallen man's gun. It's cold, but she has a moment's warmth in her yet.

She might not be able to save the world, but she can at least save herself.

It's the end of the school day and you're waiting for Jenny's mother to pick you up. A man walks up to you. He wears a coat as grey as rain, and his eyes are pale against dark skin. "You have to come with me," he says, awkward and serious at once. You recognize him, of course. You remember when he first recruited you, in another timeline. You remember what he looked like fallen in the battle at the end of time, with a gun knocked out of his hand.

"I can't," you say, kindly, because it will take him time to understand that you're not the blue woman anymore, that you won't do the things the blue woman did.

"What?" he says. "Please. It's urgent." He knows better than to grab your arm. "There's a battle—"

Once upon a time, you listened to his plea. Part of you is tempted to listen this time around, to abandon the life that Jenny left you and take up his banner. But you know how that story ends.

"I'm not in your story anymore," you explain to him. "You're in mine."

The man doesn't look like he belongs in a world of parking tickets and potted begonias and pencil sharpeners. But he can learn, the way you have.

CURSE

Samantha Henderson

1

Her son was a year grown when the dream started. Always it began in the pantry, at first—she was tallying the beer, or the bags of grain, when the first joints of her fingers started to itch. Little more than a prickling warmth, then a fierce burning, and as she twisted and scratched them for relief they sprouted fur, some gray, some brown. One by one they disjointed, split away from her hands and fell to the floor, where they scampered into the corners. She thrust her hands into the folds of her gowns to save them, but it was no use—joint by joint her fingers changed into mice and ran over her feet until she was left with nothing but two stumpy paddles.

And then she'd wake, sometimes alone, sometimes besides her husband's softly breathing body, and check her fingers in the moonlight to see if they were still there. If she was alone she'd rise and go to the cellars, checking for nibbled food and dung in the corners.

She was alone more and more. One thing she'd learned was that the smaller the kingdom, the more the king had to take into his own hands. He was away from home more often than not, now, and stayed in his own rooms most of the time when he was home, with councilors and petitions and the business of an almost-prosperous land.

Another thing she'd learned was that her business was with the beer, and the bags of grain, and the stores kept in stone-lined cisterns beneath the ground, and keeping the women a-weaving. Her business was her son, for now, and she knew that when he was grown enough

51

he would become part of the men's world with his father and learn the ways of a countrified prince.

Then it happened when she was awake, walking the halls to her rooms, leaving the candle behind and trusting to the torchlight. Her hands felt thick and itchy, and when she lifted them they fell away joint by joint, little dark bodies running to the walls and vanishing between the stones. She waited an instant to wake, then screamed when she didn't.

She staggered against the wall as a curious maid poked her head around the corner, eyes widening as she recognized her.

"What's the matter, my lady?" The maid came forward, brisk, in no sort of awe whatsoever. Because she wasn't a proper queen, she wasn't a lady, she was a miller's daughter with an odd kind of luck. So far the servants treated her with condescending sympathy.

She raised her hands, for show or to defend herself, but they were normal—strong peasant's hands with short, clean nails and losing their calluses.

"Nothing," she managed, then "nothing" again, in a tone that tried to be imperious and failed. "I just tripped, that's all."

2

The dwarf smelled her long before she came over the rise of the hill: the soap she used and the oil at the roots of her hair, and skin that never lost a touch of the sun and the faint tang of soured milk. The boy, too— the sweat of its toiling beside its mother and a diaper clout that needed changing. They paused at the crest while she sought the entrance to his dwelling in the shadow of the valley below; a shelter hacked from the living stone of the mountainside. He stood in the doorway, not bothering to conceal himself. She spotted him and stumbled downhill, dragging the tired child behind her.

"He wants me to do it again—the weaving," she said, without preamble.

"Took him a while," he replied, dryly.

She started to cry, because she knew what he was going to say and realized the truth of it the instant before he spoke. He turned inside the cave and beckoned her to follow. It was cozy inside, and roomier than she'd imagined. Red coals glowed on a long, low hearth. A squat battered kettle sat there, with a water bucket in the corner.

"He's finding a reason to despise you. He feels guilty for doing it with no justification," he threw over his shoulder.

She was such a child. She didn't know that he could hate her so.

She spoke to his back as he lifted the kettle.

"You sent them. The dreams. My fingers: mice. It was you."

He didn't turn around. She waited while he built up the fire under the heavy-bottomed copper, and folded her fingers carefully across her stomach. Afterwards he leaned against the mantle, built small to accommodate his height.

"I felt sorry for you, you know," he said. "At the beginning, even. That's why I came in the first place. Sympathy you'd have for a snail in the path, or a turtle turned over in the sun. And then, after the first night—no more than that—you started to enjoy it, the attention that you feared so much before. I could see it in you. You almost believed you could do it, didn't you?"

Were her fingers beginning to itch? She twisted them in her skirt and didn't look.

It's true, she thought. *I did think I could spin straw into gold. Not because I could, but because ugliness should serve beauty. Isn't that always the way?*

"You were quick enough to agree to the child," he said, giving her the side of his face, the silhouette of a long, gnarled nose. "And I can't blame you, for your loving man would have killed you just to make the point. That's a king's job, you know. To make a point. And perhaps he didn't want to marry you so much, for there are beautiful women enough of his own rank. But he had promised, you see. And he made his point."

"You hated me."

"Yes. For a long time." He poked at the fire and a great clot of sparks flew up, some landing on the hearth and squirming like lit worms before darkening into black ashy spots. In the corner, the boy chuckled over some toy.

"But I wouldn't have sent the dreams if you hadn't played the game of not knowing the third day. *Belshazzar, Cruickshanks. Conrad. Harry.*" His voice became burred and rough at the edges. "Three days you played me like a salmon."

She said nothing, being an inland girl. She had never tasted salmon.

3

The girl wrapped potatoes in damp clothes and pushed them into the coals banked behind the hearth. The men in the doorway were not going to go away, but she made them wait for all that. She heard one grunt softly and shift his weight.

She'd grown a lot the past year and had to bend her head to avoid hitting the arch of the fireplace, which had been built too low for human kind.

"My brother left years ago," she said, finally, still kneeling and staring at the coals. "He visits sometimes, and brings game from the forest. Less and less these days."

"Does he know who he is?" One of the men—the taller, thin one—surged forward, shrugging off the other's restraining hand. "Do *you?*"

He stopped as she turned, her eyes cold and hard and blue, so blue they were almost violet at the edges. Her father's eyes, a king's eyes, chilly and appraising. She said nothing.

The thin man flinched but stood his ground. He made an effort to gentle his voice.

"Your pardon. But your father is dying, and dying with no successor. Your brother is his heir."

She was still kneeling, still looking up at him, and now she smiled very slightly and the thin man felt that to stand over her was no advantage at all.

"His heir? What, with a miller's slut-girl for a mother, who ran away from court to return to the squalor she came from?"

The thin man swallowed and stood his ground.

"Even so, my lady."

She sighed and looked back at the coals. The roasting potatoes filled the rough-hewn chamber with the smell of clean dirt.

"He hunts," she said, finally, rising and dusting the ash off her full skirts. "Track him down in the wild wood, if you must, but don't seek him here, not if you value your lives."

They didn't move, glancing at each other nervously. The other man, who stood in the doorway, was shorter and stouter than his companion. He cleared his throat.

"We do not seek only your brother, my lady," he rumbled.

"Ah?" she was grinning now. "My own humble self? But I would not inherit; I couldn't. Perhaps my dam carried me in her belly to the manikin's house, perhaps he got me on her—isn't that what they say? You'd never prove the king's my father."

"But your mother was your mother," said the stout man. "And your mother had her gifts."

"Pieter," said the thin man to his companion.

The girl laughed: a harsh bark. "So! Straw into gold, is it? If she could, then I can? How does your master's kingdom these days, Pieter? Are there small economies? Is the wine cheap and raw in your throat? Are there discontented whispers outside the chamber of the dying king?"

The thin man turned to expostulate with Pieter, but the bulkier man pushed him aside roughly.

"I've heard enough about it," he growled, to his companion or to the girl.

"Fine threads of gold, reams of it, spilling on the floor and piling under the window. Enough to buy a kingdom, much less . . . "

"I'm useless to you, gentlemen," she returned, lifting her fingers spread like a fan in front of their faces. "For see?"

And before their eyes her fingers sprouted fur, and separated from each other joint by joint, and scampered to the floor with a squeak and a flutter, with a twitch and a shiver of bright, beady eye.

The thin man started back with a shudder; Pieter never got a chance, because a great hairy bulk loomed behind him, wrapped a beefy arm around his throat, and lifted him half a foot off the floor as he choked him.

But the thin man didn't run, not even then; it was only when he saw the footprints the girl had made in the ash and sand of the hearth that he ran—not footprints, but claw marks, a bird's foot, like those the chickens make outside the kitchen door, but huge, monstrous.

He turned and pushed past the enormous man and the gasping Pieter and vanished into the night.

The big man released Pieter, who fell to the floor in a limp bundle.

"Is he dead, Bearskin?" asked the girl.

Her brother shrugged. "Perhaps."

She returned to the fire and poked at the potatoes with the stumps of her hands.

"We have to go," she said.

"Come with me," he said. "I have places to hide you in the forest. And they will be afraid of you for a while."

"Yes," she returned, tucking the hot potatoes in her apron and wrapping them against her. "But not long enough." The cave was rustling with mice, scampering over the ashes, over the mantle, across Pieter's limp body.

She followed her brother into the forest, the potatoes warm against her thighs and the stubs of her hands, warm against the tiny fingers that were sprouting from her bloodless flesh.

CLOCKWORK CHICKADEE

Mary Robinette Kowal

The clockwork chickadee was not as pretty as the nightingale. But she did not mind. She pecked the floor when she was wound, looking for invisible bugs. And when she was not wound, she cocked her head and glared at the sparrow, whom she loathed with every tooth on every gear in her pressed-tin body.

The sparrow could fly.

He took no pains to conceal his contempt for those who could not. When his mechanism spun him around and around overhead, he twittered—not even a proper song—to call attention to his flight. Chickadee kept her head down when she could so as not to give him the satisfaction of her notice. It was clear to her that any bird could fly if only they were attached to a string like him. The flight, of which he was so proud, was not even an integral part of his clockwork. A wind-up engine hanging from the chandelier spun him in circles while he merely flapped his wings. Chickadee could do as much. And so she thought until she hatched an idea to show that Sparrow was not so very special.

It happened, one day, that Chickadee and Sparrow were shelved next to one another.

Sparrow, who lay tilted on his belly as his feet were only painted on, said, "How limiting the view is from here. Why, when I am flying I can see everything."

"Not everything, I'll warrant," said Chickadee. "Have you seen what is written underneath the table? Do you know how the silver marble got behind the potted fern, or where the missing wind-up key is?"

Sparrow flicked his wing at her. "Why should I care about such things when I can see the ceiling above and the plaster cherubs upon it. I can see the shelves below us and the mechanical menagerie upon it, even including the clockwork scarab and his lotus. I can see the fireplace, which shares the wall with us, none of which are visible from here nor to you."

"But I have seen all of these things as I have been carried to and from the shelf. In addition the boy has played with me at the fountain outside."

"What fountain?"

"Ah! Can you not see the courtyard fountain when you fly?" Chickadee hopped a step closer to him. "Such a pity."

"Bah—Why should I care about any of this?"

"For no reason today," said Chickadee. "Perhaps tomorrow."

"What is written underneath the table?" Sparrow called as he swung in his orbit about the room, wings clicking against his side with each downstroke.

Chickadee pecked at the floor and shifted a cog to change her direction toward the table. "The address of Messrs DeCola and Wodzinski."

"Bah. Why should I care about them?"

"Because they are master clockworkers. They can re-set cogs to create movements you would not think possible."

"I have all the movement I need. They can offer me nothing."

"You might change your mind." Chickadee passed under the edge of the table. "Perhaps tomorrow."

Above the table, Sparrow's gears ground audibly in frustration.

Chickadee cocked her head to look up at the yellow slip of paper glued to the underside if the table. Its type was still crisp though the paper itself threatened to peel away. She scanned the corners of the room for movement. In the shadows by the fireplace, a live mouse caught her gaze. He winked.

———

"How did the silver marble get behind the potted fern?" Sparrow asked as he lay on the shelf.

"It fell out of the boy's game and rolled across the floor to where I was pecking the ground. I waited but no one seemed to notice that it was gone, nor did they notice me, so I put my beak against it and pushed it behind the potted fern."

"You did? You stole from the boy?" Sparrow clicked his wings shut. "I find that hard to believe."

"You may not, today," Chickadee said. "Perhaps tomorrow."

She cocked her head to look away from him and to the corner where the live mouse now hid. The mouse put his forepaw on the silver marble and rolled it away from the potted fern. Chickadee felt the tension in her spring and tried to calculate how many revolutions of movement it still offered her. She thought it would suffice.

"Where is the missing wind-up key?" Sparrow hung from his line, waiting for the boy to wind him again.

"The live mouse has it." Chickadee hopped forward and pecked at another invisible crumb, but did not waste the movement needed to look at Sparrow.

"What would a *live* mouse need with a windup key?"

"He does not need it," said Chickadee. "But I *do* have need of it and he is in my service."

All the gears in the room stopped for a moment as the other clockwork animals paused to listen. Even the nightingale stopped her song. In the sudden cessation of ticking, sound from the greater world outside crept in, bringing the babble of the fountain in the courtyard, the laughter of the boy, the purr of automobiles and from the far distance, the faint pealing of a clock.

"I suppose you would have us believe that he winds you?" said Sparrow.

"Not yet. Perhaps today." She continued pecking the floor.

After a moment of nothing happening, the other animals returned to their tasks save for the sparrow. He hung from his line and beat his wings against his side.

"Ha! I see him. I see the live mouse behind the potted fern. You could too if you could fly."

"I have no need." Chickadee felt her clockwork beginning to slow. "Live Mouse!" she called. "It is time to fulfill our bargain."

The silence came again as the other animals stopped to listen. Into this quiet came a peculiar scraping rattle and then the live mouse emerged from behind the potted fern with the missing wind-up key tied in his tail.

"What is he doing?" Sparrow squawked.

Chickadee bent to peck the ground so slowly she thought she might never touch it. A gear clicked forward and she tapped the floor. "Do you really need me to tell you that?"

Above her, Sparrow dangled on his line. "Live Mouse! Whatever she has promised you, I can give you also, only wind my flying mechanism."

The live mouse twirled his whiskers and kept walking toward Chickadee. "Well now. That's a real interesting proposition. How about a silver marble?"

"There is one behind the potted fern."

"Not nomore."

"Then a crystal from the chandelier."

The live mouse wrinkled his nose. "If'n I can climb the chandelier to wind ya, then I reckon I can reach a crystal for myself."

"I must have something you want."

With the key paused by Chickadee's side, the live mouse said, "That might be so."

The live mouse set the tip of the key down like a cane and folded his paws over it. Settling back on his haunches, he tipped his head up to study Sparrow. "How 'bout, you give me one of your wings?"

Sparrow squawked.

"You ain't got no need of 'em to fly, that right?" The live mouse looked down and idly twisted the key on the floor, as if he were winding the room. "Probly make you spin round faster, like one of them zeppelin thingamabobs. Whazzat called? Air-o-dye-namic."

"A bird cannot fly without wings."

"Now you and I both know that ain't so. A *live* bird can't fly without wings, but you're a clockwork bird."

"What would a live mouse know about clockworks?"

The live mouse laughed. "Ain't you never heard of Hickory, Dickory and Dock? We mice have a long history with clockworks. Looking at you, I figure you won't miss a wing none and without it dragging, you ought to be able to go faster and your windings would last you longer. Whaddya say? Wouldn't it be a mite sight nicer to fly without having to wait for the boy to come back?"

"What would you do with my wing?"

"That," the live mouse smiled, showing his sharp incisors, "is between me and Messrs DeCola and Wodzinski. So do we have a deal?"

"I will have to consider the matter."

"Suit yourself." The live mouse lifted the key and put the tip in Chickadee's winding mechanism.

"Wait!" Sparrow flicked his wings as if anxious to be rid of them. "Yes, yes you may have my left wing, only wind me now. A bird is meant to fly."

"All righty, then."

Chickadee turned her head with painful slowness. "Now, Live Mouse, you and I have an agreement."

"That we did and we do, but nothing in it says I can't have another master."

"That may well be, but the wind-up key belongs to me."

"I reckon that's true. Sorry, Sparrow. Looks as if I can't help you none." The live mouse sighed. "And I surely did want me one of them wings."

Once again, he lifted the key to Chickadee's side. Above them, Sparrow let out a squeal of metal. "Wait! Chickadee, there must be something I can offer you. You are going on a journey, yes? From here, I can tell you if any dangers lie on your route."

"Only in this room and we are leaving it."

"Leaving? And taking the key with you?"

"Just so. Do not worry. The boy will come to wind you eventually. And now, Live Mouse, if you would be so kind."

"My other wing! You may have my other wing, only let the live mouse use the key to wind me."

Chickadee paused, waiting for her gears to click forward so that she could look at the Sparrow. Her spring was so loose now, that each action took an eternity. "What would I do with one of your wings? I have two of my own."

The other clockwork bird seemed baffled and hung on the end of the line flapping his wings as if he could fling them off.

The live mouse scraped a claw across the edge of the key. "It might come in real handy on our trip. Supposing Messrs DeCola and Wodzinski want a higher payment than you're thinking they do. Why then you'd have something more to offer them."

"And if they didn't then we would have carried the wing with us for no reason."

"Now as to that," said the live mouse, "I can promise you that I'll take it off your hands if'n we don't need it."

Chickadee laughed. "Oh, Live Mouse, I see now. Very well, I will accept Sparrow's wing so that later you may have a full set. Messrs DeCola and Wodzinski will be happy to have two customers, I am certain."

The live mouse bowed to her and wrapped the key in his tail again. "Sparrow, I'll be right up." Scampering across the floor, he disappeared into the wall.

Chickadee did not watch him go, she waited with her gaze still cocked upward toward Sparrow. With the live mouse gone, Chickadee became aware of how still the other clockworks were, watching their drama. Into the silence, Nightingale began to cautiously sing. Her beautiful warbles and chirps repeated through their song thrice before the live mouse appeared out of the ceiling on the chandelier's chain. The crystals of the chandelier tinkled in a wild accompaniment to the ordered song of the nightingale.

The live mouse shimmied down the layers of crystals until he reached Sparrow's flying mechanism. Crawling over that, he wrapped his paws around the string beneath it and slid down to sit on Sparrow's back.

"First one's for me." His sharp incisors flashed in the chandelier's light as he pried the tin loops up from the left wing. Tumbling free, it half fell, half floated to rattle against the floor below. "And now this is for the chickadee."

Again, his incisors pulled the tin free and let the second wing drop.

Sparrow's clockwork whirred audibly inside his body, with nothing to power. "I feel so light!"

"Told ya so." The live mouse reached up and took the string in his paws. Hauling himself back up the line, he reached the flying mechanism in no time at all. "Ready now?"

"Yes! Oh yes, wind me! Wind me!"

Lickety-split, the key sank into the winding mechanism and the live mouse began turning it. The sweet familiar sound of a spring ratcheting tighter floated down from above, filling the room. The other clockwork animals crept closer; even Chickadee felt the longing brought on by the sound of winding.

When the live mouse stopped, Sparrow said, "No, no, I am not wound nearly tight enough yet."

The live mouse braced himself with his tail around an arm of the chandelier and grunted as he turn the key again. And again. And again. "Enough?"

"Tighter."

He kept winding.

"Enough?"

"Tighter. The boy never winds me fully."

"All right." The mouse turned the key three more times and stopped. "That's it. Key won't turn no more."

A strange vibration ran through the sparrow's body. It took Chickadee a moment to realize that he was trying to beat his wings with anticipation. "Then watch me fly."

The live mouse pulled the key out of the flying mechanism and hopped up onto the chandelier. As he did, Sparrow swung into action. The flying mechanism whipped him forward and he shrieked with glee. His body was a blur against the ceiling. The chandelier trembled, then shook, then rattled as he spun faster than Chickadee had ever seen him.

"Live Mouse, you were rig—" With a snap, his flying mechanism broke free of the chandelier. "I'm flying!" Sparrow cried as he hurtled across the room. His body crashed into the window, shattering a pane as he flew through it.

The nightingale stopped her song in shock. Outside, the boy shrieked and his familiar footsteps hurried under the window. "Oh pooh. The clockwork sparrow is broken."

The mother's voice said, "Leave it alone. There's glass everywhere."

Overhead, the live mouse looked down and winked.

Chickadee pecked the ground, with her mechanism wound properly. The live mouse appeared at her side. "Thanks for the wings."

"I trust they are satisfactory payment?"

"Sure enough. They look real pretty hanging on my wall." He squinted at her. "So that's it? You're just going to keep on pecking the ground?"

"As long as you keep winding me."

"Yeah. It's funny, no one else wants my services."

"A pity."

"Got a question for you though. Will you tell me how to get to Messrs DeCola and Wodzinski?"

"Why ever for?"

"Well, I thought . . . I thought maybe Messrs DeCola and Wodzinski really could, I dunno, fix 'em on me so as I can fly."

Chickadee rapped the ground with laughter. "No, Mouse, they

cannot. We are all bound to our integral mechanisms." She cocked her head at him. "You are a live mouse. I am a clockwork chickadee, and Messrs DeCola and Wodzinski are nothing more than names on a scrap of paper glued to the bottom of a table."

FLIGHT

Jeremiah Sturgill

Brow lift. Neck lift. Face lift.

Blepharoplasty—not familiar with the term? Pretend I said eyelid surgery. To make them slant to the outside, that's all; the exotic look is in. Trust us. You'll love it. Rhinoplasty—a nose job, that's all. Not just a reshaping, mind you, but a *reimagining*. First, we'll add that beautiful upward tilt (yes, like hers—and hers—and hers), then we'll reduce the size and narrow the bridge. You may need to breathe through your mouth afterwards, but once we cap your teeth, you'll thank us for it.

Next is cosmetic otoplasty—that's for your ears—followed by collagen injections in your lips and cheeks. Removal of your second chin, and the insertion of an implant to help shape the first one. Permanent laser hair removal below your lower lip, above your upper lip, and for your sideburns too (I can't *believe* you have sideburns!). We may as well take off your eyebrows while we are at it. You can draw them on in the future, if you want to go retro. Or schedule a follow-up for replacements, if they come back in style.

Liposuction's next, then abdominoplasty (just another word for tummy tuck, girl, no need to worry). After that, we'll staple your stomach, reshape your buttocks, and make sure your love handles are all-the-way gone—nip and tuck and all that nonsense. You get the idea.

Of course, there's still the grand finale, the one no woman would be complete without: breast augmentation. Enlargement and reshaping in your case. In most cases, actually, but that's not important. All you have to do is show up. We mail you the bill.

The last day comes and it's done—you're done, it's all downhill from there. Just a few months of rehabilitation, followed by a simple maintenance routine. A chemical peel treatment and derm abrasion therapy every now and then for your complexion, along with the daily, oil-free, skin-exfoliating face wash. And that Hollywood all-liquid seven-day miracle diet? Why not. Couldn't hurt. Fen-Phen and caffeine pills? Sure. If anything goes wrong, you can always file a lawsuit.

All right. You've been faithful. You've done everything you needed to do, and it has worked. You can hardly believe that beautiful woman in the mirror is you.

Catching your breath in the doctor's office, you don't even mind the wait. It feels good just to sit still. Well, not *still*. Your foot keeps twitching, and you can't seem to make it stop. But why would you want to? It's good to keep moving. Helps burn those calories.

They call your name and you walk into the examination room and sit down again. Your foot keeps up its hypnotic spasming, and everything looks like it's underwater. He comes out, the doctor does, and you lift up your shirt. He pinches you with cold metal on your stomach, your back, your thighs.

"Abigail, I'm sorry," he says, and you can see it in his eyes: the news is bad. "Your body-fat index is point-oh-six." He looks like he wants to cry.

You can't help yourself. *You* cry. You deserve to feel bad, tubby. Fatso. Whale. Blimp. Pig. Point-oh-six? How could you have been so weak? Too many calories, that's the problem. You stumble on your way out of the office, ignoring the secretary when she calls out your name. You decide then and there that something's going to have to give, and isn't going to be you. You cut you intake in half—three hundred calories a day is more than enough. Decadent, even. You've worked too hard for this to end now, for it to end like this, only—

Of course it's not enough. You're still not perfect. It doesn't matter how skinny you are if you're *ugly*. Thin *and* beautiful, that's the ticket. Only you chickened out at the end, before they were finished. One last procedure, that's all. One last procedure, and you'll finally know what it's like to be pretty.

Dr. Bernstein handles the height augmentation—he always does the best job, gets all the best dwarfs. Not that you're a midget. Or are they *little people* now?

Over the course of six months, he breaks each leg three times in three different places. With the help of a special brace while they heal, he gives you another two and one-eighth inches of height. You grin and bear the pain, because it's worth it. It's so worth it. It's *gotta* be worth it.

It is worth it, for the pain pills he prescribes afterward if nothing else.

One day in his office for a follow-up exam, you pick up last month's medical science journal and see an article about hip replacements. About strong, light, titanium alloys. It seems so obvious. Why hadn't you thought of it before?

You dip into the trust fund (thankful your parents got that big life insurance policy just in time) and pull some strings, grease some wheels, sign some waivers. Three hundred thousand dollars and seven months later, 88% of your bones have been replaced by man-made parts, some lighter than the original by as much as half an ounce. The doctor even helps you pick out the supplements you need to purchase every month from the local GNC to stay healthy.

"Vitamin D," he reiterates before you leave. "It's very important to get your vitamin D."

You step on the scale and smile.

You've done it. For sure, this time. You jump up and down, squealing with delight, and clap your hands. They clank a little mechanically now, but the sound is actually quite musical, once you get used to it. Spots dance in front of your eyes. You begin to sweat. You shouldn't be exerting yourself so much, silly girl. Take a caffeine pill.

Whew, that's better. Now . . . what were you doing?

Oh yes. The celebration!

You go to your favorite restaurant—you sit at your favorite table—and the waiter, the cute Spanish one who always flirts with you, smiles and brings you your regular order. You take a long moment and smell the delicious aroma of the non-fat artificial vanilla flavoring ice cream substitute, and it's heaven. You're in heaven. You know it's the wrong thing to do, you know that it's bad for you, but you can't help yourself: you put your spoon into the ice cream, *and then inside your mouth!*

Oooohhh, everything is so cold and delicious! You let the ice cream substitute melt on your tongue, you let it run over your taste buds, you shiver in delight until—

Enough! You can't take it anymore! You run to the bathroom and rinse out your mouth with some of the bottled water in your purse. Can't be accidentally swallowing any, you naughty thing! In your haste to cleanse the badness, you spray water out all over the mirror.

But what if you were too late? What if you already had swallowed some, just a little, so little that you hadn't even noticed? You go into the stall and shut the door behind you, and you're proud for a moment that you don't even need to use your fingers anymore.

When you go to see the doctor the following day, you lift up your shirt and he pinches you with cold metal on your stomach, your back, your thighs.

He frowns. "This can't be right," he says. He looks confused. He stares at you. He helps you stand up and takes you over to the scales. He fiddles with the weights for a few minutes, but no matter what he does it still says the same thing. You smile your secret little smile, the one you smile sometimes when your face is too tired for the other one, the one others can see, and you know that the instrument is correct. You know it, but it's just not official until a doctor says so. No—the *Doctor. Capital* D. You can't wait to hear him say it. You can't wait to hear him say it, you can't wait to hear him say it. You can't wait. What the hell is *he* waiting for?

"Abigail," he says, finally giving up on the scale, "I don't understand it. How can you be six-two, weigh only fourteen pounds, and still be alive?"

You smile at him with the other smile, the external one, even though the effort threatens to prematurely wear you out. "I know, doctor. I amaze even myself sometimes."

You strut a little as you walk out of the office.

Six weeks later, you meet the man of your dreams: a multibillionaire prince in exile, who makes his home in Connecticut now that the royal family of—wherever, you were never good at geography—has fallen out of favor. What makes him so special, though, is that you like him for who he is, and he likes you for who you are. It's not your body—so perfect now, after all of your hard work—or his money and his title. No, it's the *little* things that make the two of you work so well together, like how each of you can't help but smile when you see the other and how you never run out of things to talk about. You know, the *important* stuff.

In fact, both of you were madly, wildly, truly in love (with the stars in your eyes and that warm glow in your hearts) well before it registered in your brains: it was the crotch-area that caught on first, you joke to all of your jealous friends.

Someday, if they're lucky, maybe they can find a catch half as good. The poor plain things.

Two months after you meet him, the day finally arrives. *The* day, the one you both worked so hard to obtain: your wedding day. You have on a simple white dress, no train, with very little lace work around the top. It accentuates your augmented bosom, and the rail-thin, rock-hard abdomen you sweated blood and tears and money to earn. The one extravagance in the simple ensemble is the veil—so large, airy, and white it looks like a cloud-halo around your head. That's why you bought it. He always calls you his little angel.

You step out of the limo on the big day and begin walking up the steps to the church. You take your time, resting every few steps and swallowing caffeine pills for energy when necessary. It's hard to do something so physical now that you've perfected your body, but the thought of your prince waiting for you at the top gives your blood all the strength and vigor it needs—until *it* happens.

Damn the veil. It would never have happened without the veil. You're so thin, so perfect! There would have been no purchase for the wind. But you *are* wearing the veil, and you can't take it back now even though you scream as the gust of air slams into you from the side and lifts you up into the sky.

The veil spreads out, all fifty thousand dollars of it, and it catches the wind almost as though it had been designed to do so from the very beginning, almost as though you really are an angel and the veil is your wings. You rise up into the air, higher and higher, and for a second your strained heart beats so fast that you are afraid it will burst. So you hold off on the caffeine pill you were about to swallow until it slows down again.

Your prince sees it all happen from the chapel, and he races from the church to his car. His driver speeds off while he makes a call on his cell phone, and for two whole minutes you see nothing of him at all until—it comes. The private helicopter. You smile when you see that your prince himself is there within it, right beside the pilot, shouting orders and gesturing wildly at you, his love. His princess. His *angel*.

The chopper closes in, but it doesn't work. You're far too light now, and the veil is far too efficient at catching the wind. Whenever the helicopter rises up to meet you, the gusts created by its whirling blades do nothing but send you higher and higher into the atmosphere.

Eventually the air is too thin for the helicopter to follow. You watch as it recedes, shrinking beneath you, becoming smaller and smaller—a dot—until finally, it is gone. The whole of planet Earth takes its place in stretching out beneath your feet, and you wave hello.

I'm queen of the world, you think. Smiling, you reach out with your arms and grab hold of the moon, pulling it to your bosom and snuggling close.

You wish mom were alive to see you, but she isn't and doesn't, and in fact, no one ever sees you again. Not ever. But late at night, your many friends and the adoring public that fawned so jealously after your fairy tale wedding to the prince of—wherever—often look up into the sparkling sky. Up at your legend, to stare and silently wonder at which light above was added on that blustery, almost wedding day in March.

All of them, you say in your secret voice. *All of them.*

But they don't hear you. And every time you think of using your other voice, the one they could hear, it hardly seems worth the effort.

CAPTAIN'S LAMENT

Stephen Graham Jones

My name is Quincy Mueller, but since the merchant marines I've been known almost exclusively as Muley. It has nothing to do with my character, however. Far from being obstinate or contrary, I'm in fact liberal and engaging. A more enthusiastic conversationalist you're not likely to find; sailors are lonely, I mean, and hungry for company. If anything, I suppose—and this just because I'm honest to a fault—I err toward the overbearing, as isolation is something I've had my fill of.

And yes, if you detect a hit of defensiveness in my voice, you're not far from the mark. That so much should have come from a simple misunderstanding, one night twenty years ago, is so far beyond comprehension that it's actually amusing, I think, or at least revealing of human nature.

But I get ahead of myself.

Never mind that you already know my story. That you more than likely grew up with it.

To begin, then, twenty years ago I was thirty-eight, salty and fully-bearded, recovering from a near-fatal accident which had left me convalescing for nearly fourteen months. During those weeks upon weeks in bed, the room uncomfortably *still*—I hadn't been landlocked for more than two consecutive months since my twenty-second year, when I thought marriage was the cure for loneliness—I could feel my skin growing pale and translucent, my lips becoming tender without salt to rime them. Because of the injuries to my throat, too, the doctors wouldn't allow me any tobacco; I couldn't even chew upon my pipe.

I'll spare you the fates I wished upon those doctors—curses I picked up in ports all over the world—but, looking back, I see of course that they more than likely wanted me out of their hospital as much as I wanted out myself.

Since the ninth month, I had said so little, even, that they called for a battery of tests to gauge my psychological health. Though I tried to tell them all I needed was a view of the sea, the smell of brine, still, they poked and prodded my mind until I did in fact shut down. I'm not proud of it, but, like the tarpon on the deck, his side still bleeding from the gaff, I'd flopped around as long as I could, and found that useless, so was now just staring, waiting for this ordeal to be over.

The nurses took turns rolling me from side to side to ministrate my sores and perform other indignities.

In my head, though, I was sailing. On the open sea, a boat pitching beneath me, I was beyond the reach of their needles and swabs and catheters and small, polite questions.

As the days passed, they came to my room less and less, content that my body would either heal itself in time or that I would, one day when they weren't looking, simply stop trying.

To them, I mean, even twenty years ago I was already an antique, a throwback to another century, another way of life.

And, if I'm to be honest here, yes, I did indeed stop trying, finally. But the body breathes whether you want it to or not. The heart keeps beating. Perhaps because it knows more than you do—knows that, past this experience, a whole new life will open up, and whatever infirmities persist, they can be dealt with one by one.

That's all in the future, though.

Right then, on my back in bed, miles from the shore, dose upon dose of antibiotic and painkiller pulsing through my veins, it was hard not to feel sorry for myself. To let that consume me.

It was finally a nurse by the name of Margaret whom I woke to one day. She was dabbing the wetness away from the corners of my eyes, and adjusting the various lines that went into and out of me.

"Does it hurt?" she said, her fingertips light on my right forearm.

I closed my eyes, made her disappear.

The next time I woke, however, she was there again. Evidently she'd been talking for some minutes, telling me about her social life, her family, her dreams and aspirations. I let her words flow over me like water and studied the cursive letters of her name, and watched as, in slow motion, like picture cards flipping one after the other, she pointed a syringe into one of the tubes that fed me.

How long this went on, I don't know. If I'd first seen her on a Wednesday though, her badge still new enough to be hand printed, then this was at least a Monday.

What she talked about the most was a certain boy named Billy, I think. How he'd wronged her and was continuing to wrong her, but she was going to show him.

I opened my mouth to tell her something but only emitted a rusty creak, my voice broken from dis-use.

She smiled, pursed her lips, patted my tender right arm and asked if I wanted to see the ocean?

Though I couldn't talk, still, she saw the answer in my eyes—I've always had expressive eyes—and, with the help of another nurse, maneuvered my atrophied body into a gleaming silver wheelchair, pushed me down hall after hall, my heart beating *intentionally* for the first time in months, the fingers of my left hand gripping the brown plastic armrest, her subdued laughter behind me tittering out between her closed lips.

If I could have spoken, I was going to tell her how, if she wanted, I might name my next ship the *Margo*, after her, and all the rest after that as well: *Margo II, Margo III, Margo IV*, a fleet of *Margo*s fanned out across the shipping lanes from here to the South Pacific.

But of course that was just talk—I'd never owned my own ship before, and didn't have one waiting for me when I got better.

And anyway, where she was taking me was a joke of sorts.

She finally stopped our perambulations in the waiting room, with my chair pushed up to a small aquarium with exotic fish, and, every ten seconds, a treasure chest that would burp air up to the surface.

I closed my eyes, woke again to Margaret's hand on a syringe, then slept and slept and slept.

The next time I came to she was stroking the top of my left hand and talking about Billy again.

Evidently I was supposed to have forgotten about the waiting room, about the ocean.

I can remember ever shoal in every port I've ever drawn water in, though.

I shut my eyes and shut my ears and let her have my hand. Just that.

How long this cycle repeated itself, I don't know. My guess would place it at two months; after a while Margaret became a practiced-enough nurse that she could haul me into my chair herself, just by leveraging me with her hips and the brakes on my bed, and I was a practiced-enough patient to believe that what she was shooting into me syringe by syringe was salt water, and that the dreams I had were just the ocean inside, bending itself to the moon.

Instead of going to the waiting room now, she was walking me outside, her voice drifting around me. The air was supposed to be good for me, I think. It was stale, though; there was no salt in it, no spray, and the horizon was forever blocked by trees and buildings, the sky empty of properly-winged birds.

One day, as had to happen, I suppose, Margaret asked her question again: Did I want to see the ocean?

I tried to move my left hand to indicate that I got this joke, yes, thank you, how nice, but I don't think she was looking anyway.

Back in the room this time, instead of pushing the sharp nose of the syringe into the line that went into my injured arm, she instead emptied it an inch into my mattress.

"I don't want you going to sleep just yet," she said, winking.

It made my heart beat, not with fear, but, in spite of what I knew, hope.

That night—I could tell it was night by the window—she came back for me. Her shift was over; she had her overcoat on over her thin cotton uniform.

I opened my mouth to ask a question but she just patted my shoulder and swung me down into my chair.

As you've by now of course guessed, we weren't going to the waiting room and we weren't going to the paved walking path, but the back door, and, past that, Margaret's large car.

She folded me into the passenger seat, my chair in the trunk.

"Wher—?" I tried to get out, but she guided my hand back down to my lap, eased her car down the slope of the parking lot.

Across the road there were sirens, and, walking through a pool of light, a police officer with a dog on a leash.

Margaret tensed and smiled at the same time.

"One of the slobbering maniacs, Mr. Mueller," she said, nodding to the woods. "Probably just wanted to see the *ocean*, right?"

"Muley," I tried to tell her.

Even though the road we took was more downhill than up, which is to say we were heading generally closer to sea-level, I had no illusions. After the aquarium in the waiting room, I knew I was going to be lucky to even smell the salt through her air conditioner vents, much less feel any spray on my face.

At the same time, however, if this was to be an end to my suffering, then so be it.

I pushed my back into the cup of her passenger seat and waited for whatever was to come.

As I'd expected, instead of following signs to the marina or some other place of portage, she instead wound us through a maze of residential streets I could never retrace. Billy wasn't down any of them, though, in spite of her muttering his name. Vaguely, I had the idea that her intent was to induce pity in him by pretending I was her war-addled uncle; that, for a few minutes, he was going to have to pretend to be who I was supposed to be expecting him to be. Which is to say *Margaret's*.

The profanity seeping over from the driver's side of the car, too, though vituperative and heartfelt, still it was light, amateurish. I'd heard worse in Morocco at fourteen years of age, and just over a bow line tied improperly. How that Moroccan sailor might have cursed had his intended been with someone else, it burns my ears just to think about it, and makes me smile a little too. Other people's suffering can be comical, I mean, when seen from a distance. Even mine, I suppose.

That's not to say I can't still remember the fear that rattled up through me, however, when Margaret took her car from asphalt to gravel, and then from gravel to dirt. The trees crowded around us, made the sky small. I started breathing faster, so that she had to look over, narrow her eyes.

"This isn't a good time for this," she said.

I closed my eyes.

Under her thigh was a hunting knife, the kind with a rosewood handle and a brass finger guard.

At a certain point on the dirt road, she turned the lights of her car off, and, when we saw the tail lights she evidently knew, she turned her car off as well, coasted into a slot between two large trees.

For a long time then we just sat there, the two of us, and, slowly, I tuned into a new set of sounds: the woods. And, unless as I was mistaken—as it turned out, I wasn't—the taste of salt in the now-still, un-air-conditioned air.

The sea. She was close.

I tried not to let this knowledge flash across my face.

In her lap now, Margaret had a rope. She was trying to tie a knot but making a complicated job of it. My left hand floundered over almost on its own, guided the end of the rope up and under and back on itself. She appreciated this, pulled the knot tight, nodded a reluctant thank you to me and then would no longer meet my eye. Such is the way we treat the rabbit we're about to carve for dinner, I suppose.

It had felt good though, the rope against my skin again.

Margaret patted the noose she now had and stood from the car, locking all four doors before walking away into the darkness.

What did she need me for then? The *knot*?

I stared at the spot she'd disappeared into but couldn't figure it out, and finally consoled myself trying to roll my window down to bring the sea nearer. It was electric, though, and I had no keys.

How long I sat there after she left, I have no idea. If I slept, it was only for minutes, and if I hummed, it was only to hear my own voice. In the absence of monitors and pumps and footsteps, the world was rushingly quiet, and not close enough.

At some point, anyway, Margaret strode across a bare place between the trees. The rope was no longer across her shoulder, and the knife was held in her fist, low.

I tried rolling my window down again, and was still clattering away at the button when she was suddenly at my door with the car keys.

"Your turn," she said, smiling.

Sprayed across her shirt was blood that had dried almost black.

I nodded, gave my weight to her, let her heave me into my chair, pull me backwards through the trees, dump me into a clearing behind the car I was pretty sure was Billy's.

The reason I say this is that, hanging from a thick limb above the car was a man of no more than twenty-two. A boy, really. His hands had been tied behind his back, and his throat had been carved out. From years of handling knives, I instantly understood the angles: someone had sat on his chest and worked on his neck with a blade. Calmly, deliberately.

And then he'd been strung up, with a knot only a sailor would know.

Which *was* of course what she needed me for.

She pulled the empty wheelchair back into the darkness and I looked where she was looking: to Billy's car, its vinyl roof pattered with blood.

Through the foggy glass, facing forward—away—there was a girl.

I shook my head no, no, and, because the sea was close and because it didn't matter anymore, I found the strength to pull myself forward with my left hand. It was torturously slow, however, and filled my loose pants with twigs and dirt which nettled my bed sores. But the girl. I had to tell her, had to get her to leave, to *live*.

Because I couldn't stand, I of course latched onto her bumper with my left hand, and then on the fourth try was able to hook my right under her wheel well, pull myself forward by inches.

By this time she was aware of the sound I was, had locked the door, had, even though it wouldn't help her see, turned on the dome light and started grinding the starter.

She was saying her boyfriend's name louder and louder, and then shrieking a little.

It didn't matter, though. All I had to do was pull myself up level with her window and tell her about Margaret, that we had to go *now*, that, that—

I didn't even know what. But something.

With my left hand I gripped the ledge of her back door, and with my right, the large functional hook the doctors were trying to teach me to use, I pulled hard on her door latch, my head rising even as the car started, pulling me up, up.

I couldn't hold the car there, though.

It dragged me for maybe ten feet, and then the straps on the hook let go of the stump my forearm had become and I was rolling in the dirt, Billy swinging above me, Margaret in the darkness all around, and this is how stories begin, yes.

But none of you were there for the part after the girl left, my hook clattering in her door latch, the part where I crawled arm over arm through the trees until first light delivered to me a beach, a surf, which I rolled in for hours, and have never really left since. Not longer than overnight, anyway. And, no, the name I had then, it's not the same I have now—the world is the world, after all—but my ship, my lady, she is the *Margo*. Not in honor either, but in defiance: six years after my escape from dry-dock, I read the account of that night, and found that the authorities had managed not only to scrub any reference of Margaret from the public records, but, because of the violent, infectious nature of her crime perhaps, they'd also erased the very hospital I'd convalesced in, so that all that was left for the newspaper to report was that a patient, deeply disturbed by having had to cut off his own arm off with the neck of a bottle to escape drowning, had escaped the mental hospital the town was built around, and succeeded in killing and hanging a young boy named William Jackson before disappearing, presumably, into the sea.

I'll admit to that last part anyway.

BIRDWATCHER

Garth Upshaw

I was poisoning crows the day the aliens arrived. They're smarter than you might think—crows, not aliens—and they don't go for any of the easy stuff anymore. I had some good roadkill, two squirrels and a raccoon, but I couldn't work up any enthusiasm for using it. The crows would caw and peck at the corpses as carefully as a dowager entering her bath. Nowadays, I had to mash D-Con into a virulent green powder, mix it with honey or peanut butter, and spread it on the underside of a flashy piece of metal. Crows love the sparkle and glitter, and they must know it's bad, but they pick it up anyway.

My mom's backyard stretches towards a narrow gully choked with blackberry and old-man's beard. Right before the ground drops out from underneath you, a gnarled old walnut tree stands guard. The trunk's as solid as a cement pillar, but covered with head-sized lumps that weep a yellow sap, trapping twigs, dead leaves, and insects in a sticky gruel. The branches are treacherous, thick as regular trees, and jut out at all angles like arthritic fingers. They break off with no warning, crushing the ferns and hosta underneath. The crows love the walnut tree, gathering like impudent black leaves, squawking and shouting in a raucous tumult.

That day, I watched from mid-yard, hidden behind a sheet of gray weathered plywood I'd cut a viewing slit in. A faded pink-and-green lawn umbrella cast an oval of welcome shade, but kept the air close and hot. Binoculars pressed against my sweaty face. I shifted in the folding chair, thighs constrained by the unyielding metal arm supports, and took a long swallow of tepid cherry Slurpee. The sun burned a hole in the sky like the business end of a welding torch, flashing off the pieces of Mom's hand mirror I'd shattered and arranged on a low, wide stump.

It's not worth doing a project unless you do it right, and I'd placed each piece with an aesthetic eye towards the whole effect. A landing area free of glass on the side of the stump away from me. Shards tilted different directions to send reflected sunlight 360 degrees. A central triangular piece propped so as to give a curious crow a chance for self-examination. The back of each deadly shard was slathered with my peanut butter concoction.

A dozen big crows descended from the tree, cawing and gabbling. They pranced around the stump, hopping with wings half spread, cocking their heads at the bits of mirror. Their eyes drank in the light, black and shiny as a new coat of paint. An ant crawled up my right calf, and I reached down, slowly, slowly, and ground it against my leg.

The sky flashed orange and purple, like a years' worth of sunsets had been dumped catywampus and stirred with a big stick. I looked up, surprised and mystified. Purple and orange. My high school colors. It was afternoon, four o'clock at the absolute latest.

"Doyle? Doyle, are you outside?" Mom's high voice cut through the backyard like a mosquito's whine. "What was that flash of light? I know you're there." Crows flew back to the tree, their flapping wings sounding like half-hearted applause.

I waited to answer, irritated that she'd violated my space. "I'm bird watching," I finally yelled, twisting in my chair so I could see her. She stood at the sliding glass doors, bleached blond hair cut in an expensively retro style.

"Doyle, could you come here?" Her fingers tugged at her bathrobe, pulling it tighter around her surgically enhanced figure. "Something's gone terribly wrong with the power." She cocked her head at the swirling colors still leaking from the sky. "What's all that? Northern lights?"

I sighed, levering myself out of my chair, and letting the binoculars

swing free from around my neck. "Don't be stupid. We're too far south."
A wave of petulance swept over me. I trudged towards the stump. The
afternoon was ruined.

I drew a tarp over my project, knocking a shard out of alignment
in spite of my care. I tucked the corners down, and made my way up
the lawn to the house, feeling like I was wading through hot syrup. I
stopped at the back patio, peeling my T-shirt away from my belly and
flapping the cloth to get a slight cooling effect.

A frown wrinkled the perfect skin of Mom's forehead. "If you'd go
on a diet, get some exercise, or maybe go out with a nice girl . . . "

"You said the power was down?"

"How'd your interview go?" She flashed her white teeth at me. "For
Mr. Perfect SAT scores, the job should be a breeze."

I turned, and pressing a finger to close one nostril, blew a viscous
stream of yellow snot out my nose. Most of it landed on the wilted
geraniums that fringed the patio, and I used my T-shirt to wipe the rest
off the side of my face. "What do I need money for?"

Mom flinched and retreated inside. "Dad will be home soon, and
I've been planning a pork roast." Cool air poured from the house.

"Roger loves his dead pig."

"He wants to be your friend." Mom backed into the kitchen and
took an invigorating swig from a tall glass. Ice rattled.

"Who needs friends?" I followed her inside, leaving the door open
behind me.

Mom pushed several buttons on the stove. "See? Nothing."

Détente, then. I flicked a light switch to no effect. "I'll check the
breakers."

"Thanks, dear. I knew I could count on you." Mom kissed the air
near my head.

I rummaged through the utility drawer, found a flashlight, and
checked the batteries. The breaker box was on the far side of the garage
wall, an obstacle course I was loath to traverse in the dark. "Wait
here."

The hot, stale air of the garage sucked my remaining energy away.

I played the yellow flashlight beam over the cobwebs on a jetski that blocked the breaker box, analyzing my path through the detritus of aborted recreational attempts to "bring our family together."

I'd just flipped the metal latch when a voice whispered in my ear. "Hello, Doyle."

I jumped, knocking a box of deck screws clattering across the cement floor. A clean-cut man of about forty, dressed in brown slacks and a purple and orange button-down shirt, stood beside me. I spluttered in surprise. "Who the fuck are you?"

"We arrive today." He nodded his head. Every hair stayed in place. "All at once. From far away. For everybody." He smiled, teeth shining in the gloom like a row of mirrors.

"How'd you get in?" I inched my hand closer to a plumber's wrench.

"We bring greetings, gifts for you." He held out a glowing white egg, folding my hand around its warmth, and pressed the top with his thumb.

I sucked in my breath. The garage had vanished. I stood on a beach, waves swishing in and swirling around my ankles. The cool water splashed to my knees. My arms felt firm and strong. A bright orange Frisbee sailed over my head and I jumped, catching it one-handed and flicking it back before I landed. My real father laughed and ran into the surf, diving into an oncoming wave after the flying disk.

"See?" The man's smile gleamed in the darkness. "You can choose anytime." He let go of the egg, pressing its smooth heaviness into my hand, before stepping aside and walking away, growing smaller and smaller without ever leaving the garage until he winked out and was finally gone.

I stumbled backwards, abandoning the breaker box. My heart beat so hard I thought my chest would burst. I pushed the door to the house open, brushing spider webs from my face with the hand that still held the egg.

My mother stood in the hallway, hair pressed flat on one side of her head. I looked away from her open bathrobe, not wanting to see more.

She raised her arm. An egg, twin to mine, glowed at me from her hand. Tears leaked from her eyes. "Sorry, Doyle. I haven't been the greatest mom." She pressed the top of her egg and vanished.

I sit in the lawn chair, hot air leaden and heavy on me. I try to suck more Slurpee through my straw, but I've reached bottom, and the rattling sound echoes in my ears. I can't hear any cars, and the burnt blue sky is empty of con trails. I stroke the smooth outside of the egg in my lap, and then slip it into a pocket. A crow lands on the stump, cocking its black head sideways. Its feathers are mottled, mangy. I press the binoculars hard into my cheekbones, trying to recover the sense of excitement I used to feel watching the birds take my bait.

I leap up, flailing my arms and knocking the plywood blind over. Crows scatter in a flapping black cloud, cawing their disapproval at me. I lurch to the stump and sweep the shards of glass onto the ground. The tip of one piece cuts my palm, and I bring my hand to my mouth. My blood tastes hot and salty. I hitch my shorts up and turn towards the gully, wondering if any blackberries are ripe.

THE BURIED YEARS

Loreen Heneghan

Dearest Marcella,

My love, in the course of our letters I may not have told you how distressed I become upon seeing skeletons. I find myself revolted by their empty eyes and the unhinged way they walk through the streets at dusk. A better man would be respectful, but—imperfect soul that I am—I've never put flower-crowns on the bare skulls of the dead. Why should I? Scholars have proven the dead do not care for our flowers.

While at the university, I read a treatise describing the scientific studies performed by the Institute of Eutrist. In these, a person in mourning was placed on the path walked by the remains of someone dear to them. The mourner, in their heated state, often interprets small stops and hitches in the movement of the bones to be signs of recognition. The study concluded that the dead show no more recognition for their mothers than they do for strangers. It is as old wives say: "Your dead will pause, and pass on by."

By this, some fishwife might mean it's time to give up old grief, but scientifically the phrase holds as much truth. A skeleton's only measurable intent is to walk the gods' road to the end. They only pause for those who stand in their way.

So is it odd for me to feel this way? When I see skeletons plodding back to the gate of the next world, I have never before seen them as a gentle reminder of life's transience. I see only empty people—brothers, friends, lovers—all hollowed out to nothing.

I am sure that you, my dearheart, have no fear of bones. When we met, I noted how you are as lively and clear-eyed as a jay bird. I envy that. As a physician, even one untried and fresh from the university, I should be used to the dead.

Henceforth, I shall have to be stronger, particularly in light of recent events.

Allow me to explain: I chose for us a house where the main road runs by our doorstep. I could have found a place that wasn't a thoroughfare built on one of the paths of the gods, but I do love to be in the hubbub of life. I love life far more than I hate to see the dead. I'm sure you will enjoy it here, sweet Marcella, when you return from the coastal temple and the terms of our betrothal are complete.

Here, both your family and mine have begun arrangements. Your eldest aunt has conducted several meetings of the family women. It has been made clear to me I must attend each meeting, though my suggestions on our marriage have yet to prove helpful.

Your aunt is particularly keen on the details of color and dress. She is hoping we will have caged butterflies at the service. Certainly, I can bear the expense, but I wanted first to ask you if butterflies were your wish as well as hers.

Please write to your dear lady aunt. I believe your own thoughts on insects and fabric would assuage certain arguments among the good ladies of our soon joined family.

But these small details are not why I've written. Indeed, I believe I am avoiding putting my revelations to the page.

What I truly want to tell you, my sweet one, is that a certain matter (indeed, one that has cast a shadow over our betrothal) will be resolved.

Last week I was returning from a dinner with friends from the old school. Jeoffry, you probably remember. He and I both met you in Utherdan while you were entertaining suitables.

Ah, but still I delay! No more, sweet one, for this is what has happened.

I left my companions after moon rise. The lamps along the god's road had been lit and were burning brightly. The drinking houses overflowed with noise and laughter. The sweet-cake shop was still open, though it was long past eventide. I remember feeling more at ease than I had in many years.

An old woman called to me, "Take a flower, sir? A flower for a lovely lady?"

Even though you, dear one, are far away, I felt merry. I gave the woman a penny for a boutonnière of violets and secured them to my lapel. It was pure frivolity, since they would hardly be seen as I walked away from the lamplight, singing.

The half-moon had risen. It was much later in the night than anyone would expect to see the dead. So it was an unpleasant surprise when I noted a skeleton walking toward me on the road. The the bones were translucent, not solid like the newly dead. The fragile, near-luminance of the thing made me think it had walked a long way. Perhaps the bones had risen far from the road; perhaps it walked for months along a lonely mountain path. My only certainty was that they did not rise from a soft burial on temple hill.

It may surprise you, but I knew as soon as it approached that these were the remains of a woman. I am a trained doctor, but that is not how I knew her. Recognition did not come from the hip bone or some lesson of anatomy. I knew her by the way she moved.

Skeletons move in that unpleasant way of their own, but this one also stepped with a certain grace, a rolling firm-footedness. And I recognized that walk, if nothing else.

It almost stopped my heart to see it, and I stood in the road, reeling like one struck in the head. The skeleton did not pause, and as I watched I noticed a kind of pale, phosphorus light moved within what was once a body. The light throbbed like foxfire; first caged in her ribs, then flickering in her hollow eyes. I've heard of the ghost lights, but I had never seen them before that night. Nor had I believed in them.

Usually, only a certain kind of person will say they can see the lost half of the soul caught within the mortal remains. These types are rarely reputable, being mostly fortune tellers, charm sellers, and a particularly silly species of society-girl. I am none of these things. I am a man of medicine. I know the dead cast no measurable light. It's a mere trick of the dark-adapted eye.

Yet I knew the bones as I knew the footsteps. Marcella, I tell you truly, she was all that remained of my lost Bethany.

I promised your lady aunt that I would never speak of her though I know you must have heard. Now I must confess in full. Please forgive me.

She was no one. Beth was a bootmaker's child; her family without name or property. She knew little of art or poetry, but she could carved buttons to look like unbred roses. I intended to give up everything I had for her; my family, my name my inheritance and prospects.

Instead it was Bethany who left everything behind. She disappeared as though plucked into the sky. I gave up much to be with a woman beneath my class, then lost more in her aftermath. The society of women marked me as a scoundrel. My family feared I'd again mar their name, so I was pinned carefully between the marble fortress of the university and the unsubtle chaperons who dogged my steps should I so much as stroll beyond the grounds.

There have been days I hated poor sweet Beth, thinking her faithless instead of come to harm.

But that night on the road I saw her near-forgotten movements, a full two years from the day I'd tilted between anger and despair. It had taken her far too long to rise from the earth, and there was a deep notch upon her breastbone. I believe now that she had been buried deeply and in secret.

I stepped aside as she drew close. I know there is no point in waylaying the dead, and it is offensive to do so—but my feet felt like stones as I moved away from her. I suppose my heart was breaking, but I cannot be sure. Heartbreak is, after all, a poetic condition, not a medical one.

Beth's walk did not slow as she came, but she turned her empty face to me. Her skeletal hand reached out and she paused, ivory fingertips close to my sleeve. I took her bone fingers gently, then with my free hand tore the boutonnière from my breast—three violets pinned with a paper ribbon. I wish now that I'd had something finer to give her.

Beths's remains held the twist of paper for a moment. Then she raised it to her skull and tipped it gently into the empty socket of her eye. Could such an odd gesture be random? I do not know.

Then she continued on her path, Marcella, like any of the dead. She left me for the last time.

I wept, my dear. I admit to this—I wept in the street.

It is difficult to write, my hand shakes. Forgive me for how the ink runs and pools—I push too hard against the paper—but someone did this!

Someone killed a young woman—and this was the woman I once loved. You never knew Beth, my dear Marcella, though I wish you had. She was as lively and virtuous as yourself.

I know I am now engaged and have other duties, but I am compelled to investigate this death. Justice must be sought in this world, even for the dead. Please understand, my sweet dove, this is something I must do. You deserve a husband whose heart is at peace.

However, be assured that this leaves me free—perhaps more so than I have been in years. Beth is no longer a young love you'll find me sighing over.

I have found her. She is lost.

I swear to you, this will not interfere with the arrangements for this marriage whose prospects have brought much joy to me and both our families.

Marcella, please take this into your heart—the reason I write today is to to assure you that I will be loyal. I now have no other ties in this world. Even as I must search for unpleasant truths, I swear I will keep faith with you, both as a husband and as a father to any children we may have.

In life,
Your bridegroom

THE GLORY OF THE WORLD

Sergey Gerasimov

They went upstairs, to the second floor that was actually much higher than the first. An unknown contractor had sandwiched it in between the dimly lit twenty-second and the exceptionally roomy fifty-fifth, either for fun or as a publicity stunt. As they walked up they saw through the big windows an embarrassed town changed very much by the linear perspective, refracted here and there as if seen through a huge quivering prism, scared, shiny, dark-cornered. One of the corners folded up and the rain flickering along the horizon trembled there like piano strings.

The starry heaven gaped over the clouds. The constellations and shiny dabs of galaxies wheeled there, shivering with their own beauty. Seeing this, a lady with a tame cobra around her neck frowned and strained herself to unlock the door. She was long-legged and purebred like a Great Dane.

"Savior, hold it, please," she said.

She handed him the pensive cobra, and made her hands free for a two-handed key. Savior took the snake. The cobra shook its head as if rousing itself, then squashed his hand, smiling quite cheekily and glistening as if it were smeared with stale grease. Savior put the snake into a pot with a cocoa palm and it immediately, with rumbling stomach, muzzled into the soil rich in fluoric limestone.

"Shouldn't have done that," said the lady. "Now she'll gnaw the roots. She's a snake, a predator. Understand?"

Savior presented her with a bunch of red folios, and she gave him a condescending nod. They entered.

The boss sat at a round table elongated enough to receive lots of victuals, which formed a slanted turret in the middle of it. Steamed crab legs, made of wild sardine scale, crowned the turret. A few nonentities with indiscernible faces sat nearby, so the table was empty to the right and to the left as well.

A security guard with such a muscular neck that the muscles dangled below his shoulders slept at some distance. A dog, extremely lean and long, romped on a leash staying aloof. The pet was so attenuated by hunger that you had to have a really trained eye to distinguish it from the leash. It licked off its sweat reducing the environmental pollution. Very far away three moneychangers, small end evil like avian flu viruses, played cards for curtseys with a coal-miner. A buffoon played the pipe and sold doves.

Savior froze, stunned. He had expected to see something unbelievable here, but this impossible world was anti-believable, and it had a hypnotizing music of its own at that, a shrieking sort of music that can sound inside a happy lunatic's mind; it jammed a low, quiet voice of conscience Savior had been always listening to. This world looked him over with button eyes, grinned, let him in.

"I don't believe in it," Savior whispered.

"What about getting paid?" the world asked.

"Oh. It would be nice."

"Got dyspepsia?" the lady asked and Savior started.

"No, I was just thinking."

"Yeah, thinking gives me gas too," the lady said in a brain-shrinking voice.

"Hi," the boss said, "Savior? The one? Welcome."

He held out his hand with five nails, and the Savior shook it, feeling prone to cringe.

"Well, well, I know," the boss said. "Heard much about you, you're that tough guy who cast out all them that sold and bought in the temple, and even overthrew the tables of the moneychangers. It's my house! Ye have made it a den of thieves! Piss off everybody! I can appreciate such things. But, you know, *tempora mutantur, nos et mutamur in illis.*

I mean, times change. Just in case, if you forgot Latin. Today wine maketh us merry: and money answereth all things. By the way, want to drink? No? Pity. I know everything about you because my people never lie, though I don't believe them of course. So want to hear it from you. From the horse's mouth, ha-ha. Don't be modest. Position yourself. Can fly? Or walk on water?"

The boss took from the table a forty-three-barreled cigarette lighter.

"Yes," Savior said.

"Cool. Will you fly if I throw you out of the window, right now?"

The boss brushed Savior's cheek with his fingers, quick and spidery, incompatible with his plump face.

"No, I'd be killed. The ability to fly, uh . . . comes to me, from time to time. I can try, though. Maybe, if not very high . . . "

He flew up and hovered for a minute above the table. The lady was busy putting on her nose a layer of absolutely transparent powder. The coal-sweep had already lost the game and given out all the curtseys. Being sick and tired of everything, he pressed his stained face to the wall and charcoaled a self-portrait there. Savior was hovering. His face wore a dreamy look necessary for flights.

"That wasn't bad," the boss said. "Be my friend. Meet this girl. She's Denise. A female variant from Denis. And don't meet the others. They are morons."

The lady with the key slowly winked; she was aristocratic like an oyster in spinach. Then unscrewed a stiletto-heel and picked her teeth with it.

They spoke of this and that, then the conversation turned to food and stopped at this comprehensive point. The buffoon got tired of selling the lewd doves and, being hungry, sucked at his saliva ejector. The nonentities kept doing nothing. Their gazes moved up and down Denise's legs polishing them to a mirror luster. The words stirred in Savior's mouth, losing taste like a wad of chewing gum.

"They say you can live on spirit," said the boss in a voice of a business executive opening a staff conference. "I hope that's true."

Savior was about to say something noncommercial but changed his mind and answered artlessly. "Sometimes. But I eat, as a rule. Something low-caloric. Austere repast, you know."

"Cook yourself?"

"Yes."

"By a fiat of will?"

"No. I prefer a microwave."

The boss raised his brow as if surprised at such an extravagance. "Now you listen to me, bud," he said. "I want here and now, by a fiat of will. Make for me something really delicious and special to eat."

"I can cook for you cobra's flesh. Is it okay?"

"Go on, man, go on."

Savior took a porno magazine decorating the table and flipped through. One of the women fitted perfectly: snake-eyed and resembling a piece of meat. He decided to make the dish from this picture. Tore it out, crumpled, and placed on the plate. Intertwined his fingers over it.

The boss went out of the room not wanting to wait for at least fifteen minutes. The buffoon was licking the paints off the pictures and shoving them into the proper tubes; the dog watched him with a melancholic rapacity in its heart. Denise played with a gold watch chain and moved rhythmically her wonderful eyelashes, so long and dense that they could shovel humus.

"What else can you do?" she asked and made the moment flinch.

"Everything," Savior said.

"The most difficult, I mean."

"With a single word I can make a man happy."

"It's easy," Denise said, "I can do it too. Hey, guard, I order you to be happy."

The guard woke up and burst out laughing, junked up with official delight. He was prompt to carry out the orders to sob, to fall in love, to go mad and senile, to get prodigious acne, and at last to go to sleep again. The nonentities echoed, though not at all concerned. Savior was talking, keeping his mind intent. He developed some arguments to

Denise. She was listening to him with unflagging indifference. He was so carried away that he didn't even notice the sudden appearance of a black car smelling of expensive lubricant.

The guys in the car started shooting, and a bullet plowed through Savior's spinal column. He stooped a little more, trying to remain concentrated, but the smell of the smoldering varnish distracted him. The bullet, which had popped out of his chest, was spinning on the table, before his eyes, a puffing lead corpuscle scorching the polish. Denise fired back with an enviable sang-froid and picked off two of attackers: one of them died in the driver's seat; the other got a bullet in his lung. This one fell out of the car and immersed into the green shag of the carpet. The carpet liana crawled up to him planning to suck out all his fluids except the toxins. Two non-entities were killed immediately; the third tried to flee away but died of fright on the way. The moment wheezed and wriggled on the floor. Time kept going, but away from the penal acts. Time was accustomed to such scenes, it knew what to do.

Security guards came in time splitting their sides with belated laughter, and Denise shut them up. She leaned over the dying man and eyed with curiosity the incarnadine foam on his lips. She looked like a preteen school-girl with innocent buds of breasts under a t-shirt who for the first time pressed her orbital bone against the ocular of a microscope. Her face shone like a fluorescent lamp.

"Well, now," she said in a voice of a virgin waiting for her first kiss, "we met at last, didn't we? Oh, you want to die so much, no, no, don't cheat me, you're not dying yet, want a drop of water, huh? Nuts to you . . . Gimme a rag."

A guard gave it.

She moistened the rag in the aquarium where sharky-fish shaggy with algae finned optimistically, and moved it over the lips of the dying man. A drop dropped. The man moved, moaned, and she lifted her hand.

"Nope, no way, no water today," she said in a voice of a yeanling jumping around a barn.

The boss appeared at last, sat down at the table, and started peeling a sea tomato.

"What about my meat here?" he asked, then noticed the blood and scowled at that unhygienic nuisance. The blood washed itself off.

"Almost done," Savior said. "Why is she torturing him? Let him die."

"I'd like to, dude, but no. It's personal. He is the Denis. I mean, Denise is a female name made from him. They rubbed shoulders, then, you know how it goes, rubbed not only shoulders; now they're like a dog and a cat. I don't meddle with their lives. If the torture bothers you, make him die."

"I can't make anybody die."

"I can," the boss said in a voice of inborn certainty. "Hey, you there, die!"

Three guards died and the long dog turned his heels up. The fourth guard jumped out of the window trying to escape his master's anger. The buffoon got stricken by paralysis. The remote coal-sweep escaped with severe fright. In faraway Bonzibar an epidemic of crayfish distemper broke out. The carpet liana painted itself on the carpet simulating a black and white imprint. Sharky-fish, being deaf, didn't care a cuss.

"It wasn't for you, idiots," the boss said. "I was talking to Denis. Denis, die!"

And Denis died.

The boss touched Savior's jacket and shirt. The holes were real. The flesh had already healed the wound.

"Nice," the boss said. "Very nice. The rumors were true. Those guys in the car worked for a rival firm; they wanted to blip you off. They thought I could use you. But you are so difficult to kill, aren't you? Denise is also a cool wench, good for her."

"But if they'd killed me?"

"Then what's the use for me to buy you?" the boss said. "Well done, see? Have killed three birds with one shot. Checked you up, wiped their dirty nose, and Denise gave vent to her feelings. But you're a sly guy; they knew you're worth shooting at."

Saying this, the boss looked so piercingly that he cracked in the meantime the Bermuda Triangle mystery, and eight other mysteries, not as big as that one.

"Well. How much am I supposed to pay for you?" he went on.

"Seven hundred curtseys a week . . . Pre-tax," Savior breathed out.

"Pre-tax, well, may be," said the boss. "But first thing's first. Where's my dinner? Cobra's flesh."

Savior raised his palms. The dish looked well-roasted and smelled delicious. The boss waved to one of nonentities who waddled nearby.

"You try it first."

The nobody tasted the dish. "Ummm," he purred so melodically as if he had practiced over night at a Karaoke hall. His flesh got pimpled with goosebumps. He smiled with delight, opening his mouth like a dead lizard.

"Enough." The boss tried a bit, and chewed it with concentration. "Well, it doesn't taste like glue."

He paused, busy with chewing and swallowing. His fork stirred the convolutions of noodles.

"My people can cook better," the boss said slowly, with moments of leaden silence inserted between the words. "You've put too much salt in it. Why?"

"For the lack of concentration, maybe. The noise, the shooting, I was wounded . . . "

"Give him seven hundred curtseys," said the boss in a voice of an electric meat grinder revving up, "and get rid of him right away. Drop him somewhere outside. You think, boy, you are the only one so omnipotent at my disposal? I receive eight guys like you a day. The very archbishopissimus is at my command! Lack of concentration, did you hear that? Well, I think it's the next savior at the door. Just in time. Let him in."

The door opened and bent low.

The second savior entered and presented Denise with a bunch of red folios.

"I have a talent, a wonderful thing!" the second one sang out cheerfully, positioning himself in the proper way.

"Don't take it too personally," Denise said to the first Savior, "you were a wonderful freak. But we are highly competitive, you know."

The bodies had already vanished; the cobra's flesh was eaten. The boss wiped his glossy lips.

"Savior? The one? You're welcome."

But the last guard was still falling outside. In the very beginning, he had a hope to save his life because he was an all-round diving-into-shallow-reservoirs champion who specialized in puddles. The rain had just stopped and there were lots of puddles in the streets. He flew poising himself with his long hair. But half-way down a cooling breeze gently kissed him, saying goodbye, turbulenting the hair just enough to sweep him to the concrete wall. In a few seconds, the guard hit against the wall and turned into a wet blotch.

"*Sic transit gloria mundi*," he mumbled instructively in the end. Thus passed the glory of the world. But no, the glory did not pass with him: the sunset, dense and heavy like a red-hot stone block, glared over the town. The town floundered in this light like a blowfly in sunflower oil. Only this light was real; the disheveled policemen scared of anything real fired into the sky with their authorized slingshots. They closed the left eyes at that, or both, for additional bravery.

Savior saw that as he walked downstairs. At first he thought to save the falling guard but then changed his mind: right now he didn't feel like saving anybody. There's something wrong about this world, he thought, or is it just me? Millions of people live in this flat universe as oblivious as moth-eaten scarves to what is going on. No, I'm being too picky. Where has the glory of the world gone? Or am I just an interesting freak?

He went out into the street, looked up at the blackening sky, and saw the last drops of rain, which caught the light of street lamps; they were falling slowly like confetti. Then, on buying a cheap advertiser for a half of curtsey, he started perusing the columns. But in vain: saviors were required for unqualified and poorly-paid work. To gnash their teeth off-screen in dental prosthesis commercials for example.

TEETH

Stephen Dedman

The little oblong box was made of ebony: I had to give Klein credit for a sense of irony, and possibly his knowledge of the genre. I stared at the glistening white lumps of ivory inside, and shook my head. "Beautifully preserved, aren't they?" said Klein.

"Suspiciously," I growled. "How sure are you of their provenance?"

He made a see-sawing gesture. He'd never had the looks or the range to make it as an actor (though that hadn't stopped him trying), but he was a pretty good salesman. He worked for a well-known theatrical agency, mostly getting people the stuff that they wanted that couldn't be written into their contracts. "They came from Temple's collection. Before that, I have my doubts," he admitted, "but he could hardly have asked for documentation. Body-snatchers didn't go in for paperwork."

"So you expect me trust you? Or am I supposed to try extracting some DNA?"

Klein smiled. "You could, I suppose, if you had anything for comparison . . . but you'll have to buy them first." He closed the little casket with an audible snap. "I'm not giving away free samples here. And if you look up the records, you'll find that when they disinterred Poe's corpse in 1875, the sexton noted that while the skeleton was in near-perfect condition, the top teeth had been dislodged from the skull."

I knew the story, of course. In 1873, the philanthropist George Childs had been persuaded that Edgar deserved a better monument than an overgrown grave in the Poe family plot, and paid for a new memorial. "So who collected these? The sexton?"

"Maybe, or one of the gravediggers. You could still sell teeth back then, to be made into dentures: maybe he meant to do that, or maybe he realized how valuable they were . . . anyway, one of Childs' servants found them in his collection after his death in 1894, or so the story goes, and sold them to Jules Verne. After that, the trail is easier to follow, though they were always sold in secret. Temple bought them some time in the 1980s."

I tried to look unimpressed, and refilled my glass with Amontillado, leaving his empty. "What's in the other box?"

Klein's smile became a grin, and he opened the second ebon casket with a conjurer's flourish. These teeth had been set into dentures in a wire frame, though the work was obviously primitive. "Don't touch," he said, pulling the box away from me.

"Whose are these supposed to be?" I said, dryly. "His teeth when he was a boy?"

"His mother's," Klein gloated. "I don't know whose dentures they were, but those are her original teeth."

"You can't be serious."

Klein lost a minute fraction of his smugness. "The provenance on these is a little less reliable," he admitted, "but the story is interesting. You remember Poe's story 'Berenice'?"

I may have sniffed: just because I make movies, doesn't mean I can't read. 'Berenice' is not Poe's best story, and it's most interesting for containing the seeds for 'The Fall of the House of Usher' and 'Ligeia', as well as some disturbing autobiographical elements. The obsessive Egaeus is betrothed to his cousin Berenice, but only notices her beauty when he sees her in the haunted library where his mother had died. (Poe's own mother, a beautiful actress, had died of tuberculosis when he was two: he married his cousin Virginia six months after 'Berenice' was published, and she died of tuberculosis several years later.) After Berenice dies, Egaeus breaks into her tomb and steals her most attractive feature, her teeth. When readers complained about the story, Poe actually apologized to the editor who published it, claiming that he'd written it on a bet that he "could produce nothing effective on a subject so singular" and allowing "that it approaches the very verge of bad taste"—which means it's pretty tame by modern standards.

"In 1834," Klein continued, "somebody approached Poe and offered to sell him these teeth, saying they were his mother's. Poe may have believed them, or not, but he couldn't meet their price, even though he'd just won a prize for 'MS. Found in a Bottle'. He wrote 'Berenice' hoping to raise the money, but by the time he was paid for it, the seller had disappeared. Childs' servant said he bought the teeth, and a letter from Poe describing the incident, from Lizzie Doten sometime in the 1870s, but the letter is lost. Of course, I can't really prove any of this, but since you're the biggest private collector of Poe memorabilia alive now that Temple is gone . . . and not exactly a premature burial, if I may say so . . . "

I smiled at that, involuntarily, and tried to hide it behind my glass, but I could tell that Klein had noticed. "So," I said, as blandly as I could manage, "you're asking me to pay out a quarter million based on the claims of a couple of grave-robbers, at least one thief, two fantasists—one of them the creator of a celebrated hoax—and a poet who claimed to be channeling the dead, and now a dealer in stolen artwork, and God knows how many fools and liars in between."

Klein shrugged: he didn't need to look around at the bookshelves, the bust of Pallas above the door or the mummy case in the corner to know how obsessed I was with Poe, horror's patron sinner. "You must be used to that."

He was right, of course—everybody in Hollywood lies constantly, if only to themselves—but that didn't stop it sounding like an insult, and I hate being insulted. "You've seen them," he continued, smirking. "Sleep on it, and decide for yourself, but don't take too long. I can always find another buyer: do you want to spend the rest of your life wondering what you could have had?"

———

Poe said it better than I could, of course: *And the evening closed in upon me thus—and then the darkness came, and tarried, and went—and the day again dawned—and the mists of a second night were now gathering around—and still I sat motionless in that solitary room—and still I sat buried in meditation—and still the phantasma of the teeth maintained its terrible ascendancy, as with the most vivid and hideous distinctness it floated about amid the changing lights and shadows of the chamber.*

Of course, I didn't spend all of that time motionless or meditating: I wasn't able to sleep for long without dreaming of adding those teeth to my collection, but I made the effort. I remembered to eat, and wash, and while I didn't need to leave the house, the phone and fax machine was never silent for very long: I had another two films in pre-production and one in post, so I had plenty to occupy my time if not my mind. But I kept returning to the library and staring at the treasures of my collection. The teeth, if I bought them, would have to go in the safe: if they were fake, then the fewer people who knew I had bought them and been fooled, the better. But if they were real, the idea of them belonging to someone else was unbearable.

I picked up a collection of Poe stories, and leafed through it, hoping he would give me an answer.

Klein was grinning again, or still, as he walked into my office at the studio on Friday night, opened his attaché case, and produced the boxes again. "I was sure you'd call," he gloated.

"Sure enough that you didn't try to sell them to anybody else?" I murmured.

He faltered slightly at that, but his insulting smirk returned as I handed him a glass. He gulped it down as though it were water, and I poured him another. "Yes," he admitted. "I knew you could pay more, and sooner."

I nodded, and opened the attaché case to show him the stacked banknotes, then snapped it shut again. "You have them?"

He opened his own case, removed the ebony caskets, and placed them on my desk. I looked inside both boxes, and nodded. "The old law of Hollywood: give 'em what they want." I drew a deep breath. "What do you want, Klein?"

"Well, I'd like to be paid," he said dryly.

"You will be, I promise . . . but what do you do with your money? Do you collect anything?"

"No, not in the way you mean it. I mean, I like to have the best, but so does everybody, right?"

"The best of what?"

"The usual stuff. House, car, clothes . . . you know."

"Anything you wouldn't sell for a profit?"

"No, I guess not. Why?"

"So what really moves you is money?"

"Well, sure, same as everybody. So what?"

"Have you read much Poe, Klein? 'The Cask of Amontillado', perhaps? 'Hop-Frog'? 'The Conqueror Worm'?" Somehow, looking at his triumphant sneer brought that one instantly to mind. "'The Premature Burial'?"

"I saw some of the films."

"A poor substitute for the genuine article," I said. "And a man in your line should be able to tell real from fake." I pulled the small pistol from my pocket and pointed it at his stomach. "Take this, for example."

His eyes widened. "What—"

"This might just be a prop," I said, "and if it is, then you can just grab that case and run out of here and tell people how you managed to take me for a quarter mill. But it might not be: sometimes it's cheaper to buy the real thing than fake it." I grabbed the case, and nodded at the door. "There's something I want to show you."

It was so satisfying him seeing him walk down the corridor, hands clasped behind his head, that I almost took pity on him—but if I did that, I'd be finished in Hollywood. I steered him towards the soundstage where the crew had reconstructed a used crematorium. I pressed the buttons to open the door, and another to start the burners. "For example," I said, "is that fire really hot enough to actually destroy a body?"

Klein was sweating by now, and I doubted it was because of the flames. "If it helps, it would need to be about 1600 degrees not to leave any identifiable remains. But paper burns at a third of that." And I threw the attaché case into the oven.

Klein squawked, then stared at me. "You're crazy!"

"Crazy enough to throw away a quarter million on a whim? Maybe I am . . . but then, that's not my money: it's yours. All you have to do is go and get it—but don't take too long."

He stared into the flames. "You're bluffing. The money's fake. Counterfeit. Copies. Whatever."

"Maybe," I said. "Maybe not. But to me, that money's worth less than the possibility that these teeth are real. What's it worth to you? Do you want to spend the rest of your life wondering what you could have had?"

He turned to look at me, hoping for some clue in my expression, then leapt into the flames. I pressed the button to close the door, and stood there for a few minutes half-hoping to hear a cry of "For the love of God, Montressor!"—but there was nothing but silence.

I waited for two hours, reading e-mails and script outlines on my Blackberry, before turning the flames off. When I returned to the studio on Monday, the oven had cooled down, and the crew was emptying it out.

Maybe I shouldn't have gone down to the soundstage to watch them, but I had to make sure there was nothing left that could be identified, no tell-tale hearts or anything of that nature. Klein was right about the money, of course: most of it was fake, but he'd probably never had a chance to find out. Fortunately, nothing in the ashes resembled a banknote, or the attaché case. Just some small fragments of bone indistinguishable from the others we'd used to decorate some of the sets, and some lumps of molten metal that had once been his Rolex and his belt buckle.

One of the stage hands picked some white lumps out of the ashes, and looked at them curiously. Teeth. Human teeth. My heart grew sick, but then he tossed them into the bin with the other rubbish. I smiled to see them there, but my smile failed as the teeth seemed to form themselves back into Klein's familiar smirk. Another shovel-full of ash landed on top of them, but I could still see them glistening there. I see them still.

A BUYER'S GUIDE TO MAPS OF ANTARTICA

Catherynne M. Valente

Lot 657D
Topographical Map of the Ross Ice Shelf (The Seal Map)
Acuña, Nahuel, 1908
Minor tear, upper left corner. Moderate staining in left margin.

Landmass centered, Argentinean coast visible in the extreme upper quadrant. Latitude and longitude in sepia ink. Compass rose: a seal indicating north with her head, east and west with her flippers, south with the serrated ice floe on which the beast is situated. Legend in original handwriting. Ross Ice Shelf depicted with remarkable precision for the era, see Referent A (recent satellite imaging) for comparison.

The 1907 expedition to the Antarctic continent was doubly notable: it was on this virgin crossing that young Nahuel Acuña, barely free of university, lost his right foot to an Orca in estrus, and by simplest chance the good ship *Proximidad* employed an untested botanist by the name of Villalba Maldonado. Maldonado, himself a recent graduate of no less note than his illustrious shipmate, worked placidly as a cook to gain his passage, having no access to the funding that pursued Acuña through his career like a cheerful spaniel.

One may only imagine an unremarkable Saturday supper in the ice shadows and crystalline sun-prisms in which Villalba, his apron stained with penguin oil, his thinning black hair unkempt, his mustache frozen, laid a frost-scrimmed china plate before Acuña. Would he have removed his glasses before eating? Would they have exchanged words? Would he have looked up from his sextant and held the gaze of the mild-eyed Maldonado, even for a moment, before falling to? One hopes that he did; one hopes that the creaking of the *Proximidad* in one's mind is equal to its creaking in actuality.

Acuña's journal records only: *seal flank and claret for supper again. Cook insists on salads of red and white lichen. Not to my taste.*

The famous Seal Map, the first of the great Acuña Maps, offers a rare window into the early days of the rivalry, and has been assessed at $7500US.

Curator's Note: Whiskey stains date from approximately 1952.

Lot 689F
Topographical Map of the Ross Ice Shelf (The Sun Dog Map)
Maldonado, Villalba, 1908
Single owner, Immaculate condition.

Landmass low center, no other continents visible. Latitude and longitude in unidentified black ink. Compass rose: three-horned sea-goat, a barnacle-crusted tail indicating south, upturned muzzle designating north, vestigial fins pointing east and west. Sun shown centered, with rays embossed in gold extending all the way to the ice shelf. Parhelion is indicated, however, in the place of traditional concentric circles, two large dogs flank the orb of the sun, apparently Saint Bernards or similar, their fur streaming as if in a sudden wind, embossed in silver. Their jaws hang open, as if to devour the solar rays; their paws stand elbow-deep in the seawater, creating ripples that extend to the shoreline. The Map Legend explains that the pair of dogs, called Grell and Skell, may be found at coordinates *(redacted)* and that they require gifts of penguin feet and liverwort before they are willing to part with a cupful of the sun, which if carried at the end of a fishing pole and line before the intrepid polar *conquistador*, may burn with all the heat and pure light that he requires.

Offshore, a large, grinning Orca whale is visible, with a severed leg in her mouth.

When Maldonado returned from the *Proximidad* expedition, he arranged, presumably without knowledge of any competition, for the dissemination of his maps in parallel to Nahuel Acuña's own efforts. The printing of the Sun Dog Map, illustrated by Maldonado himself, was funded by the daughter of Alvaro Caceres, best described as a sheep and cattle magnate in the grace of whose shipping interests the *Proximidad* functioned. Pilar Caceres was delighted with the Maldonado sketches, and sold an ornate necklace of onyx and diamonds (Lot 331A) in order to finance this first map.

While the phenomenally precise Seal Map made Acuña's name and allowed him a wide choice of whalers and naturalists eager to avail themselves of his guidance, the Sun Dog Map stirred a mania for all things Antarctic in Buenos Aires. Nevertheless, Maldonado was not able to fund a second expedition until 1912, while Acuña booked passage on the *Immaculata* the following spring, confounded by the popularity of a clearly fraudulent document. He gave a lecture on the necessity of precision at the Asociación Cartographica Argentina in December of 1908, declaring it a ridiculous matter that he should be required to address such an obvious issue. He was, however, interrupted by vociferous requests for more exact descriptions of Grell and Skell.

Maldonado himself declined to appear before the Asociación despite three invitations, and published the Toothfish Map (Lot 8181Q) in early 1909 without their stamp.

This first and perhaps finest example of the cartography of Villalba Maldonado is one of only three remaining copies and has been assessed at $18500US.

Lot 699C
Map of the South Orkney Islands
Acuña, Nahuel, 1911
Sun damage throughout, fair condition.

Four large islands and sixteen smaller isles lie in the center of the map. Isla Coronación is the only named landmass. Latitude and longitude demarcated in Mediterranean octopus ink. Thirty-two point compass rose, crowned with military arrows wrapped in laurels, and bearing the archaic *Levante* designation on its eastern arm. See Referent B for satellite comparison.

The comparatively moderate climate of the South Orkney Islands (now the Orcadas) allowed Acuña to remain there throughout the war, returning his maps to the mainland via Jokkum Vabø, an illiterate sealer and loyal friend of the cartographer. The two men built the cabin in which Acuña worked and lived, and Vabø made certain that they smoked enough seal-meat in the summer months to keep his friend breathing, returning with costly inks and papers when migrations allowed. This was to prove the most prolific period of Nahuel's life.

From 1909 to 1918, Nahuel Acuña walked the length and breadth of the South Orkneys, polishing his teak prosthetic with the snow and grasses of the coast. He built a circular boat of sealskin and walrus-bones (Lot 009A), paddling from island to island with a gargantuan oar of leather and Orca-rib, a tool he must have found rich to use. He grew a long black beard that was said to glint gold in the sun, and never thereafter shaved it. He claimed later to have given Maldonado not the slightest thought during this hermitage, though Vabø would certainly have reported his rival's doings during his visits, and as the coyly titled Seal Pot Map details just this area, there is some dispute as to whether Maldonado might have actually managed landfall during his 1912 expedition aboard the *Perdita* and met cordially with Acuña. It is not possible to ascertain the authenticity of such rumors in either direction, but it is again sweet to imagine it, the two bearded mapmakers seated upon a snowy boulder, sharing lichen-tea and watching the twilight fall onto the scarlet flensing plains. It is a gentle pleasure to imagine that they had no enmity for one another in that moment, that their teapot steamed happily between them, and that they discussed, perhaps, the invention of longitude, or methods for slaughtering walrus.

First in the *Orcadas* series, this prime specimen of Acuña at his height has been assessed at $6200US.

Lot 705G
Map of the South Orkney Islands (The Seal Pot Map)
Maldonado, Villalba, 1914
Single owner, very slight water damage, lower right corner.

Five large islands and twenty-six smaller isles lie in the center of the map. All are named: Isla Concepción, Isla Immaculata, Isla Perdita, Isla Proximidad, Isla Gloriana, Isla Hibisco, Isla Sello Zafiro, Isla Pingüino Azul, Isla Cielo, Isla Pájaros del Musgo, Isla Valeroso, Isla Ermitaño, Isla Ocultado, Isla Graciento, Isla Mudanza, Isla del Leones Incansable, Isla Sombras Blancas, Isla del Ballenas del Fantasma, Isla Zapato, Isla del Mar de Cristal, Isla del Morsas Calvas, Isla Rojo, Isla Ónice, Isla Embotado, Isla Mentira, Isla del Araña Verde, Isla Abejas, Isla del Pie de la Reina, Isla Acuña, Isla Pilar.

All ink sepia, compass is a seal's head peeking out of an iron pot, her flipper pointed south, the pot handles east and west, and her head, capped by the pot's lid, indicating north. Smaller versions of this creature dot the island chain, their faces intricately inscribed. The legend claims that these Footless Seals can be found on the sometimes-green shores of Isla Graciento, on the long Norwegian flensing plain that occupies most of the island: *When the Iron Try Pots left to render Seal Fat are left to boil until Moonrise, it occasionally Happens that a severed Seal Head which has a Certain blue Tinge to its whiskers will Blink and open its Eyes, and with Cunning Hop Away into the surf, carrying the Iron Try Pot with it as a new Body. If an Explorer is very clever, he will leave a few of his campfire Embers burning and pretend to Sleep. If he is an Excellent Feinter of Slumber, the Queen of the Seal Pots whose name is Huln will come to rest upon the dying Fire and warm Herself. If he has brought three Pearls as tribute, the Queen will allow him to dip his Spoon into the Pot and drink of her Broth, which is sweeter than dandelion honey, and will keep him Fed and Happy for a fortnight and more.* (translation: Furtado, 1971)

Unable to convince the skeptic Alvaro Caceres to fund a second expedition despite the popularity of his work, Villalba Maldonado contented himself with the attentions of Pilar Caceres. Portraits (Lots 114 & 115A-F) show a handsome, if severe woman, with a high widow's peak and narrow eyes. She continued to sell her jewelry to print his maps, but no amount of necklaces could equal a southbound vessel. However, she became an expert in the preparation of sheepskin parchment, and in this manner became all the more Maldonado's patroness. She wore red whenever she met with him, and allowed her thick hair to fall at least three times upon his arm. With the grudging consent of Alvaro, Villalba and Pilar were married in April of 1911. She wore no jewels, and her dress was black sealskin. She was soon pregnant, and their daughter Soledad was born shortly after Maldonado departed on the *Perdita* in 1912. Pilar arranged for him to stay on through 1915 as a nominal military service, and thus both cartographers walked the ice floes during the Great War, far from each other and as ignorant of the other's activities as of the rest of the world.

Six maps were printed and distributed between 1908 and 1912. Each was received with ravenous acclaim, and applications for passage to Antarctica tripled. "Paquetes" were sold at docks (Lots 441A-492L), wooden boxes containing "supplies" for a successful Antartic expedition: desiccated penguin feet, bundles of liverwort, fishing poles, sheets of music to be sung at the ice-grottos of the Dream-Stealing Toothfish, cheap copies of the six maps, and three small pearls. However, most enthusiasts found themselves ultimately unable to make such a perilous voyage, and thus Maldonado's reputation grew in the absence of Acuña or any definite rebuttal of Maldonado's wonderful maps.

Not to be confused with the plentiful copies included in the *paquetes*, this original Caceres-issue map has been assessed at $15900US.

Lot 718K
Map of Queen Maud's Land
Acuña, Nahuel, 1920
Single owner, immaculate condition.

Landmass right center, Chilean coast visible in top left quadrant. Latitude and longitude in iron gall ink. Compass rose is the top half of a young woman, her head tipped up toward north, her arms open wide to encompass east and west, her hair twisting southward into a point. See Referent C for satellite comparison, Points 1, 4, and 17 for major deviations.

Curator's Note: Obviously Queen Maud's Land was not the common appellation at the time of Acuña's map, however, his own term, Suyai's Plain, was never recognized by any government making a claim to the territory.

Upon returning from the South Orkneys in 1919, Acuña was horrified by the *paquetes* and Maldonado's celebrity. The sheer danger of packing penguin's feet instead of lamp oil made him ill, and he immediately scheduled a series of lectures condemning the cartographer, challenging him to produce either Grell or Skell (he did not state a preference) on a chain at the Asociación banquet, or Huln, if the dogs were recalcitrant.

Attendant at these lectures was a young woman by the name of Suyai Ledesma. In imitation of her idol, Suyai had begun to produce her own maps of the *pampas*, the vast Argentine interior where both she and Acuña had been born. She presented her research at the Asociación banquet in a modest brown suit, her voice barely audible. She concluded with a gentle reminder that "the cartographer's art relies on accuracy as the moon relies on the sun to shed her own light on the world. To turn our backs on the authentic universe, as it exists beneath and before us, is to plunge into darkness."

Though Ledesma and Acuña never married, they were not often separated thenceforward, and she accompanied him along with their two sons on the *Lethe* expedition to Iles Kerguelen in 1935.

However, until the 1935 expedition, Acuña felt it was his duty to remain in Buenos Aires, to struggle against Maldonadan Antarcticana and its perils, and to rail against his rival whenever he was given a podium and a crowd with more than two folk to rub together. These philippics were eventually assembled and published posthumously by Carrizo and Rivas under the title *On Authenticity* (1961). One copy remains outside of private collections. (Lot 112C)

Maldonado responded slowly, as was his habit in all things. In 1922, his sole rejoinder was a small package, immaculately wrapped, delivered to Acuña's home. Inside was long golden chain attached to a crystal dog's collar (Lot 559M) and a note (Lot 560M) reading: *As you see I do not, as I see, you disdain. It is big enough.*

But fate would have her way, and in the end the Antarctic was not quite big enough after all. In January of 1922, three young men were found frozen to their ship on the Shackleton Ice Shelf, still clutching their *paquetes*, in possession of neither a cup of sun nor the Queen of the Try Pots. In May, Acuña had Villalba Maldonado arrested for public endangerment.

This pristine map of Queen Maud's Land, produced at the height of conflict, has been assessed at $6700US.

Lot 781A
Map of the South Pole (The Petrel Map)
Maldonado, Villalba, 1925
Significant damage, burns in top center portion

Landmass center, eastern Antarctic coast visible. Latitude and longitude in walnut ink, black tea, and human blood. Compass rose: a snow petrel rampant, her claws demarcating southeast and southwest, her tail flared due south, her wings spread east and west, and her head fixed at true north. Beneath her is emblazoned: Seal of the Antarctic Postal Service—*Glacies Non Impedimenta.* (Ice Is No Impediment.) Alone of the Maldonado maps, color of indeterminate and probably morbid origin have been used to stain portions of the interior red, differentiating zones of "watermelon snow," fulminating plains of lichen grown bright and thick, bearing fruits which when cracked open are found to be full of fresh water, more and sweeter than any may ask. The red fields encircle a zone of blue ice, frozen rainwater enclosing a lake of brine. Upon this rainwater mantle, explains the map legend, sits the Magnetic Pole, which is a chair made of try pots and harpoon-blades. The Pole sits tall there, her hair encased in fresh, sweet water gone to ice, her eyes filmed. Her dress is black sealskin, her necklaces are all of bone and skulls. *Grell and Skell they are Her Playmates, Her Guardians Dire, and Huln she is Her Handmaid, but Never moves She, even Once.* (translation: Peralta, 1988.)

She is waiting, the notations go on to state, for the petrels which are her loyal envoys, to deliver a letter into her hands, written on sheepskin, whose ink is blood. What this letter will read and who it may be from, no whaler may say—it is for her alone, and she alone may touch it.

The Petrel Map was produced in Maldonado's third year in prison, delivered to the printer's by his bailiff and repaired there, as the original document was created using unorthodox methods, owing to Villalba's lack of access to plentiful inks. The viciousness and length of his incarceration and Acuña's uncommon success in enforcing the sentence may be credited to many things: the influence of the spurned Asociación, the corrupt bureaucracy which was prone to forgetting and misplacing whole cartographers, the persuasiveness of Acuña and the pregnant Suyai as to the menace of Maldonado and his clearly deliberate deceits. Nevertheless, the summer of 1925 saw the first map in three years, and a new rash of *paquetes* eagerly broke the docks, the Shackleton incident all but forgotten. Stamps of the Antarctic Postal Service were now included, along with stationary and "ice-proof" pencils.

The Petrel Map was completed from memory, according to Pilar, a testament to an extraordinary intellect bent on total and accurate recollection. Public outcry warred with the Asociación on the subject of Maldonado's release, and funds were mounted for a *Proximidad II* expedition, but there was no one to receive it, the Caceres-Maldonado accounts having been frozen, and the usual half-benign institutional fraud absorbed the money once more into the body of the state. Meanwhile, Acuña's tarnished star rose, and he was commissioned by the British Navy to deliver maps of the subcontinent.

By 1928 Maldonado was in complete isolation. He was not allowed visits from his wife, or perhaps more tellingly for our purposes, letters. Acuña was recorded as visiting once, in 1930, with his young son Raiquen. It is not for us to imagine this meeting, so far from the decks of the *Proximidad* and salads of lichen, far from claret and the green shadows of the *aurora australis*. However, after this incident, Acuña arranged for Maldonado to be moved to a special penitentiary in Ushuaia, on the southern tip of Argentina, with the shores of the South Shetlands in sight, on very clear days.

The Great Man looked up from his bread and held the eye of the Naval Cartographer. Their beards were both very long, but Acuña's was neatly cut and kept, while Maldonado's snarled and ran to the stone floor.

"I promised you, my friend," he said, his voice very rough, "that it was big enough. Big enough for us both to look on it and hold in our vision two separate countries, bound only by longitude."

"What's big enough?" little Raiquen asked, tugging on his father's hand, which had two gold rings upon it.

But Acuña did not answer. For my own part, my heart was filled with long plains of ice receding into eternity, and on those plains my prisoner walked with bare feet and a cup of gold.

—Keeper of the Key: The Autobiography of a Prison Guard, Rafael Soto, 1949

Villalba Maldonado died at Ushuaia on June 4th 1933. Acuña lived, feted and richly funded, until 1951, when he drowned off the shore of Isla Concepción. Suyai and her sons continued in residence on the islands, producing between them twelve maps of the area. (Lots 219-231H) Raiquen relocated in middle age to the mainland where he lives still in well-fed obscurity.

The Petrel Map was Maldonado's final work, and as such, has been assessed at $57000US.

Lot 994D
Captain's Logbook, the *Anamnesis*, disembarked from Ushuaia, 1934

Here is presented the logbook in which Soledad Maldonado signed her name and declared her cargo—an iron coffin lashed to a long sled. She left her ailing mother in Buenos Aires and sailed south as soon as tide and melt permitted, and Captain Godoy deposited her on the floes of the Weddell Sea per instructions. His full account of the voyage and Soledad's peculiar habits, studies, and intentions will be released only to the buyer, however, his notes conclude thus:

I watched the young lady amid her supplies, her sled, her eight bristling dogs, her father's long, cold coffin. She gave me a cool glance in farewell and turned southward, towards the interior ice. She waited for a long while, though I could not think what for. It was drawing on night, and there were many stars showing when it happened, and I must insist that I be believed and not ridiculed, no matter what I may now write.

Two great dogs strode out from the long plains of ice, enormous, thickly furred, something like Saint Bernards. They pressed their noses into her hands and she petted their heads, scratched behind their ears, let them lick her face slowly, methodically, with great care. The huge hounds allowed her to yoke them at the head of her team, and without a whip she directed them inward, onward, hoisting aloft as they flew a long fishing pole, at the end of which was an orb of impossible light, like a cup overturned and spilling out the sun.

The Log Book has been assessed at $10700US. Bidding begins at noon precisely.

AFTER MOREAU

Jeffrey Ford

I, Hippopotamus Man, can say without question that Moreau was a
total asshole. Wells at least got that part right, but the rest of the story
he told all wrong. He makes it seem like the Doctor was about trying
to turn beasts into humans. The writer must have heard about it third-
hand from some guy who knew a guy who knew something about
the guy who escaped the island by raft. In fact, we were people first
before we were kidnapped and brought to the island. I was living in a
little town, Daysue City, on the coast in California. Sleepy doesn't half
describe it. I owned the local hardware store, had a wife and two kids.
One night I took my dog for a walk down by the sea, and as we passed
along the trail through the woods, I was jumped from behind and hit
on the head. I woke in a cage in the hold of a ship.

People from all over the place wound up on the island. Dog Girl
was originally from the Bronx, Monkey Man Number Two was from
Miami, and they snatched Bird Boy, in broad daylight, from a public
beach in North Carolina. We all went through Moreau's horrifying
course of injections together. The stuff was an angry wasp in the vein,
and bloated me with putrid gases, made my brain itch unbearably. Still,
I can't say I suffered more than the others. Forget House of Pain, it was
more like a city block. When you wake from a deep, feverish sleep and
find your mouth has become a beak, your hand a talon, it's terrifying.
A scream comes forth as a bleat, a roar, a chirp. You can't conceive of
it, because it's not make believe.

Go ahead, pet my snout, but watch the tusks. No one wants the

119

impossible. What human part of us remained didn't want it either. It was a rough transition, coming to terms with the animal, but we helped each other. After we had time to settle into our hides, so to speak, there were some good times in the jungle. Moreau could only jab so many needles in your ass in a week, so the rest of the time we roamed the island. There was a lot of fucking too. I'll never forget the sight of Caribou Woman and Skunk Man going at it on the beach, beneath the bright island sun. The only way I can describe it is by using a quote I remember from my school days, from Coleridge about metaphor, "the reconciliation of opposites." I know, it means nothing to you.

We all talked a lot and for some reason continued to understand each other. Everybody was pretty reasonable about getting along, and some of the smarter ones like Fish Guy helped to develop a general philosophy for the community of survivors. *The Seven Precepts* are simple and make perfect sense. I'll list them, but before I do I want to point something out. Keep in mind what it states in the list below and then compare that to the dark, twisted version that appears in Laughton's film version of the Wells' novel, *Island of Lost Souls*. Monkey Man Number One and a couple of the others took the boat to Frisco, and by dark of night robbed a Macy's. One of the things they brought back was a projector and an 8-millimeter version of the flick. I believe it's Bela Lugosi who plays Speaker of the Law. I'll refrain from saying "hambone" for the sake of Pig Lady's feelings. That performance is an insult to the truth, but, on the otherhand, Laughton, himself was so much Moreau it startled us to see the film. Here are the real Seven Precepts, the list of how we live:

1. Trust don't Trust
2. Sleep don't Sleep
3. Breathe don't Breathe
4. Laugh don't Laugh
5. Weep don't Weep
6. Eat don't Eat
7. Fuck Whenever You Want

You see what I mean? Animal clarity, clean and sharp, like an owl's gaze. Anyway, here we are, after Moreau. We've got the island to ourselves. There's plenty to eat—all the animals that resided naturally and the exotic beasts Moreau brought in for the transmission of somatic essence—the raw ingredients to make us them. A good number of the latter escaped the fire, took to the jungle and reproduced. There are herds of suburban house cats that have wiped out the natural ostrich population and herds of water oxen that aren't indigenous.

Actually, there's also a tiger that roams the lower slopes of the island's one mountain. Ocelot Boy thought he could communicate with the tiger. He tracked the cat to its lair in a cave in the side of the mountain, and sat outside the entrance exchanging growls and snarls with the beast until the sun went down. Then the tiger killed and ate him. The tiger roared that night and the sound of its voice echoed down the mountain slope. Panther Woman, who lay with me in my wallow, trembled and whispered that the tiger was laughing.

She also told me about how back in the days of the Doctor, when her tail and whiskers were still developing, she'd be brought naked to his kitchen and made to kneel and lap from a bowl of milk while Moreau, sitting in a chair with his pants around his ankles, boots still on, petted his knobby member. I asked Panther Woman why she thought he did it. She said, "He was so smart, he was stupid. I mean, what was he going for? People turning into animals part way? What kind of life goal is that? A big jerk-off." We laughed, lying there in the moonlight.

Where was I? I had to learn to love the water, but otherwise things weren't bad. I had friends to talk to, and we survived because we stuck together, we shared, we sacrificed for the common good. Do I have to explain? Of course I do, but I'm not going to. I can't remember where this was all headed. I had a point to make, here. What I can tell you right now is that Rooster Man went down today. He came to see me in the big river. I was bobbing in the flow with my real hippo friends when I noticed Rooster calling me from the bank. He was flapping a wing and his comb was moving in the breeze. Right behind him, he obviously had no idea, was a gigantic alligator. I could have called a warning to him, but I knew it was too late. Instead I just waved goodbye. He squawked bloody murder, and I finally dove under when I heard the crunch of his beak.

Tomorrow I've got tea with the Boar family. I ran into old man Boar and he invited me and Panther Woman over to their cave. The Boars are a strange group. They all still wear human clothes – the ones that can do anyway. Old man Boar wears Moreau's white suit and his Panama hat. It doesn't seem to faze him in the least that there's a big shit stain in the back of the pants. I've shared the Doctor's old cigars with Boar. He blows smoke like the boat's funnel and talks a crazy politics not of this world. I just nod and say yes to him, because he puts honey in his tea. Panther and I crave honey.

The other day, when he offered the invitation, Boar told me under his breath that Giraffe Man was engaged in continuing experiments with Moreau's formulas and techniques. He said the situation was dire, like a coconut with legs. I had no idea what he meant. I asked around, and a couple of the beast people told me it was true. Giraffe couldn't leave well enough alone. He was injecting himself. Then a couple days after I confirmed old Boar's claim, I heard they found Giraffe Man, on the floor of what remained of the old lab—a bubbling brown mass of putrescence.

We gathered at the site and Fish Guy shoveled up Giraffe's remains and buried them in the garden out back. Monkey Man Number Two played a requiem on the unburned half of the piano and Squirrel Girl, gray with age, read a poem that was a story of a tree that would grow in the spot Giraffe was buried and bear fruit that would allow us all to achieve complete animality. Everybody knew it would never happen but we all wished it would.

When I loll in the big river, I think about the cosmos as if it's a big river of stars. I eat fish and leaves and roots. Weasel Woman says it's a healthy diet, and I guess it is. How would she know, though, really? As long as I stay with the herd of real hippos, I'm safe from the alligators. There have been close calls, believe me. When standing on land in the hot sun, sometimes I bleed from all my pores to cool my hide. Panther

Woman has admitted this aspect of my nature disgusts her. To me she is beautiful in every way. The fur . . . you can't imagine. She's a hot furry number, and she's gotten over her fear of water. I'm telling you, we do it in the river, with the stars watching, and it's a smooth animal.

If you find this message in this bottle, don't come looking for us. It would be pointless. I can't even remember what possessed me to write in the first place. You should see how pathetic it is to write with a hippo paw. My reason for writing is probably the same unknown thing that made Moreau want to turn people into beasts. Straight up human madness. No animal would do either.

Monkey Man Numbers One and Two are trying to talk some of the others into going back to civilization to stay. They approached me and I asked them, "Why would I want to live the rest of my life as a sideshow freak?"

Number Two said, "You know, eventually Panther Woman is going to turn on you. She'll eat your heart for breakfast."

"Tell me something I don't know," I said. Till then, it's roots and leaves, fucking in the wallow, and bobbing in the flow, dreaming of the cosmos. Infrequently, there's an uncertain memory of my family I left behind in the old life but the river's current mercifully whisks that vague impression of pale faces to the sea.

That should have been the end of the message, but I forgot to tell you something. This is important. We ate Moreau. That's right. He screamed like the bird of paradise when we took him down. I don't eat meat, but even I had a small toe. Sweet flesh for a bitter man. Mouse Person insisted on eating the brain, and no one cared to fight him for it. The only thing is, he got haunted inside from it. When we listened in his big ears, we heard voices. He kept telling us he was the Devil. At first we laughed, but he kept it up too long. A couple of us got together one night and pushed him off the sea cliff. The next day and for months after, we searched the shore for his body, but never found it. Monkey Man Number One sniffs the air and swears the half-rodent is still alive on the island. We've found droppings.

DEBRIS ENSUING FROM A VORTEX

Brian Ames

SD is back, guiding Blake to another memory. There is a grin on SD's lips. Blake's medicine smiles as wide as a black-green sky spinning over a storm. But this is a *good good good* thing, this bird's mouth that feeds its young his recollections back one by one. The worms of foundation laid upon Blake's tongue.

Imagine that you are he. You live in a world you have forgotten. Every day people and places assume familiarity with you, but you aren't having it. A female person called "Ginger," for example, expresses some tenderness toward you. You fail to remember. You are taken through a place whose walls and angles are wholly foreign. People who populate it seem to know where they are, but you don't.

What Blake once knew flew away on a violent night wind.

Put yourself into the date that happened. Search for a clue. Find out why Blake's forgotten more than you've ever learned. Discover who this SD character is. Linger in a whorl of his fingerprint, suckle at the dugs of his DNA, worry through the pattern of his loss. Then you'll know. Then you can help him, too, as SD does, or tries to do.

The night Blake's roof came off began as most did, with his return from work. The night his walls were sucked skyward featured a light supper of spinach salad, grilled tilapia wrapped in a tortilla with hot sauce, yellow peppers and onions, a cold beer. The night his furniture, wall hangings, stove, carpet, washer and dryer, hot water heater, books, autographed baseball collection, weight set, lamps, blender, alarm clock, refrigerator, rake and broom, toothbrush, candy dish, Johnny

Cash record albums, commemorative program for the 1987 World Series, nose-hair trimmer, fireplace flew five ways off into space had him situated in a nest of undisturbed progression of positive trajectory, on an unmolested life path suddenly fucked by chance.

All of those things suctioned into vortex. All that mattered nabbed by an F4 funnel thief. A spinning highwayman of random act stole his possessions. And in his possessions, the fundamentals of his memory.

The news channels had made their seductive promise of dangerous weather. The sky had darkened and thrown its cloud-to-ground lightning. Thunder pealed urgently, proximately. A supercell, crushing air into heat, warped heaven. Windchimes on Blake's porch toned merrily, anomalously. Rain gathered then dropped.

As everyone living in flyover country knows as well as the palms of their own hands, a supercell thunderstorm takes the name *mesocyclone* when the National Weather Service, using Doppler radar, detects cyclonically rotating air. A tornadic vortex signature appears on the radar image as an area within the storm with changing wind directions of high periodicity. A tornado warning goes out to those in the path. Sirens go like mad. The lost-sheep television bleats.

F4: 207-260 mph on the Fujita Scale. Devastating damage: Houses and other small structures can be razed entirely; automobiles are propelled through the air. Memories are sucked into the supervortex. Blown bookpages explode into flames.

Blake's failure to appreciate his evolving emergency results from his fascination with bright lights, shiny things. Lightning is smack to him. Watching it strike is akin to filling a vein. Mainline this energy. Let these synapses crackle with delicious dopamine fulminations. Hope for a bolt out of the blue.

But too late—Blake's ears pop like pistol shots as pressure plummets. Through the torn membranes of his eardrums: the runaway locomotive roar, shingles tearing away, rafters splintering, wallboard cracking, electrical wiring hissing free from its stays, copper pipe shrieking apart, glass bursting into spray, the vast universe-filling rise of everything and all.

The loss, and then the quiet as the sky opens into calm, brilliant blue.

Blake peers over the lip of the bathtub. His mind is a rubblescape like that which unfolds before him. He can scarcely blink as his stares out from his sanctuary. He remembers that this is a tub, that water will drain from a tub in a certain coriolis direction depending on whether the observer is in the Northern or Southern hemisphere. But as memories go, that's about it. Sooner or later, emergency workers show up looking for the dead and living. There is question—even today—as to which camp Blake is in.

But SD will help Blake find his memories, yes? Though Blake's possessions are strewn across three counties, SD will guide him to them—and the recollections dwelling in each found object—over the course of several months. A broken picture frame discovered in a field near St. Paul puts Blake in mind of a man who was his father. A fragment of crystal at a crossroads near Blackjack makes him remember a college date that went unexpectedly well. There is the spare Michelin tire half submerged in Peruque Creek—Blake remembers being promoted at his firm.

"Have I shown you this?" SD asks, and Blake sees the weather-soaked, bloated pages of a collection of short stories by Jeffery Deaver. Blake smiles. He had a daughter—or was it a niece?—once.

But SD must exact a price, too. His services don't come free. Blake's memory finder, the redeemer of his mind, must also bring back those bitternesses, those aches, those turn-aways we'd rather all forget.

For Blake was a dog-kicker. A yellow-piss-soaked sycophant in the hierarchy of his corporation. A liar, cheat, thief. An apostate. A black-hearted cynic. A denier of culpability. A finger-pointer. A mocker of principles and a hater of fellows.

All of these things, too, must and will come back. SD will reveal them as Blake's lost things are found.

We can all judge whether he would have been better off dead, blown upward into the vortex. But only SD can help him navigate.

Self diagnoser. Sad doppelganger. Sin doll. Systolic diastolicist.

Simulacrum demon. Sharp-tongued dagger. Sainted dalliance. Stained dumpling. Shattering destroyer. So-called doorway. Sabertoothed dancer. Skull donkey. Sabotage dilettante. Spiritual desperado. Sagging dopefiend. Sex-crazed deathmonger. Suck dream. Surely damned.

Shit Disturber.

WHEN THE GENTLEMEN GO BY

Margaret Ronald

It wasn't a sound that woke her this time, nor the soft slow lights that came dancing through the curtains. She thought in that first wakening haze that it might be a scent, like the "bad air" her mother had talked about, creeping in to announce their presence. Then full wakefulness and knowledge struck her, and her only thought was *Not yet.*

Laura rolled out of bed, making sure not to disturb Jenny, who'd crawled in about an hour after bedtime. Toby, in the crib, slept like a swaddled stone. The nightlight cast a weak gold glow over them, but the first hints of blue had begun to creep in, cool and unfriendly. She glanced back once at the sound of Jenny's whimper, then turned her back on her sleeping children.

At least their father wasn't here.

It was an old bargain, old as the Hollow at least. With bargains you had to uphold your side; she'd learned that early, probably before she even knew about the Gentlemen.

Her bedroom in her parents' house had faced the street, and when she was five the changing shapes of headlights across the far wall had fascinated her. One night she woke to see a block of light against the far wall, flickering in all the colors of frost. When the light stayed put, as if the car that cast it had parked outside, she sat up in bed, then turned to the window.

The light was just outside, on the strip of green that her father liked to call the lawn. She crawled out of bed, dropping the last couple of inches to the floor, and reached for the curtain.

"Don't look."

Laura turned to see her mother standing in the doorway. "Mumma?"

Her mother crossed the room in two strides and took Laura into her arms, cradling her head against her shoulder. "Don't look, baby, don't look."

Obediently, Laura laid her head against her mother's shoulder and listened as something huge or a hundred smaller somethings passed by with a thunderous *shussh*. Her mother's eyes were closed tight, and she rocked Laura as if she were an infant again, even though Laura had two little brothers and hadn't been rocked since the first one was born. The sleeve of her mother's bathrobe was damp with a thousand tiny droplets.

In the morning, she tried to talk about it. "I had a dream last night—" she said at the breakfast table.

"I expect we all had dreams," her mother said, pouring milk over her Cheerios. "What with all that pizza last night. Bet you had them worst of all, right, Kyle?"

Her brother Kyle, six years old and indeed the one who'd eaten the most, shook his head and began to cough.

The light was stronger in the living room. Soon it would be strong enough for her to read by, if she'd ever had the urge to do so. Laura closed the bedroom door behind her, making sure it latched, and picked her way through the maze of toys that covered the carpet. She watched the blue-edged shadows rise over the edge of the couch and drew a deep breath. *I wonder what they'll bring,* she made herself think over the rising dread in the back of her mind. *And to whom they'll bring it.*

They bring gifts. I have to remember that. They bring gifts too.

It wasn't till she reached second grade, just after Kyle's funeral, that she found a name for them. It was in a book of children's poems, the old kind that usually read as if they'd been dipped in Karo syrup. But this one, "The Smuggler's Song," wasn't like that at all. It made the room seem darker when she read it, and darker still when she thought about it. Even after she learned that the poet hadn't ever set foot in Brooks' Hollow, she still secretly called them the Gentlemen, after the poem.

Five and twenty ponies/ trotting through the dark . . .

She waited until her father took her remaining brother out to play baseball before talking to her mother about it. "Mumma," she asked as they washed dishes together, "why did Kyle get sick?"

Her mother's hands paused, wrist-deep in sudsy water. "Well," she said after a moment, in that careful voice adults used when they didn't know how to say something, "people in the Hollow get sick sometimes. It's just something in the air."

"Oh."

"You don't need to worry, sweetie. I won't let anything—" She stopped, her lips pressed together, and went on in a different tone. "You know what the pioneers used to say about our land? Good land, bad air. They might have been right about the air, but we had the best farms for miles. Still do. The Hollow's a good place, Laura. I want you to remember that."

Later that evening, after the boys had settled in to watch football, her mother took her by the hand and led her upstairs, where she rummaged in the back of the closet until she found an old cardboard box. "I thought you might want to try this on," she said, and took out a fragile crown, woven out of hair-thin wire and stones like gleaming ice, so delicate it chimed in her hands. She set it on Laura's head and held up a mirror. "Don't you look just like a princess, now."

Laura caught her breath. "I do! Mumma, I do!"

"I thought you might." Her mother smiled.

———

Laura shivered to remember that crown. It was here somewhere, in the boxes she'd packed up after her mother's death, but she hadn't ever gone looking for it. She sometimes dreamed of wearing it, and woke up with bile in her throat.

She reached up and took down the little blue notebook from its place above the television. It had pages of notes about the sound the Gentlemen made: pines in the wind, highway traffic very far away, heavy rain, but none of them quite caught it. She'd been keeping the notes ever since she could write, first on what it looked like when the Gentlemen went by, then—later, as she grew up and began to understand—the annotations.

And the more she watched the indistinct shapes through the curtain, the more she felt as if her whole life became only watching. Her second brother's death, her graduation, the strikes at the cabinet factory—all images apart from her. Even now, she was at a distance, watching herself sitting huddled wrong-way-round on the couch, a patch of drying formula stiff and sticky under her left forearm.

Sometimes they brought things, she told herself again. A crown, a song, a whisper in someone's ear. And their trail was thick with flowers, even when they passed by late in October.

And the Hollow was a friendly place, after all. It seemed there was always a family to bring a casserole; it seemed there was always a service "for those taken from us" at the little church that was the only official marker of Brooks' Hollow, and the pews were always full.

But you didn't talk about it. You shrugged, and blamed bad air, and made sure your child's last months were comfortable, treating them like a stranger the whole time, and then you buried them in the good rich earth of the Hollow.

The light grew, shimmering like opals, and with it came a faint scent: greenery, growing things. But there was an edge to it as well, something like grass clippings left in the rain and then rotting in the sun. Something green gone wrong. Laura held the book tight against her chest, as if it might hide her, her and her children. "The Smuggler's Song" was inked in blue on the inside flap, an addition she'd made just after her wedding.

Them that asks no questions isn't told a lie./ Watch the wall, my darling, when the Gentlemen go by!

In her senior year at the county high she met Rich. Rich came from the north of the county, and he played guitar, and when he smiled at her Laura felt her heart come unstuck. For the first time in ages she felt as if she could be part of the world again.

She was worried at first what her parents would say. Some of her girlfriends had had to move out of the Hollow because their parents had kicked them out for any number of reasons—going out with boys, going out with only one boy, getting pregnant, not staying pregnant. Her parents turned out to like Rich, though, and they even helped them find a place to live.

They got married on the hottest day of the year. But the sky was clear, the beer was cold, and Rich looked at her like she was the sun come to earth. At the reception, she tore her hem dancing and had to go looking for her mother. She finally thought to look for her in the bathroom, only to find her talking to an old friend. "Rich tells me they've bought a trailer down in the Hollow," said Laura's old babysitter.

"It's a nice little place," Laura's mother said. Laura shrank back against the door.

"That ain't right, Missy. Bringing someone new into the Hollow ain't right, especially not a good sort like Rich. Why didn't you send her away?"

Laura held her breath. "She's all I got," her mother said after a moment. "I can't send her away."

"Oh, Missy. That's no way to treat a good girl. You know what the Hollow's like—that's why we've been sending our girls out. I know. You get sent or you get taken, and that's it."

"Or maybe you spend a good long life in the Hollow, like me and Bobby." Laura's mother sniffed. "Maybe that's what I want for my girl.

You think of that? Besides, the way you keep sending your girls out, there won't be hardly any families left, and it'll be harder for anyone who stays. You think you're doing it for the whole Hollow, but it's just for yourself."

"That's not it," Laura's babysitter insisted. "That's not why. There's things a girl should know, if she's going to be a mother in the Hollow. You think she can handle that? *I* can't handle that, and I'm twice her age. It's not worth it."

" . . . she's all I got."

The other woman sighed. "Well, God keep you both."

Laura hesitated a moment longer, then thumped the door as if she'd just opened it. "Mumma?" she called. "I need some help with my dress."

"Be there in a moment," her mother said.

Not worth it. She formed the words, but couldn't make herself push the breath behind them. It was easy to forget, sometimes, amid the gifts tangible and intangible. No woman in the Hollow ever miscarried. No plants died in the ground, no house ever caught fire, no one ever quite starved. When you looked at the uncertain world, you could be forgiven for thinking that maybe Kyle's life had been a good trade.

At least Laura hoped you could be forgiven.

What was it the union man had said, just before she'd had to leave for Toby's birth? "The contracts need to be renegotiated," he'd said, and there was more. Most of it she hadn't paid attention to, being nine months pregnant and having what her friend Charlene called "baby brain." She'd thought it was dumb at the time—you make a bargain, you stick with it—but that had been before Rich came back.

Maybe bargains went bad, sometimes. Maybe they went bad and there wasn't anything you could do but stick with it and hope for the best.

The closest anyone ever came to saying anything out loud was just after her mother's death (no Gentlemen, just three packs of

Marlboros every day for twenty years). A lawyer in a rumpled blue suit had arranged for a big town meeting, and he'd gotten nearly the whole Hollow to attend on the promise of free barbecue. He had charts, and maps, and he talked excitedly about disease clusters and the factory up the road. And after half an hour of silence from the good folks of the Hollow, he'd asked them to join in a class action suit.

The minister of First Church, acting for all of them, had smiled and nodded and escorted him to the door. "A lawsuit can't help us," he'd said, "even if you knew who to sue."

It was right after he closed the door that someone could have spoken, could have broken that throat-tightening silence and actually said who was to blame. But the lawyer drove off, the silence won out, and the minister shrugged and sighed.

Rich went to the war. Rich came back. Laura had written him about Toby's birth, and it made her heart fly free again to see him smile. But the look he turned out the windows was haunted, and with more than just wartime ghosts. He couldn't drive any more, not without pulling over and putting his head down every few miles. So he spent more time in the Hollow, and the Hollow clotted around him.

In April, after the Gentlemen's spring visit (which would later be annotated with Ashley Irvine, 6, 4 mos. after G.), they had a fight. It wasn't even a real fight; she'd dropped a glass, and he'd charged into the kitchen so fast he almost knocked over Toby. He yelled at her, she yelled back, both scared and angry at each other for being scared, and Laura didn't even see the slap coming until her cheek was already burning with it. She raised a hand to her face, disbelieving. Rich stared at her as if she'd grown horns, then turned and ran out the door, heedless of Toby's yowls.

Laura didn't go after him, even when dinner and sunset passed without his return. She took extra time putting the kids to bed, and didn't get up when she heard the front door open.

When she came out from the bedroom, she found him sitting at the kitchen table, staring at his hands. She sat down across from him, and after a while, he began to talk.

"They told me I might have trouble, coming back," he said, and this time he didn't move away when Laura took his hands in hers. "And I think I was okay, for a little while . . . But something about here, it's like, like I keep seeing things I oughtn't, and it just keeps getting worse. Like something keeps poking at my head." He glanced out the window, as if something was watching him.

Laura said nothing, only thought of how smart Rich had been in high school, how quickly he saw things that it took her ages to notice, and how she should have known that wouldn't change.

"Let's get out of here," he said, and kissed her fingers. "I don't know where just yet, but we can live with my folks a while."

Laura unknotted her hands from his and went to stand by the window. "This is my home," she said.

Rich's eyes went wide and broken. "I know, babe, but it's not a good place. We need to get out."

I do. But you get sent or you get taken, and that's it. "So," she said, "either I go with you, or you go alone."

"What? No, that's not—"

"I know." She turned and smiled at him, blinking back tears. "I'm sending you away, Rich. I'm sending you out of my life." *And out of the Hollow.*

The divorce wasn't pretty—it couldn't have been, with the two of them still in love. Rich called her and left messages, angry or maudlin or pleading, and she'd listened to them all, hugging herself so tight there would be white marks in her arms when the message ended. Toby began to fuss more, and Jenny started to crawl into bed with her at night.

But Rich was free. Rich was out of it, and she could never, ever hand him over to them. Even if she sometimes woke and cried over the cold side of the bed. Even if she was back watching her life again.

The lights hadn't changed, and the whispering had stilled. And now Laura had to admit it, had to see that the Gentlemen had come to her house. *Oh, I tried, I tried,* she thought. *I could have sent the kids away, I could . . .*

But would it have done anything? The old women, like Lara's babysitter, had sent their kids away. And some had then died alone and unnoticed, so successful at cutting the ties between their loved ones and the Hollow that they'd cut their own lifelines. Even that wouldn't have been enough.

She'd gotten as far as the border of the Hollow, car packed to the gills and kids in the backseat, before the strength left her limbs and she found herself unable to leave. She'd even thought about ringing the house with iron and salt, the way one woman had back in '09, but that woman's family had all died in a gas explosion two months after. The Gentlemen took their claim. You had to carry out a life to them, and you had to let them carry that life away.

It was an old bargain, old as the Hollow at least. And you had to keep bargains.

A soft trill shook the window panes, traveling from them down to the tips of her fingers through some malign conduction. Her first instinct was to categorize it, and she thought of flutes, screech owls, mourning doves, before she quite heard it, and hearing it was lost.

This was right, the cry said. Children die, and if one of them had to, who better to choose than their mother? She sat up—looking, had she known it, very like her mother—then got to her feet.

She ghosted into the bedroom and gazed at her children. *Toby,* she thought, *he's too young to really understand about being sick. No, Jenny, because she's had at least some time. No . . .*

Something burred against her consciousness, a wrong note in the Gentlemen's music.

Decide. You have time. Just decide.

But the burr remained, coming through in bursts like—*like a phone,* she realized, and glanced over her shoulder in time to see the harsh red light of the answering machine flick on.

"Uh. Hi. It's me," Rich's voice said, crackling over the tape. "Look, I know you're not awake—Jesus, I hope I didn't wake the kids, I'm sorry—

but I had to talk to you." He went on, but Laura was no longer paying attention. His voice was harsh and ragged and so unlike the Rich she'd known, but it was enough to drown out the Gentlemen's echoes.

Laura looked back at her children. She could let herself walk into the room, as she was doing now, let herself pick up a child and go outside. And she could tell herself later, when her child died, that she hadn't really done it, that she'd just watched herself do it.

She thought of the crown, and of Kyle.

Jenny shifted, putting out a hand to the empty space where Laura had slept, and sat up. "Mumma?"

"Stay inside, sweetie," Laura said. She crossed her arms, denying herself a last hug in case her resolve failed. "Stay inside and under the covers. I'll be back—" She caught the lie between her teeth and shook her head. "Sleep tight, sweetie. Love you."

She turned her back, ignoring Jenny's scared squeak, and closed the door. The last moments of Rich's message cut off, cut short by the tape, and Laura touched the answering machine as she passed. "Love you too."

Finally she closed her eyes, opened the front door, and stepped out into light. The trill sounded again, closer, all around her, and she opened her eyes with a gasp. Two dozen sets of eyes regarded her, wide and unblinking.

They didn't ride horses, of course; at the back of her mind she was proud of herself for having figured that out. They rode owls, giant white faces staring at her without curiosity. That was the only thing recognizable about them; it was as if the owls, strange and gigantic as they were, were a concession to reality.

They were made of light, and they shone, oh they shone. For a second she thought they could be angels, but the memory of the little blue notebook tainted that thought. One of the riders—white and blue, and human only in shape—leaned over his reins toward her and gestured toward the house.

"No," she said aloud. "You didn't get Rich. You don't get them. You get me."

The rider slashed one hand across his chest: rejection. Others agreed, some agitating their mounts so that the huge birds hopped from one foot to the other.

She shook her head. "I don't care what you want. You don't get to choose. And I choose this. I choose me." She leaned forward, and was rewarded by the sight of the head rider leaning away from her.

You think you're doing it for the Hollow, but it's just for yourself. The words were her mother's, but the head of one of the Gentlemen moved, as if speaking her thoughts.

Laura shook her head. "No. For the Hollow. For the dead of the Hollow." All the services, all the casseroles, all the dead then and now.

There came a familiar prickling on the back of her neck. If she turned now, she knew, she'd be able to see Jenny at the window, nose mashed up against the glass, mouth open in the beginning of a sob.

She didn't turn, not even to say goodbye. *Watch, darling. Watch.* "This bargain is ended," she said. "We will not be renegotiating."

The head rider motioned to the others, and they advanced on her, cruel hooked beaks clashing. Laura held her ground. It always hurt to break a bargain; there was always something that got lost. But it was worth it, if the contract was no good.

The owls took her by hand and foot and hair, and their beaks were sharp. The first cut came, and with it a rending deeper than her skin, deeper than her heart: the Hollow breaking, breaking so that it could never be repaired, and her blood turning the rich soil to useless swamp.

Watch. Oh, watch.

THE HUMAN MOMENTS

Alexander Lumans

12:12. "We will glorify war—the world's only hygiene."
There are too many dead from the new flu pandemic, and the earth-movers bring bodies by the tons. One never thinks to consider a human population in tons: the weight of geological formations, of the Huns, the Visigoths, the Million Man March, the weight of knowledge that bears down on the shoulders of Western gods.

Every hundredth body that arrives to be broken down in this Cryogenics Lab, the video monitors change lenses and take slow-motion thermal video of the sonic ruin. I must review these videos as my position requirements dictate, no matter the level of inadequacy.

This time the video runs even slower. Frame after frame I watch the still-life body of a woman become crystals in space, and I am reminded of Duchamp's *Nude Descending a Staircase*. Notice the fracturing of time, how the person has been smeared across the staircase; she doesn't really exist in one place at any one time, just like quantum mechanics describes the electron. *Clothed Standing until Detonation*.

I stand, walk to the room's one bare wall and press the one green button. On a tray, hot chocolate pours out into a Styrofoam cup. It's the little things, the human moments. *Bewildered Drinking His Spirits*.

12:41. "We intend to exalt aggressive action, a feverish insomnia, the racer's stride, the mortal leap, the punch and the slap."
It's Tuesday. Work on the dead continues. This lab is below the world's surface and I have not seen the sun for eight months. But in this small

sanctuary there is a cot and an instant hot chocolate dispenser and an over-the-shoulder sense that someone else is taking stock of the situation. The city of Drammen, the University of Oslo, Norway's President Gunvar Haldor, *der Fuerher*, they spare no expense for the Cryogenics Lab. I am a division of a division in Sector Quad of the Jotne/SB *Verksted*, additional funding provided by the ATLAS Organization—bald, birthmarked men who fear how they will die more than Death itself. They do not want their pale skin to sag off, their eyes to go agape. But I hunt Death here, I the young lion, Death in black fur and pale crosses, running before me under the violet sky ceiling, palpable and living. Death's cold sense comes from the blast chamber I monitor through the one window and into the control panel that whirrs awake in my hands. LEDs flash in coded patterns, tell the time in green, and catalog the laser's diamond cells. Every two-stage He-3 Cryostat cools radiation shields, heat switches, and the superconducting magnet system connected by OFHC thermal copper wire. All for the love of the engine. I have been culling this love for years, ever since Uni and my studies in comparative mythology, art and technology, the history of contemporary Father Italy.

From my chair, I freeze the dead and shatter their frost bones with high frequency waves, searing enough to make dogs bleed from the ears. I redistribute radiation and sound sensor orbits. I match temperature gauge readings in the WRONGSCAN handbook to Kelvins sensitivity: absolute zero. Another body comes and I take comfort when I press the "Commence to Atomize" button. The laser looks phallic. I name it ADAM. Private Ansgar, out.

10:58. "Art, in fact, can be nothing but violence, cruelty, and injustice."

By dumb waiter, meals always arrive on a wax plate with plastic forks and knives. It is always green beans, sauerkraut and pan-fried moose on Wednesdays. Fridays are surprises, but surprises imply security breaches. They use plastic because they are afraid of exposing the metal to beta particle radiation.

Today, a telegram comes on its own wax plate. The yellow paper resembles crude library cards (if there are any left in the world) and it reads: "Ansgar. Position: redundant. Humanoid Robot LIO-7 Prometheus to resume control of Cryostats for absence of error. Replacement: effective immediately." The telegram means human error—the kind is that expendable.

Your odds of dying in a fireworks discharge: 1 in 340,733; in accidental electrocution: 1 in 9,968; in an air/space incident: 1 in 5,051. By falling: 1 in 218. Suicide: 1 in 121. Down here, the odds are equal: 1 in 1. My own death is certain, and so my name is no longer vital. Names are traceable. Out.

4:17. "We intend to sing the love of danger."

Ancient life was all silence; sounds were attributed to gods. Here, the Liquid Argon and Nitrogen tanks sing to me. I do not speak, but follow the erratic strike of keyboard keys, blips on a radar module. Words in the manifestoes I read between deliveries: F. T. Marinetti, Umberto Boccioni, Giacomo Balla. And when my brain tells me my retinas are burning up the way particles do on re-entry to the atmosphere, even I, the futurist, must break down and find beauty in the speed of a pencil tip.

I take out an old E.T. lunchtin from under the counter and place it in my lap. (I salvaged it from the stiff hands of a young American lad.) Inside the tin: 4 X 4 foot sheet of high-resolution, professionally bleached paper folded into squares of 1 X 1, a Number 3 Pencil (tip sharpened with ADAM—an after-hours success), a planchette of cedar set on casters, and the forthcoming hours. Between atomization of a Ukrainian nationalist with no legs below the knees and an Indian woman whose belly is swollen with twins, I take readings from the crude wooden tool shaped like a heart. I slide the pencil down into the center hole, unfold the paper, and place the planchette on top. Even this simple machine has a sound. The cedar creaks, the unoiled ball bearings whine, and the graphite drags.

Step 1: Close your eyes.

Step 2: Place both hands on opposite sides of the planchette.

Step 3: Receive a Question from the back of your brain and do not speak it. The medium is aware.

Step 4: Open your eyes.

I sometimes do not remember the question. Words it has provided before: "Aleph," "Nadir," "Extra Fine," and "Vituperation." I look down at the paper now and the word "Break" stares back at me. The pencil's graphite is cracked and I cannot breathe with that word in my head. Reset ultra-low-noise IF amplifiers to ultra-low DC Power. The secondary air purification system for the primary air purification system kicks on with the chug of a man choking on salt water. 76.5% Nitrogen, 22.4% Oxygen, 0.00433% Carbon Dioxide, 0.0018% Neon, 1.09387% Lime Scent. Death is domestication; someday I will die and something new will steal my carbon; "Prometheus" is the word I am inundated by in this No Man's Land. Prior to his arrival, will I program this installation to freeze my bones and shock me into shards?

Addendum: Who else waits for technology to take their place? Do birds?

3:49. "Time and Space died yesterday."

Friday. The phrase "Abysmal Water" will not leave my mind. It glows in bright blue neon strips; electricity is a blue thing. My ears have begun to bleed on the hour, every hour, to the extent that I use my government-issued nylon sleeve to soak up the streams. Another telegram arrives by way of dumb waiter and it reads the same as the previous message, except that my position has now been downgraded to: "inadequate."

I am Sysphysian in dexterity and Dionysian in gall.

I watch the video monitors. Three are trained on the body in the blast chamber. One monitor looks on me. I cannot see my eyes and that instills a fever in me. Most dead we receive here in Drammen still have their eyeballs, and I am reminded of how I once saw the photo of a young *hibakusha* onto whose iris an infinite image of the Father Bomb had been burned, grafted, cut and sealed like a newly minted coin from the planchet, a coin meant to commemorate the outnumbered survivors.

7:48. "Why should we look back, when what we want is to break down the mysterious doors of the Impossible?"

Twenty-six separate ice ages have occurred on Earth and I am ushering in the twenty-seventh with the repeated press of a button. Today is the day I lose count of how many times I press that button and it is the same day I begin counting how many times I blink. The average man blinks at five second intervals and each blink lasts one-third of a second; the eyes are closed for four seconds every minute. I do not like that I neglect the monitors for a total of ninety-six minutes every twenty-four hours. That's ninety-six minutes during which Prometheus may arrive, and I cannot afford to even blink when he comes through the one locked door and bleeds dry what human moments are left. Prometheus, I assure you, finds a certain salvation in firm number averages. My survival is as unlikely as Heracles passing by Mount Caucasus on a second course. Prometheus is coming and he has no liver upon which I may set an eagle to devour.

I take out the lunchtin again and use the pencil's broken end to write a number on the bleached paper. The digit looks strange when made by a human hand, even one that is surely my own, so strange that I cannot discern where it sits on a number line. The Egyptians once used a decimal system of seven symbols. One is a single line. Ten is the drawing of a hobble for cattle. One hundred, coil of rope. Ten thousand, a finger. One million is the figure of a god with arms raised above his head. Perhaps I have not drawn a number here on the white paper, but rather an arm, an arm whose fingers are so tiny that they escape the sharpest eye. I crush the paper into a ball before putting it back in the lunchtin. This many-fingered god is what I imagine Prometheus to be, and man has not yet eaten god.

11:11. "A typewriter is more architectural."

The overhead fluorescent bulbs have turned off. I miss their humming that once sounded so much grander than a field of crickets. The lights in the blast chamber, the tracking stroboscopic patterns around the Argon Tanks remain on; I must continue the work. Another fine mist of ice falls to the chamber floor like snowflakes which science has discovered are not all atypical, but there must be some flaw in the prismatic rainbow that arcs across the room, a pattern which tells me more about Prometheus' arrival and my departure.

I cannot recall what letters make up my name—I will sign with three coils of rope and a dove's tail over a broken window.

Also: my ears have stopped bleeding, but that means I have finally been hemorrhaged dry. The dumb waiter dings. The third telegram I read by barium glow:

"Do not drink the hot chocolate. Continue Atomization as needed. LIO-7 en route, *en masse*. Prepare for transportation."

The dumb waiter door shuts and I swear laughter echoes from the ceiling, though it is only the conveyor belts' hydraulic engines high up in the facility.

The first thing I do is press the one green button on the one blank wall for a fresh Styrofoam cup of hot chocolate. This is my third since midnight. Even the most human of moments become mechanistic in sequence. I look up at the dark ceiling and drink. I have outlived a use, and it occurs to me, with hot chocolate in my mouth, that we do not have an initial use. We exist to make more exist, to one day transport ourselves away from ourselves. I swallow. I order a fourth cup.

Of special note: other definitions of "transport" that appeal to me more: *to send to a penal colony overseas, or a state of overwhelming usually pleasurable emotion.*

0:00. "Injustice, strong and sane, will break out radiantly in their eyes."

The lights have not turned back on and the green digital clock has reset and not begun again. A man in corduroy pants and a leather jacket torn at the shoulder stands in the focal array zone of ADAM, and I refuse to press the "Commence to Atomize" key. His clothes are too familiar to disintegrate. I'm afraid the man looks like me, pallid and hopeless, though I have not seen a mirror's reflection in over one year. At one point in his life, he too wrote down a number he did not recognize and threw it all away.

Abysmal Water. The Great Possession. The Cauldron. The Clinging.

These phrases boom through me. For the last time, I open the lunchtin and place the planchette on the control panel. I make a fist, hold it down against the wooden tool, and then raise my arm above my head and smash the heart-shaped implement into pieces.

The splinters I pull from my hand grab at the wrinkles and pull the inside out before all feeling slips away. Pain is an adaptation that keeps us alive through nerve stimulation: mildness, localization, distress, debilitation, agony. This is a good kind of hurt, a human hurt, as if more is learned about the body and soul by the reaction to acute mortality. I do not want Prometheus to find me in this injured state, so I uncrumple the wad of paper and wrap it around my hand like dressing a wound. The frozen man in the chamber assures me that someone is definitely watching.

0:00. "We want to hymn the man at the wheel."

My own desperate mission to build a Prometheus. Fourteen Styrofoam cups stacked on top of each other to make a Styrofoam figure, the removed splinters hold the arms and antennae together, a stiff old cosmonaut. The white pile of rounded ribs glows in the dark. They make brittle bones, but bones nonetheless.

Again, I turn around to face the camera that once captured the back of my head. I pause the monitor's feed and return to the front screen: my features I can only describe as humanoid, no longer flesh and blood. The laugh lines are ninety-degree angles. The broad forehead is a solar panel. The intersection of royal nose, pencil-thin eyebrows, and ridged skull in pale crosshairs follow the limits of the Golden Mean. All beauty is mathematics, the Greeks pronounced, and all beauty has been reduced to a ratio: 1.618 to 1. The Man Alive to Dead and

Frozen and Dusted: 1 to Omega. Even the dimensions of my clenching teeth are based on Phi, not even a whole digit. By fundamental laws, we are base equations, and as perfection comes at the highest price, my squinted eyes tell me the cost is not worth the vastness. I turn the monitor off, shiver in my seat, and slowly pick at the holes in my hand. This is a quiet room.

0:00. "There was nothing to make us wish for death, unless the wish to be free at last from the weight of our courage!"
The bell chimes, the door opens, the fluorescent lights turn back on. But there is no man nor humanoid nor even a complete thing:

1. scalene triangle for hat
2. blue pipe of a nose
3. a head no more than a large washer turned on its edge—the hole facing me
4. a barrel body of faded red wood and a waist carved into a bulky skirt—three holes bored through the chest like lobotomies gone awry
5. a vague avian nature to every angle—the albatross around my neck
6. this machine stands seven feet tall on one peg leg

No Golden Ratio commands this creation. I cannot look away. With two arms that have no hands, it carries a 200-watt flashlight and a green toolbox.

"Are you Prometheus?" I ask.

He says nothing. He blocks the one way out.

"Are you my replacement?"

In a motion that is anything but fluid, a mouth opens in its chest with the sound of small gears turning, this pale jaw lowering like a drawbridge at the helm of a thousand tiny fingers. The hole in its head is cold, black. Its blank stare is far worse than any frozen man's face. This, of all things, is my surrogate, and I am desperate to shrink and disappear. But instead of reciting a preprogrammed command or a string of Euclidean distances or an inventory of spare parts and services, the chest's electrolarynx reads vibrations from its internal systems and speaks in low pitch: "Beat."

"Beat?"

"Beat." And this is all it can say. "Beat." The one phrase that booms through that head, body, and heart. Seventy-two in one minute. This is how it keeps its heart rhythm constant, and the same as counting blinks, blinking every time I count the next one. But where the number of blinks may vary in a minute, this machine's consistency is inhuman and perfect and beautiful, and I do not know whether to throw myself at its feet or slam the door on its lowered jaw.

I say, "You cannot count any faster or slower."

"Beat."

"And you have one task to fulfill."

"Beat."

"And you cannot swerve from that task."

"Beat."

I face the maker, Codename: Cloak and Dagger, and realize that the only important pattern is the lack of pattern. Not even the dumb waiter or the cups of hot chocolate fit into a meaningful sequence. The lights go off again and Prometheus turns the flashlight on. The light is jarring, as if it indicates an oncoming train, and so what Fascism did to Italy's rail system, Prometheus will do to our cryogenics facility by flashlight. Perfect time keeps my atomization process on schedule. I remember how my face looked in the video monitor, how my name is now distant, and I feel the eagle at my own liver. I babble to the idol:

"Weather balloon. Dual currents. Pitchfork. Water fountain. Caldera. Speaker magnet. Cutlass. Kanji dictionary. Hair trigger. Phase diagram. Wand. Convolution integral. Camera. Harpie. Flywheel. Tower crane. Turntable. Scylla and Charybdis. Follicle. Resonant frequency. 3/8 inch drill bit. Oslo. Carabiner. Abstract. Dynamic. Extremely transparent. Brightly colored and extremely luminous. Autonomous. Transformable. Dramatic. Volatile. Odorous. Noise-creating. Explosive."

On impulse I say these words and even then, I find myself describing Prometheus as a god. We futurists give skeleton and flesh to the invisible, the impalpable and the imperceptible. We find abstract equivalents for every element, and combine them to make our world more pleasurable. These dissimilar words, these are the human moments I've been looking for, and in this once dull white room, I find comfort in speaking because my voice is my own, still full of lifts, drops, and errors.

"Beat," says Prometheus.

"Camelia blossom. Disguise. Atomic mass," I say. Via ADAM, Prometheus and I have already scattered a thousand treasures of force, astuteness, and raw will-power; with fury, we've thrown them impatiently away, carelessly, unhesitatingly, breathless. Let it be proclaimed that the word "Norway" shall prevail over the word "Freedom." Look at us! We are still untired because we do not ever stop.

THE SECRET IN THE HOUSE OF SMILES

Paul Jessup

Jack cut up pictures of girls with thin razors and then glued the most pleasing body parts together onto a single white sheet of paper.

A leg, snip; an arm, snip. Eyes, snip. Perfect hair, snip.

And then the assemblage. Glue spread across the floor and the sound of glossy pages being stuck and unstuck together. Like Velcro and leather.

The trance was finally broken when the door burst open, slamming against the fragile dormitory walls. Jack jumped but did not stop. Snip, snip, snip. Stick, stick, stick.

Standing in the doorway was Alice in a black dress and green striped stockings. She had her bookbag slung over her shoulder. "Hey hot stuff. Want to go vampire hunting with me? I've got a good one."

Jack did not turn. Did not move. His body was still, rock still, stone still. Meditation. Concentration. The last sorcerer's apprentice. He had to reverse it, to change it back to what it once was.

Alice looked down and saw what Jack was doing. "This again?"

Alice sat down on the floor next to him Indian style, draping her arms across his shoulders. She felt his bones beneath his shirt, his skin hot and sweaty against hers. Jack did not respond. He had found a page with the perfect waist.

She walked over to his dorm window and looked at the campus outside. It looked cold. Night. The pathways between buildings were covered in a quilt of red and brown leaves, illuminated by the sparse golden light of the streetlamps.

Alice sat on his bed. Jack liked seeing her on his bed. Her body accented against the green blanket.Her stockings almost matched. Jack screamed. Alice jumped in surprise. He spit, he swore. He pushed the glossy pages across the floor. Kicked the half-finished girls in anger, destroying all his work. "It's no good, it's no good," he said, "I can't do it. I shouldn't have performed that magic trick. It was all wrong.. Now pieces are missing. Gone."

He looked up at Alice, her staring back. "Come on," she said, "Let's go and do something else. I hate it when you get like this."

Alice picked up the phone, the music of the dialtone singing in her ears. It was time to make a call, time to get Jack out of the dorm room and do something important, something worthwhile. Some vampire hunting would do them all some good.

The walls were red brick and coated with posters. One advertised a local illusionist who was performing for the student government. He wore a top hat and cape, and a waxed moustache that curled to either side of his head like a cartoon villain. In the distance they heard the showers, splashing and laughter.

Jack looked at the wall and grabbed a poster. It was a girl in a bunny costume, holding up two connected brass rings. A simple trick. "Her ears! Her ears! I feel like I'm back on top again. I can almost see her in my mind—moving in and out of vision like a pale ghost. I have to cut off these ears. They are her perfect ears."

Jack rubbed his stale glue laced hands together. It sounded like sandpaper grating. "It will only take a second. Just let me cut off her ears and shove them into my pocket. Come on pretty please, come on."

Alice tossed the poster to the ground and glanced up and down the hallways. No one was here. This didn't feel right. "Hurry up," she said, "Before someone sees us."

Eagerly Jack reached down, pulled out his razor. Snip, snip, a perfect ear for his pocket. Shaped like a conch shell.

"Ok, let's go."

They walked briskly down the hall, their footsteps echoing to the sound of the rushing water and bathing.

Jenny sat on a large orange beanbag chair, her legs crossed and her eyes staring at a large flat screen television she had on the facing wall. A circus show. With artistic clowns prancing about and bemoaning on the nature of existentialism. One threw a pie at the other, and proclaimed all actions absurd.

Jenny wore a dirty purple shirt, stained with ketchup and grease. Her hair was piled up above her head and tied in place with twine and wilted flowers. She wasn't wearing any pants. Just panties and bare legs riddled with shaving scars. She nodded as they walked in. "Some fucked up sideshow," she said, "Have a seat and watch it with me. They're going to bring out the freaks next. My favorite part is when the geek cuts the Siamese twins in half. It's a kick."

They all sat on the floor, facing the large screen television. Alice saw the fridge over in the corner, pushed up against the wall. It opened from the top, like a trap door to a stage. She heard it humming from across the room.

Jenny put her arm around Jack. Her skin was corpse cold, white and pale against his spray-on tan skin, but she was not the true queen.

"Hey, sweetie. Want to do me a favor?"

Jack laughed, nervously. "Sure," he said, pushing her arm away and standing up abruptly.

"Go and get me a beer from the fridge. And maybe take out a pizza and put it into a microwave. You guys hungry? Thirsty? Want a beer or something?"

They all grumbled sure, yeah, of course.

"Good idea," Jenny said, "And Alice—stop looking at my legs. Got it? These are not for you. I've already told you that you're not my type."

Alice laughed a tittering hee hee hee laugh as on the verge of mania. She watched as Jack walked over the fridge. He wore a long yellow raincoat. Alice thought he looked ridiculous. Like a giant bumblebee detective.

The televised twins howled, and there was a sound of tearing meat. "Oh," Jenny said, "This is my favorite part. It always gets me hot. Watching them tear these girls apart. Damn. I am so horny."

Alice turned her face from the television and looked directly at Jenny, keeping her eyes on Jenny's round and acne scarred face. "Did I ever tell you my major?"

Jenny scoffed. "Do I even know you? You just came along with the boy. Why do you think I care about you?"

Alice was unphased. She had done this a thousand times. "Come on," she said, "Take a guess."

Jenny sighed. "I'm missing the best part. I don't care."

"Just guess?"

Jenny tried to hide her anger. "Quantum Physics? You look like a super geek."

Alice pointed to her nose. "Exactly. But not quite. It's a branch of quantum physics. I'm a vampire hunter."

Now Jenny was interested. She turned off her television and turned her gaze to Alice. "A vampire hunter? What does that have to do with quantum physics?"

Alice put her finger to her lip and chewed on the calluses as she spoke. "Well, it's kind of like a vampire observer, really. See, reality is a binary state, right? You can be alive, or you can be dead. One or the other. Vampires, on the other hand, are a superposition of both states. That are both and neither at the same time. Like a supernatural Schrödinger's Cat."

Jenny inched in forward. "I don't get it. So vampires are, what? Super posit wats?

"Superposition. See, in quantum computing a qbit can hold three states while a regular bit holds two. The third state is actually all states and no states at the same time. It's kind of like the inverse of zero. Vampires are the same way—they are a qbit."

Now Alice was excited. She reached over and grabbed Jenny's hands. Her eyes were red. "So, the only way you can tell what a quantum particle is, is by observing it. When you observe it then it tells you what states it is in. But it changes depending on *how* you observe it. Isn't that wild? That's why I'm a vampire observer. I perform tests to see if the state of something living could also be dead. If they are just living or just dead, then they aren't quantum vampires. If they are living with the possibility of being dead, then they are vampires."

Jenny frowned. "I don't get it."

Jack put a pizza into the microwave and turned it on, and tossed a beer at Jenny. Jenny quickly spun around and grabbed it. "Thanks," she said.

"It's crazy, I know. But here. If I have a mirror, and I hold it up to you, and you don't reflect I am performing a test. I am observing you, and if you have the possibility of being a vampire, then you would not have a reflection. Like this."

Alice held up a small makeup mirror. The glass glinted in the neon lights that flickered on the ceiling, casting its own mirror light in the room. Jen stared at it, stared through it, trying to peer into herself. No reflection. Jenny ran out of the room screaming.

Jack hummed and rocked back and forth. Hummed like the freezer in Jenny's apartment. He then darted beneath his bed and pulled out his little perfect pile of magazine parts and glue.

Jack ignored Alice. She did not exist to him. She'd been trying to get his attention all day, all night, for the past month.

He had an ear to affix. He wanted to use his special glue stick for this. It was black and white, like a magic wand. Stick, stick, stick.

She looked at Jack, watched him drool over the perfect ear. No, she did not know why she was still with him. Maybe it was convenience?

Jack screamed. He threw the razor against the ground and scattered the pictures. "The ear is wrong! I thought I had seen her—a glimpse. But no, fading. Fleeting. A mist. It's gone. This trick went south."

He turned and looked at Alice. "There was an audience, you know? They watched the whole thing. Yet no one knew what really happened. And she was smiling the whole time."

Alice did her nervous laugh. Hee hee hee. "Come on Jack. You're just worked up, is all. Take a breath, forget about it all for a moment. You need to relax a little."

Jack rubbed his hands together. Stuck pieces of magazine parts grinding. Arm and leg and stomach and mouth, pushing and rubbing between his hands in an orgy of glossy body parts. "I know of a secret. Hidden in the house of smiles."

Alice leaned forward. "Yeah? What's that? House of Smiles?"

Jack crawled under his bed. His head and waist disappeared under the mattress. Legs wiggled as he searched. Alice heard plastic boxes moving. More things moving. How could he be taking so long? There was barely any space underneath their beds.

Jack scurried out form under his bed. He had a shoebox covered in a plastic bag. He removed the bag, pulling the box out. It was decorated with pictures of rabbits running and a picture of a fox stalking in the green pine trees.

"Here," Jack said proudly, "Here it is. Here, here, here. She smiled like a saw. Big teeth, cutting things apart. The last of the great stage performers. Queen vampire, in hidden stasis." Jack pulled off the lid with a flourish and a tada! Inside was a diorama. Careful, tiny little pieces collected together. Hand made, hand painted. Perfect little pine trees. Perfect little cabin. With a large cartoonish smile painted on the side. And behind, bathed in a cold blue winter light was a perfect tiny freezer chest. Closed and grey.

Excited, Jack turned over the lid. There was a map. It was a detailed map, one written by hand, with directions scrawled across it. Strange directions, turn left at the burning towers, if you've walked past the giant's legs, you've gone too far.

"Where is this at?" Alice asked.

Jack pointed, moved his finger. Made humming sounds. Like a low flying plane. "Not far, not far. Just the woods outside of the University. Could walk there from here. There is a shack and all these abandoned apple trees. A whole orchard left to rot and misery. Whoever owned it must've left in a hurry."

Alice grunted. "Good." She said, "Let's get going then. I can collect everything we need and get going."

Jack shook his head, slamming the book shut. "No, not yet. We can't go yet."

Now it was Alice's turn to have a headache. She just couldn't keep living life like this. Always on the edge of some strange madness.

"Why not," she asked, exhausted.

Jack pointed at the mismatched photographs.

"Because she is not finished yet. I have to remember her, I have to love her. Then we can go back. Then we can use the freezer."

Alice slouched his shoulders. Resigned. "Ok," she said, "All right. Jackie boy, let's construct your perfect girl, shall we? And then—then what? We go to the woods?"

Jack pounded his fists into the floor, drumming the wood. He spoke as he drummed. "You don't understand. Ghosts are more important than food. Ghosts are more important than anything. If you forget them they are erased. Stolen, vanished. Faceless things looking for masks in the rain. You cannot deny me this. You cannot deny her this. Ghosts are more important than vampires. Than dreams. Than water or light. And the ghosts of the saw are the hardest to please. Half finished ghosts, covered in smiles and torn apart."

When he stopped drumming they sat in silence for a minute. "Fuck Jackie," Alice said, "Just tell me what to do, and I'll do it."

She helped him find posters. Find magazines. She cut with him and glued with him and he was happy because he started to see her again. In the glimpse of still life, he caught her. Caught her in fleeting moments, flying and trying to escape.

Alice didn't know it. She could not know what Jack was looking for, who Jack was trying to piece together out of old sticky pages and glossy photos. All she knew was that there was a vampire, in the woods, one that she could observe, one that she could hunt.

She helped Jackie-O Jack perform a bit of magic. Perform a bit of now-you-see-me, now-you-don't. This was a special kind of magic.

Backwards magic. Most magicians were in the art of taking things apart, taking things away, making them disappear and cut into tiny pieces. Not Jack—no, the Jack man had a plan. A new kind of trick. He was going to put someone back together. Reverse that saw, take the blade out and piece her back together again.

A little bit of Now-you-don't-see-me, Now-you-do.

And she would be happy. She would be thankful. And she would say she forgave him, and say that he wouldn't have to be sorry or feel guilty anymore. That was ok, what he did all those years ago. That she was happier now, better now. In a place where queens and puppets dance. And she would be whole again. Setting him free.

They each had pockets filled with picture pieces. Photograph slices, body parts and different snatches of text that Jackie-Jack man thought would come in handy. Special words. Magic words, printed on the page but not to be spoken aloud. When spoken aloud they lose their magic.

Out past the University. The lights and the towers dim glows behind them now. Like distant earth stars, slowly going supernova and fading out.

Pine trees. From his dream, no—his memory. They surrounded them. Sticky, they smelled of sap. The knotted and spiny branches webbed around them, catching them. Claustrophobic. Leaves plastered to their feet with mud. In the distance they heard dogs barking in the cold and Alice shrieked.

Jack did not care. Let Alice scream. Her screams would only echo through the air, and no one could hear them now. Not in the land of the saws. Not in the land of the dead.

Alice reached over and held his face. Her lips were like wet pomegranates. He smelled the seeds on her. Very slowly she said—"I think we are being followed. Do you understand? We are being followed by someone. I think it is Jenny. Vampire Jenny."

Jack nodded, but didn't care. He kept right on walking. Alice dragged behind him, her eyes looking out into the trees, searching and finding faces everywhere, blinking in and out of existence.

He was laying seeds along the ground, and everyone would have to come. Follow, follow. To the house of smiles!

Here was the place, the memory hole, the memory whole, the whole thing. The shack. Grey shack, shingles broken and smashed. Dead shack, undead shack, shack like a home brought back from the dead. Windows were holes, eyes like empty caves. Big smile painted on the side. Cheshire smile, haunted smile. Ghost smile.

Welcome, welcome it said. Welcome to the house of smiles. Welcome to the quantum gateway, the world between binary states. Let the saws sing out the chorus of the heavens.

Jack had a cape. Where did he get the cape from? Nobody knows but Jackie. So they laid the magazine parts down and asked him, now what? He walked over to the freezer in the back and inspected it. It hummed. He walked behind it, pulled out a saw and then approached Alice with heavy footsteps.

Everything fit together now.

"Open Your Pockets!" he commanded in his best magician voice.

She opened her pockets and let the cut up pieces flutter around like butterflies, like broken and dead leaves. He opened the freezer with a flourish and a Tada! And a wave of the magic wand. Inside, inside.

Queen of the House of Smiles. Cut up, wrapped in plastic. Each piece, each part. Crammed in. But some parts were missing. Some parts were always missing. He hated that. How could he remember her with all the parts missing? Sawed off and stolen. The trick that went south. The too sharp saw, grinning as it cut into her, and her all smiles the whole time, even in that pain, the audience applauding.

And then her asking him—Jackie—please, put me back together again. She whispered it as she smiled, teeth together. He wanted to stop sawing, that Jackie-O did—he wanted to. Keep cutting as the crowd applauded.

The pages fluttered, stuck and unstuck. They flew over and stitched themselves onto parts, stitched everything together. The missing pieces made whole out of magazine skin and magazine eyes and magazine faces.

In the trees faces crawled out, sat down to watch the show.

Saw, saw, saw. The vampires applauded and Alice was all smiles. She could not stop grinning, could not stop laughing as each part of her body was removed, magazine pieces representing her waist, her eyes, her hair fluttering around her as he cut into her.

The body rose slowly from the freezer chest tomb. The body was her. The sorcerer's last apprentice. Dressed in plastic, the distorted clear making her even more real in the moonlight. Living, alive.

Time to dance like half-dead cats. Presto!

A DANCE ACROSS EMBERS

Lisa Mantchev

In the clearing where it was always-spring, Grandmother Bear took Milena's hand in her paw and smiled. "I am to be married today."

"Again?" Milena laughed. Grandmother Bear was forever getting married to someone or other. "Will there be mummers and fire-dancers? Will we drink rosewine and dance until morning?"

"Of course," said Grandmother Bear. "That is how these things are done."

Milena pointed to a lovely thing of white mist, woven from spidersilk and woodland lace. "And will you wear your veil, Baba Metza?"

"Yes, I will," said Grandmother Bear with a laughter that was sunshine and tears that were the soft, sweet rain. The soon-to-be bride rose and took up a ceramic dish filled with wheat, coins and a raw egg. Then she tossed it over her head.

The dish smashed on the forest floor in a hundred-thousand pieces and Milena skipped over them to retrieve the veil. It was not as tricky as fire-dancing, but it still brought very good luck indeed.

It was a sunshine-on-snow morning. Brilliant white light poked fingers through the curtains, but Milena knew better than to put her bare toes on the floor. They'd freeze, sure as anything, and she'd be stuck there until spring. Her suspicions were confirmed when she poked her nose out from under the covers like a little brown wood-bunny and an icicle formed on the end of it.

Somewhere in the basement, the furnace grumbled to life. It

gobbled up coal in shovels-full, its chin hovering over the bin like an old person eating soup; even under the covers Milena could hear it chewing with its furnace-door mouth hanging open, belching smoke and sooty cinders. She could also hear Tatko listening to the morning news on the television.

And Mama opened the door to her room. "Good morning, darling."

"Did you have a nice time at your party?"

"Of course." Mama, with her face turned to the curtains, didn't sound as if she was telling the whole truth.

"Can I come with you next time?" Milena pressed.

"It's not that sort of party." Mama patted the hump of blankets that covered Milena's knees. "Did you have pleasant dreams?"

"I didn't sleep last night; I went to a party too. A wedding." Milena tasted her quilt when she answered. "Grandmother Bear got married."

"Again?" Mama turned, and her smile warmed the room as much as the radiator which clanked and hissed like a tea kettle. "Who did she marry this time?"

"Father Time." Milena rubbed at her sleepy eyes with her fists. "He's old, with a long white beard and crinkles around his eyes. But she likes him ever so much. So they married, and I was the best girl."

"But, of course! And then what?"

"There was sunshine and rain, all at once. And when the stars came out, she tucked me into the big bed in the middle of the forest," Milena said. "I didn't want to sleep there because the ghosts might take me in the night."

Mama froze as though icicles had grabbed her elbows. "The ghosts?"

"The ones that take people from their beds in the middle of the night," Milena told her. How silly of Mama to not know about the ghosts! "Ventsei told me—"

"Yes, well, your friend Ventsei shouldn't say such things." Mama had the frown-line that cut her forehead in half. "Get dressed now. Breakfast is waiting."

Milena pulled and stretched her sweater like it was saltwater taffy until her head popped through the opening at the top. Then she skipped down the stairs. "Good morning, Tatko!"

Her father greeted her at the table with a smile like warm chocolate. He kissed her with a loud smacking of his lips, and his moustache sprinkled her with drops of coffee. "Eat!" he commanded.

"All right, all right." Milena reached for her napkin and wiped off the offending coffee. Her plate held slices of spicy *lukanka* sausage around the edge, with a buttered *pitki* alongside a soft-boiled egg. While Milena ate, her parents talked, words tossed back and forth over her head like the red rubber ball on the playground.

"Another one taken in the night," Milena's father said with his eyes on the paper. He had his mouth full of caviar and toast.

"Shush," Mama told him. "Not in front of the little one. The words are sparrows; once released, they cannot be caught."

"We should tell her, before she hears at school. It was the fire-walker—"

"Ivan?" Mama said with a sharp intake of breath.

"What about the *nestinar*?" Milena asked. Ventsei's grandfather performed the ritual every year on Saint Constantine and Helena's Day.

"The glowing coals are a bridge between the village and the patron saints and venerable ancestors," he once told her, then winked. "Some hail me as a prophet, but most just call me crazy."

No one in Ventsei's family went to the parties, so Tatko didn't like Milena to visit Ventsei's house.

"He . . . left last night," Milena's father told her with a rattle of his silverware.

"Did he disappear like a magic trick?" Milena asked. "Magicians can make people disappear with a poof of green smoke and nothing's left but a rabbit." She swung her legs against the rungs of her chair. "Maybe it was the ghosts. They steal people from their beds. Do you know where they take them?"

"You'll be late," her mother interrupted. "And put on your coat."

161

"Yes, Mama." Milena slid out of her chair and ran for the front door.

"It's not so important that I am well," her father was saying in the kitchen, "but that my neighbor is worse off than I."

Milena pulled on the heavy wool coat, the one with fur around the collar. She strained her ears to hear what Mama would say.

Normally that phrase—*but that my neighbor is worse off than I*—made Mama laugh, but she wasn't laughing now.

"Indeed, they are worse off this morning for certain."

Something in her voice prickled Milena's throat, and she decided she didn't want to hear anymore. She reached for her hat, scarf, and mittens of pink yarn. She shoved her slipper-shod feet into her overshoes and lifted her voice to bellow down the hall, "Ciao!"

"What is wrong with your own Bulgarian, eh?"

Milena called back, "*Divizhdane!*"

"Have a good day!"

Milena saw Ventsei trudging up the first hill. He'd gone on without her.

"I thought of a new riddle!" she called as she struggled through the snow to catch up. They played this game every day on the walk to school. "As small as walnuts, they sit in a low place but reach to the skies. What am I?"

He didn't answer, and he didn't stop to wait for her either. Instead, he plodded through the snow with his chin tucked against his chest and his coat collar turned up against the chill of the morning. She skippity-skipped up next to him and nudged him with her book bag.

"*Dobro utro*, Ventsei."

Ventsei shook his head. "No, it's not a good morning." His nose was red just as it was every morning, but she could tell from the way he swallowed hard that he'd been crying.

"What happened?" she asked, then she remembered the rubber-ball words her parents had exchanged. "Is it about your grandfather?"

"I don't want to say."

That was a first. Milena blinked at him. "Are you all right?"

"No."

They plodded in silence for a few minutes. Only their boots, scuffing through the snow, murmured *tsh-tsh-tsh* to each other. Ventsei's breath came in short pants and the crystals hung in the air long enough to freeze in ugly misshapen imps. He shoved them away and seemed to make up his mind about something. "The ghosts came last night and took him."

"I thought he left," Milena said.

"No, they stole him right from his bed."

The imps snapped and snarled and then dove headfirst into the snow banks that lined the road. Milena stopped and stared at her friend, but he kept marching forward, and she had to run to catch up.

Milena's coat blew open, and the icy wind rattled her bones. "Did you see it happen?"

Ventsei shared a bed with his grandfather because their house was old and small and there wasn't enough space for everyone.

He jerked his chin up and then down. "They were all in dark suits, and they had guns."

"Now you're exaggerating," Milena said. It was a big word, but she used it with confidence, having been told on occasions too numerous to count by her parents and her teachers that she exaggerated too. "Ghosts are white. And they carry chains."

"Not these ones." Ventsei came to a standstill in the snow; with his pale face and blank expression, Milena thought he looked more like a ghost than the ones he'd described. "He never thought they'd come to the house because of the *stolinina*—"

Milena gasped at the idea of the ghosts rummaging through the icons, rearranging the votives, or maybe even tapping on the drum. The little chapel in the back of Ventsei's house held the icons of saints and the sacred drum, and all the villagers considered it holy. "Did they touch anything in it?"

"No."

She put an arm around his shoulders and squeezed him as hard as she dared. "Why didn't you stay home today?"

Ventsei shook his head. "My mother thought it would be better if I got out of the house and away from the trouble there."

"And your father?"

"He didn't say anything." Ventsei's hands doubled over into fists. "But I think he went to look for my grandfather."

Milena didn't know what to say to that. She scuffed the snow with the tip of her boot. "Did you have any breakfast this morning?"

"I don't remember."

"Come on. Silviya's window is open. Let's get *banitchki*."

Ventsei hung back. "I don't have any money with me this morning."

"I have coins." She tugged him across the snow and to the blue-shuttered window. Lelya Silviya's house leaned just a little to the left, like a tired old woman resting on the way home from the market. Its wooden shingles slanted this way and that, the plaster walls crumbled a bit around the edges. But Silviya's oven was hot, and her wizened hands rolled the finest pastry in town.

Milena reached up on tiptoe to slide her coins over the timber-framed windowsill. The smell of melted butter and hot baking pans set her stomach rumbling. "Two please, extra hot."

"Every morning you say that, Milena," Silviya grumbled, "and every morning I give you a *bantitza* that is hot as the sun blazing down on Rose Valley in June. I am not a doddering old woman to forget such a thing. These just came out of the oven. Be careful you don't burn your mouth. You too, Ventsei."

"Yes, Silviya," they chorused as they each juggled a hot pastry from one mittened hand to the other. Steam rose off them like smoke from Tatko's cigars, but they smelled infinitely better. Milena took a bite before she ought and, of course, scorched the roof of her mouth.

Ventsei saw the water rise in her eyes and admonished, "You do that every time."

Milena huffed around the molten cheese and danced from foot to foot. "I know."

"Then why not wait a moment longer?" he scolded without any real heat. "And the answer to your riddle? Small as walnuts, sitting in a low place but reaching for the skies?"

"Yes?" she said with a happy grin, glad to stand in a sure place for the first time since leaving the house.

"Your eyes," he answered. "Now one for you. What is the sweetest and the bitterest thing in the world?"

She thought on it as they ambled down the street, taking careful bites. "Sugar is sweet, but not bitter. Maybe lemonade?"

"Close, but no. It's the tongue that is the sweetest and bitterest thing in the world."

Milena didn't know what to say after that; she wanted to comfort her friend, to say something about her visit to Grandmother Bear and the ghosts that roamed the forests. Instead, she picked the phyllo-dough crumbs from her mittens as they neared the schoolyard.

At the gate, Ventsei grasped her by the elbow. "Don't say anything to anyone else, all right?"

Milena lowered her voice. "About the ghosts?"

He nodded. "It's not safe right now. Nothing is."

"Maybe . . . " Milena hugged her book bag to her chest. "Maybe we should ask Baba Metza. She'll know where they've taken your grandfather."

Ventsei stared very hard at something overhead. Then he looked down the street and up. And finally he nodded. "Come on; let's go."

They turned the opposite direction and headed for the forest. The ringing of the teacher's bell gave chase but could not catch them.

All the rain that had fallen during Grandmother Bear's wedding had frozen in glittering rainbow-orbs that rolled and crunched underfoot as they picked their way through the forest. The trees were no longer bedecked with flower-garlands but reached skeletal arms toward the dour, gray sky.

"Baba Metza?" Melina called as they entered the clearing that was her bedroom. "Are you here?"

"I am." There was a rustle in the frost-speckled bushes, and then she ambled in on all fours. At first Melina thought the snow clung to the shaggy silk of her coat, but when Grandmother Bear got closer, Melina could see that white hairs threaded through the brown. Swirls of snow started at the corners of Baba Metza's lovely dark eyes then whorled over her shoulders and down her back.

Melina's hand twitched toward Grandmother Bear's fur, but such a thing wouldn't be polite unless invited. She twisted her hand behind her back instead. "Are you quite all right, Baba Metza?"

"Just a little tired." Grandmother Bear settled back on her haunches and looked them over. "What brings you here in the daylight?"

"Ventsei has a problem."

Grandmother Bear's shaggy head swung towards the boy. "Is that so?"

Ventsei didn't answer; he was trying too hard to keep the tears from falling, so Melina answered for him. "His grandfather was taken by the ghosts."

Grandmother Bear didn't look surprised. Just sad. "Yes, I hear the whispers on the wind."

Ventsei found his voice. "Where did they take him?"

"The bees are sleeping, but even in their sleep they whisper to me." Grandmother Bear's ears twitched toward the wild beehive ensconced in the oak tree. The buzz of a thousand creatures snoring rose louder for a moment, then faded back. "Far away, little one. And your father has joined him."

"Oh, no." Milena covered her mouth with both hands, but Ventsei only looked grim about the mouth.

"I thought that might happen," he said to Milena's surprise. "Can you ask the bees, Baba Metza, what I should do?"

Milena listened again, squeezing her eyes shut and concentrating very hard. She heard the ice crackling on leaves and the gray of the sky and even the promise of grass under the snow, but she could not make out the conversation between Grandmother Bear and the hive-mind.

"Even the bees don't know the answer to that," Grandmother Bear finally said. "But they bid you pile the logs high and burn them down to glowing coals. Then dance across the embers. And when you go into the fire-trance, you will be able to hear the voices of your father and grandfather. And they will tell you what to do next, *nestinar.*"

"Ventsei . . . the *nestinar*?" Milena said. "But . . . he's too young to be the fire-dancer!"

"I am not!" he blazed at her. "I'm nearly nine and older than you!"

"Only by two months," she argued.

"Ah," Grandmother Bear held up her paw, "but his soul is far older than yours, Milena-my-love."

"How can his soul be older than mine?"

"He has heard more, seen more, knows more." Grandmother Bear stood up on her back legs and reached into the hive. Her massive paw extracted a chunk of honeycomb that she broke into two dripping-gold pieces. She handed one to each child, but her eyes were always on Ventsei. "He understands the changes coming better than you, with your head full of fairytales and loveliness."

"You make that sound like a bad thing." Milena moved honey and wax around in her mouth. "I'd rather my head be full of nice things than ugly ones."

Ventsei shifted his honeycomb to one hand and licked his fingers. "I would too."

"As would we all." Grandmother Bear shook her head; the swirls of white spread down her back to meet the snow on the ground. The flakes began to fall, thick and fast. Milena blinked them off of her lashes as fast as she could. The clearing was dusted with powdered sugar snow and icicles clung to Grandmother Bear's fur.

"Baba Metza?" Milena could hardly see her for the white.

"Children, you must stack the wood high and let the fire burn bright . . . " Grandmother Bear said as a bearded man—Father Time—

appeared between the oldest of the oak trees. Grandmother Bear nodded to him. "One moment more, my love."

"We must leave," he told her. "It's not safe to linger here. I have heard gypsy bells in the woods, and I will not let them catch you."

Milena glared at him. "Where are you going?"

"Deeper into the woods, further up the mountain." All the rich brown of Grandmother Bear's fur was gone now. Against the falling snow, it was nearly impossible to see her. "Closer in time to spring and closer to the stars in the heavens."

"Don't go!" Milena started to run forward, but Ventsei caught her by the back of her coat. "I don't want you to go."

"Go I must. My husband calls to me.

"When will you be back?"

"She's not coming back," Ventsei said. "Are you, Baba Metza?"

"Clever boy, clever boy," Grandmother Bear said with a chuckle under her sadness. "I would tell you, before I go, about the eagle. He is a creature that flies between the worlds, from the mountain heights to the underworld depths. He drinks from the lake of the water of life that lies at the end of the earth. And he is the helper of heroes."

The last thing Milena ever saw of Grandmother Bear was her honey-sweet smile as Baba Metza said:

"Watch for the eagle, Ventsei."

When they got to Ventsei's little house, his mother was hurriedly shoving clothes into suitcases. She'd sewn her lips shut with white thread and wouldn't say anything to either of them. She handed him a packing case and gave his shoulder a push.

Milena tiptoed behind and held her breath as they passed the *stolnina*. The little alcove held burning candles in red votives even during this rip-and-upheaval. The icons hanging on the walls returned Milena's tentative glance with black eyes rimmed in gold paint.

She hurried to follow Ventsei to the little back room that had been his grandfather's. He knelt by the dresser and opened one of the drawers. Milena stayed in the doorway; she hadn't been invited in, and anyway, the room smelled of ashes and burned-up secrets.

"Will you take your trains?" she finally asked.

"No."

"Your teddy bear?"

"I don't think so."

"What will you take then? I'll help you pack."

"It can all stay."

"Then what are you getting?"

"His matches." Ventsei put them in his pocket and backed out of the room. He took her by the elbow and pulled her through the kitchen. Great tears rolled down his mother's cheeks, but she paid them no mind, not even when they dripped on the photographs she held in trembling hands.

The children went into the little yard behind the house.

"Will you help me with the wood?" Ventsei asked.

"But you should be packing—" Milena started to argue, but he cut her off with a sharp look.

"Baba Metza said to pile the wood high. And that's what I'm going to do, with or without your help." Ventsei filled the wheelbarrow full and rolled it over the packed snow with a bump-bump-bump around to the front of the house. Melina hefted a log under each arm and followed him.

Ventsei's house formed one side of a small square; he headed to the very center, and Milena added her logs to the pile he made. Ventsei restacked the wood the way his grandfather had, criss-crossing logs so they would burn hot and even. Then he got to his feet, knees crusted with ice, and headed back to the woodpile. Milena trotted after him, not wanting to stay in the square by herself.

By the time they came back with more wood, Ventsei's neighbors had ventured out. Wearing hoods and scarves, silent and grim, they appeared with more logs and helped with the stacking. They worked alongside the children, at first saying nothing but eventually driven to speak.

"For Gavril," Yuliana said.

"For Krasimir and Pavil," Ianka added.

"The *nestinar* will speak to them when the fire burns down, yes?" Zlatka asked.

"I don't know," Ventsei said, his voice low. "But I will try."

"Ask," Zlatka said with a hard swallow under her many headscarves, "if they are well."

"Ask," Ianka said, "if they will ever return."

"You know the answer to that," Yuliana scolded. "Ask instead what we should do without them."

Milena trotted back and forth until her legs and back ached. Splinters riddled her mittens, and her whole skin prickled. But she didn't stop, driven as she was by the desperation and grief of those around her.

And all the while, she wondered if her own Tatko or Mama would be taken away by the ghosts that had visited all the others. Fear hummed in her blood; perhaps they'd been taken during the day, and her house would be dark and empty, the door standing open . . .

She swallowed a sob, and Ventsei looked up from the mountainous stack of wood. His dark hair fell into his eyes; when he brushed it back, it was as though he peered into her soul.

"They'll be fine. They're—" but he bit off the words with a glance around him and didn't finish.

Milena fell to her knees next to him. "They're what? Tell me, Ventsei. Please. What were you going to say?"

"They're safe. You don't have to worry." He reached out and squeezed her arm. "They're members of the Party."

Milena thought of her parents' party clothes: the black suit and the coat with fur around the collar. Mama's diamond necklace. The long, dark car like a sleek panther that came for them. How tired they often seemed, and stuffed full of secrets after a night at a party. She'd always thought parties such fun. But no more.

"Ventsei," Milena held his hands in hers. "Are you certain you can do this? Walk across the fire, I mean. What if you burn up?"

"Don't ask questions," Ventsei said as he struck a match and held it to the pyre. "Simply watch and believe."

More people gathered as darkness fell: those who had been at school and at work. A few scuttled indoors like roaches afraid of the light, but most of the neighbors formed a ring around the bonfire. Bagpipes crooned and wailed. The memories of loved ones taken gathered in the smoke; wavering figures in gray that sent shudders down Milena's back.

Ventsei disappeared into the press of people and returned carrying the ceremonial drum. "I will not use the icons . . . but I would have you play this for me." And he handed it to Milena.

She accepted the instrument with great reluctance. "I'm too little."

"Those are not the words of a girl who talks to bears," Ventsei chided. By now, the fire had died down and only the embers remained. "I would have you do it. You can't make nothing out of something—"

"But I can make something of nothing," Milena finished.

"So make a loud noise for me." Ventsei took a deep breath, and he stepped out onto the coals.

Milena found her heartbeat and his in the drum. She pounded the taut-pulled leather with the flat of her hand, unable to look away. Ventsei tread in the short, even steps of the *tipane*, on the whole length of his feet.

She didn't disappoint him; the beat of the drum was strong and loud. Milena lost herself in it, as Ventsei lost himself in the dance. Everyone else was chanting, holding up their hands. Voices climbed in the old songs. Young and old called to those who had died, to those who had been taken.

The ghosts gathered along the edge of the crowd and watched with empty holes for eyes and grim mouths. They wore the dark shadows like cloaks, and the sight of them startled Milena so that she nearly missed a beat; heartbeat, drumbeat. Her breath was in her throat, and she wanted to scream to Ventsei to run. But her friend looked at her, into her, through her. His lips moved—

Drum harder. Drum faster.

And because he was older, because Grandmother Bear trusted him so, Milena did as he told her.

"Speak to us!" someone cried. It might have been Zlanka or Yuliana. And one by one, the hazy gray memories moved forward to embrace those who mourned them, to whisper in the ears of those left behind.

Ventsei reached out and grasped her by the hand. With a swift tug, Milena too was on the embers. And then they were running down the road, past the school. They tossed riddles like red, rubber balls over the stone walls, but they did not stop. They galloped over cobblestones and onto the dirt path through the forest. They dodged trees and leapt over fallen logs until finally they stood on the top of the hill behind Grandmother Bear's forest.

The eagle hovered overhead and then dipped down. Ventsei's mother clung to its neck, and she motioned to her son.

"I have to go." Ventsei's words matched Milena's thudding heartbeat and the memory of her hand against the drum.

"How will I find you, when I grow up?" Her tears were rainbow orbs that rolled down the mountainside.

"One last riddle, then." Ventsei clung to the eagle and smiled down at her. "A world without people, cities without houses, forests without trees and seas without water."

She knew this one, and each tear she shed held a laugh. "A map."

"There is no hero without a wound." Ventsei touched a finger to his chest. "Mine is in my heart, leaving you. Don't forget me."

"I could never—"

But the eagle flapped its mighty wings, and they were gone, borne aloft on the wind. Milena blinked once, twice, and they were gone over the horizon.

And she was back on the village square, with the drum still in her hand, looking at the empty space where Ventsei had danced across the embers. The villagers had fallen silent. The ghosts were gone, thwarted by Ventsei's escape.

Milena hit the drum. "For Gavril." And twice more. "For Krasimir and Pavil." And one last time. "And for three generations of *nestinari* taken from us."

Her parents pushed through the crowd, and Tatko caught Milena as she fell, exhausted, into his arms. Mama took her by the hand and cried big, silent tears.

"What happened?" her father demanded as he bore her through the deserted-night streets.

"Ventsei left," Milena told them. "He's gone where the eagle flies." She looked up at the night sky, where only one star burned. "And I will go to meet him . . . as soon as I find the map."

THREADS OF RED AND WHITE

Lisa Mantchev

Ventsei hiked the hill trails to remind him of that place long lost to him. The fragrant spruce and fir were the same as those he'd left behind, and their roots reached for the heart of the mountain with gnarled, patient fingers.

Time had passed since the eagle had landed on foreign soil and deposited a young boy and a woman who could not speak. The boy wandered far, the soles of his feet still burning with the dance. His mother followed three steps behind, a silent shadow whose grief faded-to-lingering with each step.

They drifted both north and west until they found a place where Ventsei could breathe without the air catching in his throat; a place where both the mountains and trees whispered "home" in his adopted language.

Tereza looked from mountain to forest, and she pulled out the first of the stitches that sealed her lips shut. Every year after that she removed one more, until the only thing that prevented her from speaking was her decision to swallow her words rather than give them voice.

Twenty stitches pulled; twenty years gone, as though they were no more than a series of heartbeats, a hand coaxing a rhythm from the stretched-skin surface of the ceremonial drum.

Ventsei counted out twenty paces and turned to look back at the lone set of footprints he'd left in the snow. He had the park to himself when the others scattered during the lunch hour. It sounded too fanciful to say that he'd rather feed his soul, and so he said nothing when he put on the pair of sturdy boots he kept under his desk.

Today, the boughs filtered the thin light of winter's-end, and he was glad of the down-filled jacket over his starched cotton shirt. Spring was a dream to this place, still decorated in blue-tipped frost, and most of the wildlife had not yet roused from under that blanket. Though there were claw-marks high in the trees, they were not fresh.

The bears still slept.

He hoped that among them was a once-brown bear now white with snow and sorrow; that Baba Metza had also found her way to this tranquil place—

"*Dobar den.*"

He spun about, feet skidding on the ice. "*Izvinete* . . . I mean, excuse me."

"No need to translate for me, Ventsei." An old woman sat upon a rock—one he'd passed only moments before. Wearing innumerable layers and a frown, she leaned on a stick of forged iron and looked about her with an air of condescension. "You have done well for yourself here, the winds tell me."

"I'm sorry for not greeting you by name," Ventsei apologized, wondering how someone so old and so crooked could have climbed the incline. "Are we acquainted?"

"We are that," she said but didn't elucidate. "You're a doctor, the winds whisper. A specialist."

"An internist, yes."

She harrumphed, but her breath did not crystallize in the freezing air so much as it danced away in a flurry of snowflakes. "Internists know everything, but don't know how to do anything."

"My grandfather used to say much the same," Ventsei said, with a smile despite himself. "And surgeons don't know anything, but know how to do everything."

"And there are those who both know nothing and can't do anything," she added. "So maybe better to be an internist, eh?"

"I thought so, Baba . . . " He allowed the word to trail off, waiting for the stranger to supply her name.

"You don't recognize me? You've been gone too long, too long." He didn't answer fast enough for her liking, and the stranger's stormy expression summoned thunderclouds. "You walk these paths and see the other forests, the other mountains."

Ventsei nodded, though his neck was stiff. "That is true."

She slanted a gaze at him that was sharper than a kitchen knife. "You wonder if that silly bear escaped the hunters' rifles and the gypsies' leashes."

"I don't deny it, although how you know—"

She interrupted with a rush of words that was like an ice-fed stream down his back. "And your thoughts stray to little girls with pink mittens. You wonder what it would be like to have married a nice Bulgarian girl, one who speaks the language you confine to your dreams."

Ventsei flinched as though she'd struck him and bit his tongue to keep from answering; his mother's son, indeed.

The stranger cackled with unexpected laughter that called back the sun. "You have nothing to say to Baba Marta, eh?"

The chill spread along Ventsei's limbs. "My apologies, Grandmother March."

She snapped her wizened fingers at him. "Hold out your hand." Ventsei did as she bade him. "Twenty years without wearing a *martenitza*, it's a wonder you're not dead from bad luck." She tied threads of red and white about his wrist as she hummed. "White for purity of snow, red the setting sun." She tied the knot tight. "It must be worn until you spot the first stork of the year."

It must be worn to appease her, so that winter passes and spring arrives. "There are not many storks here, Baba Marta."

She turned Ventsei's hand over and his gold wedding band glinted. She hissed and shoved him away. "Stupid thing, what have you done?"

He rubbed it with his thumb, as he often did to reassure himself it was still there. "You are wise. I doubt I need explain it to you."

Grandmother March rose from the boulder and slapped him twice in quick succession. "Once for forgetting the rites of the season."

Ventsei rubbed the burning spot on his cheek. "And the second?"

"I intended you for another," she said as she hobbled away. "You made promises to her."

Yes, he had made promises. And his regrets about those left behind had a way of tinting all his memories; his past was the same crumbling brown of old paper, and as likely to fall apart if handled roughly.

Grandmother March didn't take her leave of him, but she added, "She will be disappointed."

Ventsei had to step off the path to give chase.

The blood ran, as did he. He slid down the mountain, ripping his jacket down one arm and scratching his face on naked thorns.

In the ravine, the forest lost all familiarity. The trees Ventsei had counted as friends were now strangers, and the river—a crooked finger when viewed from above—showed hairline fractures in its frozen surface.

Grandmother March could not be wholly displeased if the ice was melting, but the *martenitza* tightened around his wrist.

"Who will be disappointed, Baba Marta?" Ventsei called as he threaded his way through the firs: the slender *elha*.

"You think to keep pace with lightning?" Grandmother March taunted him from the other side of the stream.

Ventsei rested his hands against his thighs as he tried to catch his breath. "What are you doing here? Now, after so long?"

"There was no reason to come any sooner," Baba Marta said. "She traded me twenty years, and twenty years I collected."

"Who traded you twenty years?" But he knew.

Baba Marta's face crinkled with a sly smile. "Your Milena made a beautiful *samodiva*."

"You changed her into a wood nymph." It was not for him to question, he who had counseled with bears and escaped upon the eagle's back.

His fruitless searches were now explained, why no one knew what had happened to her. "In exchange for what, Baba Marta?"

She whistled low through her teeth. "You were the one so fond of riddles. '"A world without people, cities without houses, forests without trees and seas without water.' Answer your own question."

The wound on Ventsei's heart opened just a little. "A map."

Baba Marta raised a hand. "I offered gold." Coins spilled through her wizened fingers. "And I even offered back the years." The coins turned into discs: pocket watches dangling by thin chains before they hit the snow and disappeared with a hiss. "But she would have nothing but the map. So I gave it to her. And now she's come, looking for you."

Ventsei took a step forward and heard the ice crack under his boot. "Milena's here?"

"What do you care?" she demanded. "You, with your doctoring and your ring and your new life? You, with your forgotten promises?" She pointed her walking stick at the stream. The ice broke, and cold flooded into Ventsei's boots and socks. "You'll need deeper water than that if you wish to drown out the past."

"There were no promises—" He jumped to keep from falling in and landed beside her on the far bank. "Except the ones you made to trick her."

Grandmother March tucked her arm in his, delighted by his accusations. "No tricks, no tricks." She cupped a hand about her ear. "Can't you hear her singing?"

Ventsei held his breath. There was a sound, thin and silver, that might have been a voice calling to him.

"Come," Grandmother March coaxed. "She is just down the river and across the bridge."

"There's no bridge in this park, Baba Marta."

"Oh no? Then how to you explain the *mostovi*?" She drew him around an outcropping of rock.

"You didn't—"

She had. The Wonderful Bridge rose high overhead. Once-high river water had transformed the stone into vaulted arches that spanned the canyon.

But it had no place here. It belonged in another valley, another time. Ventsei stared at it, aghast. "You had no right to bring it here."

"I was doing you a favor, stupid boy. Your true love is just on the other side." She tried to pull him forward with her.

"Milena was a childhood friend." He stood fast, refused to be budged. "I married my true love."

"Cross the bridge," Grandmother March urged him as though he'd said nothing at all. "You can go back."

"I can't. I have a life here. A daughter—"

"A mongrel child." Grandmother March spat into the snow. "Not a child of kings."

"There aren't any more kings, Baba Marta. All the kings are dead. The princes stand alongside the peasants." Ventsei shook his head. "Enough. This folly keeps me from my work and my home. Go back where you belong, and take your threats and your bridges and your fairy tales with you."

Baba Marta chuckled. The mist crept around her ankles like baggy, wrinkled stockings. "If you will not go to her, I will bring her through myself. Come across, dear Milena. See how he speaks to your godmother."

Tiny whirlwinds stirred the loose snow. Sparkling crystals stung Ventsei's eyes and then the blizzard cleared.

"It is you!" someone cried and kissed him with her cold lips. The woman was a stranger to him, but she wept diamond tears with Milena's brown eyes.

She wore a loose-fitting shirt and gown, a green leather belt and a sleeveless jacket. Every garment was decorated with feathers. Ventsei reached out with a tentative hand and brushed back a strand of her hair. Loose and wild, it reached down her back and the ends were tipped silver with ice.

"You've changed," he said.

Milena stepped back, as if she needed the extra room to take in his height. "As have you."

"There now." Grandmother March beamed, and the sudden flood of sunshine-on-snow blinded him again. When Ventsei blinked, she was gone. But Milena remained.

"Take me to your house," she demanded, clasping his hand with the impetuousness of the child he remembered. "I want to see everything."

Ventsei wondered how he would explain this woman, so oddly dressed, arriving without warning or luggage or money. How would he explain it to his mother, who would surely remember Milena's eyes?

Milena shivered in her thin garments, and he knew whatever trouble it might cause to bring her home, he couldn't leave her to freeze in the park.

"Of course," he said, because it was the only thing he could say. He shrugged out of his down jacket and placed it over her shoulders. "My car is this way."

She followed him up the mountain, nimble as a goat.

Ventsei paused on the porch to stamp off his boots. He inhaled the sweet breath of night and . . . not wood smoke, but the scent of roses. Droplets of oil fell from Milena's fingertips and onto the steps.

Another thing to explain.

Kimberly looked up when he opened the back door, her expression startled. She had the phone cradled between her neck and her ear.

"No, he's here. Never mind." She set the phone back on the cradle. "That was the office. They've been calling since you didn't come back after lunch." Her eyes traveled from Ventsei to Milena, then back to her husband to demand an explanation.

"This is a friend," he said in English. "From the old country."

"Ah." Kim smiled and gave him the look that meant *the house is a mess, I wasn't expecting company, we'll discuss this later and you won't enjoy it* before she turned to Milena. "*Dobar vecher.*"

Ventsei switched to Bulgarian. "Milena, this is my wife, Kimberly."

"Good evening to you as well," Milena said as the scent of roses filled the room.

Kim shook her head. "I'm sorry, my Bulgarian isn't as good as it should be." She wiped her hands on the back of her jeans. "I'll go get your mother, Ventsei. She'll want to greet your guest."

Milena turned to him as Kim left the kitchen. "She's upset."

"The little one tires her." The kitchen was hot, crowded though it was just the two of them.

"Little one?"

"Our daughter, Damascena."

"A child named for the roses," Milena said, her voice low. "It is lovely."

Then there was only the soft tick-tick-tick of the clock on the wall. Ventsei stared at it so he wouldn't have to look at anything else. The clock was new, but painted to look old and cracked. Kimberly shopped at thrift stores and brought home scuffed and rusted bits she called 'antiques' that were the source of much gentle teasing on his part.

Kim's fascination for collecting things that would otherwise be fodder for tetanus shots both puzzled and delighted him. But how would their house, their odd collection of furnishings, look to an outsider?

To one of my oldest friends, he amended.

Milena looked from the kitchen table, where none of the chairs matched, to the cheerful curtains cut down from an old tablecloth, to the wood-burning stove that produced a constant glow. "It's just like home."

A drop of oil fell from her extended hands to land on the hot metal with a hiss and sizzle. A smoke-flower bloomed atop the stove and was gone.

"Milena."

Just like the clock, the voice was flecked with rust; the sort of thing that would scratch deep if handled carelessly. Ventsei turned to see his mother standing in the doorway to the kitchen, Damascena balanced on her hip.

His mother had broken her long silence.

The child in her arms crowed with surprise. "Baba!"

"Yet another Grandmother," Milena laughed. "Congratulations are in order. *Chestito!*"

Tereza poured into the room like sparkling wine after a cork. A stream of welcoming words flowed from her: well-wishes about Milena's journey to this place and Tereza's own happiness about her marvelous grandchild.

Milena looked at Damascena with solemn eyes. "*Nazdrava*, little one. To your health."

The child held out her fat arms and went to Milena. Face-to-face, Ventsei could see they shared the same curve of the cheek, the tilt to the nose—

His daughter so resembled the Milena that he'd left behind, that he could hardly breathe. The tightness was back, squeezing his chest with fears and longings he thought he'd abandoned.

Kim saw it too. She hovered in the doorway as though the shared joy and memories of the other women prevented her from entering. When she turned, he followed and caught her halfway down the hall.

Kim spoke to her own ghosts. "In all the years, your mother has never spoken a word to me. Not a word to her granddaughter. But she says another woman's name and it's like some magic spell has come undone."

Ventsei caught her hand in his. "She's homesick."

"This is supposed to be her home." Kim swallowed hard enough that Ventsei could see all the things stuck in her throat. "What about you? Would you go back, if you could? Would you wish things to be different than they are?"

He would not lie to her, so he said nothing.

"Our baby looks like Milena." Kim's tears glinted in the dim light. "How is that even possible?"

"It's my fault," Ventsei said, drawing her into his arms. "I thought about her so often . . . "

"You thought about her?"

"She was the girl I couldn't bring with me, the girl I couldn't save."

"She wasn't yours to save." Kim pulled away. "And now she's here."

"Yes."

"Why?"

"I don't know."

"For how long?"

"I don't know that either."

"What *do* you know, then?"

The argument was like the automatic gunfire he remembered hearing, huddled under the quilt of his Grandfather's bed; it didn't require forethought, aim or skill but the words hit their targets all the same.

Ventsei wanted to tell her that he loved her, but the words would mean less than nothing now. "Come back to the kitchen. We'll have dinner, and visit. You can get to know her—"

"I'm tired, Ventsei. I spent my afternoon nursing the baby and folding laundry and wondering if you were dead in some damn ravine." Kim went up the stairs two at a time to get away from him as fast as she could. "I don't speak the language, and you have more important things to do than play translator."

"I don't mind—"

"But I do. Just go keep an eye on her."

Kim closed the bedroom door behind her, and Ventsei didn't ask which 'her' Kim meant.

Tereza and Milena had cleared off the little table and set it in the center of the kitchen. Next to the woodstove, a cinnamon-coated bear lay stretched out, claws extended. Damascena sat on her squat little behind in the middle of the fur, chewing her fist and burbling in a language all her own.

The bear opened one eye to look at Ventsei, then closed it again and smiled at the excited chatter of the two women. If bears could smile, that is, and Ventsei wasn't sure he wanted that many teeth on display near his daughter.

"A paint brush for an artist," Tereza was saying. "Scissors for the tailor."

"A pen for a writer." Milena stirred the contents of her junk drawer with her hands. "Money for the banker."

"It's been a long time, firedancer." Grandmother Bear shifted her bulk carefully so as not to upset her precious burden.

Ventsei was glad Kim had barricaded herself upstairs; a bear at the hearth would shake the last leaf from the tree. "It has."

"Your *martenitza* looks a bit tight."

"It is that." He tried to fit a finger under the binding threads, but found there was no room. "Where is Father Time? How is your husband?"

"He elected to remain on the Bridge." Her ears flicked back at the baby, who was blowing spit bubbles and pulling at Grandmother Bear's thick coat.

"You left him there," Ventsei guessed.

"Better that time should stand still tonight." The bear smiled. "You have traveled far, but the road has circled back. Perhaps the embers were only banked and not extinguished, eh?"

"You are most welcome here, Baba Metza," Ventsei said as scooped up his daughter. "But I will thank you to remember that this is not your forest, but mine." He turned his back on the bear and whispered to the child. "What big mess are your Baba and Auntie making?"

"You remember this, surely," Milena said with a laugh. "We'll let Damascena walk to the table, and whatever she sees first, she will be when she grows up. It should have been done as soon as she started to walk!" She looked to Tereza. "What did Ventsei pick?"

Tereza smiled. "A stethoscope."

"You see? It was his destiny." Milena slanted a look at him that cut.

"The eagle carried you far," rumbled the bear by the woodstove, "but you could not outrun that which had been decided."

The *martenitza* scored the skin now, tightening in a delicate thread-noose. Ventsei put the baby in her high chair and handed her a toy before going to the refrigerator and pulling out a carton of yogurt.

"I don't know if we have a round loaf of bread," Tereza fretted. "A square loaf won't roll, and she must chase it."

"It can wait until the morning," Ventsei said. He filled a plastic bowl and found one of the baby spoons that looked so ridiculously tiny in his hand. "I can go to the store."

Milena laughed at him. "Oh-ho! Such an important person, to buy bread instead of making it."

"*Proshtupulnik* is an old tradition," Ventsei said. His pulse throbbed in his fingers with each heartbeat, each word. "Perhaps one best left in the past."

The two women stared at him, while the third tugged at his beard and stuck her fingers up his nose.

"The child should know where she comes from," Tereza said after a long moment.

"Yes." After twenty years of silence, he did not want to dismiss her precious words. "And you will tell her the stories and sing her the songs. But she alone will decide where she is going." Ventsei fed Damascena a spoonful of yogurt, most of which ended up on her chin, her cheek and down her front. "I won't have you telling her 'you chose a pen, you must write' or 'you must travel the world because you took the globe.'"

Milena shook her head, whether in disappointment or disapproval Ventsei couldn't tell. The feathers had thickened along the fluttering edges of her dress and belt. "It's harmless—"

"It's not!" He brought his fist down on the table and everyone jumped. Damascena puckered her face and began to cry, and it took several frustrating seconds to extricate her from the high chair's safety harness. By the time he had her on his shoulder, she was alternating wails with hiccups.

Ventsei patted her heaving back, swaying a bit and trying to soothe her as the back door opened to admit a third Grandmother.

"Tell them about the nightmares, *nestinar*." Grandmother March leaned heavily on her stick. "Or did you lock them away with your language and your traditions, firedancer?"

If he hadn't cradled his daughter, trying to calm her, he might have punched the wall. "I dream that the ghosts come, that they pull my wife from our bed, our child from her cradle. I dream that my life here is the dream, and that reality burned the night I danced on the embers."

Kim was back, summoned by the noise. "I heard her crying." His wife's eyes were red from doing the same. "Why are you shouting?"

Ventsei didn't answer her. Instead, he divided his anger between his mother, his friend, the bear and the crone. "I will not be dragged into the past by the whims of others."

Kim tugged at his arm. "Stop screaming over the baby. Give her to me."

"You will never see a stork here," Baba Marta shrieked. "This land will never again know the spring!"

Damascena shifted in his arms, and Ventsei looked down at the naked, creased folds of her neck. A cluster of veins stood out on her skin, dark pink against the white-as-snow.

Kim tugged at his arm again. "What are you staring at? Give her to me, Ventsei!"

"What did they call this mark at the hospital?" he asked. He pitched his voice very low, very soft. "I've forgotten how to say it in English."

The clock on the wall counted off the seconds. Tick-tick-tick . . .

Kim looked at the birthmark and wiped at her running nose with her sleeve. "It's a stork bite. Please give her to me."

"The stork has already been and gone." Ventsei raised his chin at Baba Marta. "The spring will come anyway, with or without your say-so." His eyes passed over Milena as he turned to Kim. "She has no hold on me."

He didn't explain which 'she' he meant.

Baba Marta threw her head back and keened. She hit her walking stick against the floor; once, twice. Her stick came down a third time, and she was gone.

Ventsei gave the baby to Kim. "I'll explain when I get back."

Kim jerked her chin at Grandmother Bear. "And perhaps you'll explain that, too."

"That, too," Ventsei agreed. He went down the hall to the closet to retrieve a camping lantern and another jacket.

By the time he returned, the kitchen door stood open. His mother sat on the floor, her hands over her eyes. Kim hugged the baby close, but didn't say a word. She only kissed him on the cheek with lips as warm as the Rose Valley in June.

Both Milena and Grandmother Bear were gone, and two sets of footprints led away from the house.

To hike back into the park by moonlight was to step into a black-and-white photograph. Ventsei found Milena and Grandmother Bear at the edge of the bridge that led back to his homeland and his childhood.

Milena had her back to him, one hand stroking Grandmother Bear's head. "I should never have come."

Ventsei moved to stand next to her. "Not true. My heart dances, knowing that you survived. And you don't have to leave."

"This place has its own spirits." She'd shed his coat. The dark feathers along her arms were tipped silver with starshine and ice. "My mountains and my forests are on the other side of that bridge, and the old country needs the *samodivi*."

"And what about you, Baba Metza?" he asked.

"I don't see why I can't stay a while." Grandmother Bear sat on her haunches and studied the claw marks high in the trees. "When Damascena gets old enough, she can visit me in this forest."

"Will you get married again?" Milena asked in her little-girl voice. "Will you wear your veil?"

"I am already married," Grandmother Bear reminded them, "and too old to wear white." She unwound the hidden scarf and offered it to Milena. "Take my veil back with you, find a use for it. Wear it in good health."

Milena put it on with a laugh; the spidersilk and woodland lace covered her with a layer of frost. "I will that."

Ventsei found his voice. "Take something back for me too."

"A message?" Milena turned to him. "Will you bind it to my leg with golden thread?"

"No." Ventsei opened his pocket knife and slid the blade under the red and white threads. He cut through the *martenitza*. He could have tied it to a fruit tree, giving it health and luck, or he could have buried it under a stone. Instead, he wrapped it about Milena's wrist. "May each spring be lovelier than the last."

"*Leka nosht*, Ventsei."

Good night.

"*Dovizdhane*, Milena."

Farewell.

EXCERPT FROM A LETTER BY A
SOCIAL-REALIST ASWANG

Kristin Mandigma

I apologize for this late reply. Our mail service has been erratic recently due to a spate of troublesome security-related issues. I don't think I need to elaborate. You must have read the latest reports. These government spooks are hopelessly incompetent but they (very) occasionally evince flashes of human-like logic. I expect it will only take them a matter of time before they figure it out, with or without their torturous diagrams, at which point I may have to seriously consider the advisability of having one of our supporters open *another* German bank account. As a diversion, if nothing else, and I have had nothing entertaining to watch on cable television (which I believe has also been bugged because it persists in showing me nothing but Disney) for a while. Just between the two of us—I do believe that if fatuous, single-minded politicians were not an irrevocable fact of life, like having to use the toilet, we would have to invent them.

Now, to your letter. I confess to having read it with some consternation. I am well acquainted with your penchant for morbid humor and yet the suggestion that I might write a short "piece" for a speculative fiction magazine struck me as more perverse than usual. What on earth is speculative fiction anyway? I believe you are referring to one of those ridiculous publications which traffic in sensationalizing the human imagination while actually claiming to enrich it by virtue of setting it loose from the moorings of elitist literary fiction? Or whatever? And by elitist substitute "realist," I suppose. You argue that speculative fiction is merely a convenient "ideologically neutral" term to describe a certain grouping of popular genre fiction, but then follow it up with a defensive polemic on its revolutionary significance with regard to encapsulating the "popular" Filipino experience. To which I ask: As opposed to what?

I believe, Comrade, that you are conflating ideology with bourgeois hair-splitting. When it comes down to it, how is this novel you sent along with your letter, this novel about an interstellar war between monster cockroaches and alienated capitalist soldiers, supposed to be a valid form of social commentary? I do not care if the main character is a Filipino infantryman. I assume he is capitalist, too. Furthermore, since he is far too busy killing cockroaches in godforsaken planets on a spaceship (which is definitely not a respectable proletarian occupation), his insights into the future of Marxist revolution in the Philippines must be suspect, at best. And this Robert Heinlein fellow you mention, I assume, is another imperialist Westerner? I thought so. Comrade, I must admit to being troubled by your choice of reading fare these days. And do not think you can fob me off with claims that your favorite novel at the moment is written by a socialist author. I do not trust socialists. The only socialists I know are white-collar fascist trolls who watch too many Sylvester Stallone movies. Sellouts, the lot of them. Do not get me started on the kapre, they are all closet theists. An inevitable by-product of all that repulsive tobacco, I should say.

With regard to your question about how I perceive myself as an "Other," let me make it clear that I am as fantastic to myself as rice. I do not waste time sitting around brooding about my mythic status and why the notion that I have lived for five hundred years ought to send me into a paroxysm of metaphysical Angst for the benefit of self-indulgent, overprivileged, cultural hegemonists who fancy themselves writers. So there are times in the month when half of me flies off to—as you put it so charmingly—eat babies. Well, I ask you, so what? For your information, I only eat babies whose parents are far too entrenched in the oppressive capitalist superstructure to expect them to be redeemed as good dialectical materialists. It is a legitimate form of population control, I dare say.

I think the real issue here is not my dietary habits but whether or not my being an aswang makes me any less of a Filipino and a communist. I think that being an aswang is a category of social difference—imposed by an external utilitarian authority—like sexuality and income bracket. Nobody conceives of being gay just as a literary trope. Do they? To put it in another way: I do not concieve of my biological constitution as a significant marker of my identity. Men, women, gays, aswang, talk show hosts, politicians, even these speculative fiction non-idealists you speak of—we are all subject to the evils of capitalism, class struggle, the eschatological workings of history, and the inevitability of socialist relations. In this scheme of things, whether or not one eats dried fish or (imperialist) babies for sustenance should be somewhat irrelevant.

I would also like to address in more depth your rather confused contention that the intellectual enlightenment of the Filipino masses lies not in "contemporary" (I presume you meant to say "outdated" but were too busy contradicting yourself) realistic literature, but in a new artistic imaginative "paradigm" (again, this unseemly bourgeois terminology!). As I have said, I would emphatically beg to differ. Being an aswang—not just the commodified subject, but the fetishistic object of this new literature you speak of—has not enlightened me in any way about the true nature of society, about modes of production, about historical progress. I am a nationalist not because I am an aswang, but despite of it. You only have to consider the example of those notorious Transylvanian vampires. No one would ever call them patriots, except insofar as they speak like Bela Lugosi.

Before I end this letter, I must add another caveat: my first reaction upon meeting Jose Rizal in Paris during the International Exposition was not to eat him, as malicious rumors would have you believe. In fact, we spoke cordially and had an extended conversation about Hegel in a cafe. I do think that he is just another overrated ilustrado poseur—brilliant, of course, but with a dangerous touch of the Trotskyite utopian about him. I prefer Bonifacio, for obvious reasons.

In closing, let me say, as Marx does, that "one has to leave philosophy aside." You must inure yourself against these pernicious novels about cockroaches and spaceships (and did you mention dragons? all dragons are either Freudians or fascists) for they can only lead you to a totalizing anthropogenetic attitude towards the world. Concentrate on the real work that needs to be done, Comrade.

(For all that, let me thank you for the sweaters. I can only hope you did not buy them in that cursed cesspool of superexploitation, SM Shoemart. It is getting quite cold here in America, hivemind of evil, and it has been increasingly impractical for me to fly out without any sort of protective covering.)

Long live the Philippines! Long live the Revolution!

THE RIVER BOY

Tim Pratt

There once was a woman who wanted more than anything to have a child. She was old, and had outlived her own sons and daughters, and their sons and daughters, too, and since her grandchildren had all been excessively taken with modern ideas and upstart temperance religions, there were no great-grandchildren. Her family name—which was very beautiful and meant "those who dwell on the banks of the great river" in an old forgotten language—was withered and almost gone, and she could not bear to be the last of her line. She knew many secrets and mysteries—that was how she'd achieved such long life, a life that had seemed a boon when she was young, but was more and more now a misery—and so she made a plan.

A few months before the snows were due, she left her cottage on the cliffside, with its medicinal garden and curmudgeonly half-wild goats, and hiked two slow days through the woods. She fended off wolves with her walking stick and highwaymen with her glares, and by shaming them with the names of their mothers—one of her many powers was to know the name of everyone's mother, even yours, little one.

Finally she reached the bank of the river where her ancestors had been born, a mighty water so vast and long that for most of its length it had no need for a name other than "The River" or sometimes "Big River." She had, in her youth, traveled the river, from source (a bubbling crack between two rocks in the mountains) to mouth (a fishing village that had grown into a vast port during the decades of her middle age). But this modest spot, a bend in the river with bare trees and browning long grass, was the particular place where *she* came from, so she made camp, and dipped her toes in the muddy placid reedy water's edge, scaring frogs and prompting the slow process of alarm that passes for startlement in turtles.

"Oh river," she said, "You are all the family I have left. Your waters flow in my blood, and I'm sure the blood of my many relations runs diluted in you. I am too old to bear more children of my own, and stealing away bright children from unfit parents can have troublesome consequences. Please, great river, if it be in your power, give me another child, and I will devote myself to him forever." She knelt on knees creaking from her long journey and drank the silty cold water of the river until her belly was cold and hard as a stone. Then she rolled over, wrapped herself in a cloak by the fire, and slept.

When she woke, it was no longer autumn, or even winter, but spring, and the sun shone down on her grassy bed surrounded by purple wildflowers, and a tiny baby boy dozed placidly on her chest. She sat up, ravenous, but pulled the baby to her chest with old instincts, baring her breasts. The baby nuzzled, clutched, and latched, sucking. The old woman was amazed she could produce milk at all, though she supposed that was no more miraculous than the fact of the babe himself. But when he dropped his head down, sated, she saw a trickle not of colostrum or milk but of clear cold water from her breast. She shivered, rose unsteadily to her feet, and looked at the wide empty channel of cracked earth where the river had been. She looked down at her baby, and he opened his eyes. They were the rich deep brown of river mud.

"Drought," she said firmly, scowling at the riverbed. "A little rain will put it right, I'm sure." She looked at the baby, her expression softening, and whispered "You're mine." She began the long hike back to her cottage, baby clutched close.

The old woman named her son River, and he grew quick as marsh reeds. His eyes were changeable, brown to blue and back again, and he loved it when she sang him all the songs of her youth, and the songs learned in her many travels from delta to tributaries to alluvial plains.

She sang him the songs boatmen sang, and the songs dock loaders sang, and fisherman songs, frog gigger songs, washer-woman songs. He drank the water from her breasts until he was old enough for goat's milk, and later honey from her hives and vegetables from her garden, and he sang, too, almost even before he could speak. The old woman felt dry places inside her blossom, felt fissures in her spirit heal, every time the boy called her "mother."

And she never, ever thought about the land beyond her mountain cleft, and she never, ever ventured over the hills to the river valley beyond.

When River was ten years old, he began to have nightmares. He would wake, shouting, and the old woman would rush from her pallet to his hammock, where he would twist and gasp like a fish in a net. At first, he was simply inconsolable, but after three nights he began to tell her about his dreams. "I see boats titled on dry sand," he said. "I see women with cracked lips. I see strong men sitting idle on heaps of crates. I see lines and hooks twisted in tree limbs, and an empty city, and a dozen dead villages, and more, and more, and more."

The old woman closed her eyes. It was possible, she knew, to grow as old as she had grown and yet still not become wise. But she *was* wise, even if she had let her knowledge guide her to troubling places. "Tomorrow," she said, "We'll take a journey, and see what we see."

River was excited, as boys will be, at the prospect of a trip. It was spring, so there were no hungry wolves, only songbirds and butterflies, and River whistled at the one and chased the other, all nightmares forgotten. After two days they reached the spot where River had been born, or gifted, and the flowers were dead, the trees dying, the bare riverbed a stretch of misplaced desert.

"Ten year drought," she said, and River yawned mightily.

"I'm so *sleepy*," he said.

"It was a long journey. Come, lay down here in this dry place." She led him to the center of the riverbed, and he followed, trusting as always. She returned the bank and watched him settle to the ground, expecting a miracle in reverse. But he just slept, and she thought perhaps her own power was too strong, that she'd doomed the land of her ancestors with her own one life's need. She wept then, and the tears rolled in clear fresh rivulets down her cheeks, breaking into waves when they struck the dry earth, and in moments the riverbed was filled bank to bank with a welter of mother's tears, and her boy sank without a ripple.

"My son is drowned," she thought, and sat unmoving as night fell, seeing no need to rise from that spot ever again, knowing even her own long life would end in time if she did not eat or drink.

The water lapped the bank in a long slow rhythm, and frogs—already frogs!—began a counterpointed croaking, and with a slow dawning kind of awe she realized the river and the frogs were, in a way, singing; an old song of consolation for men and women whose loved ones had died and been sent floating down the river; a song she had taught her son just that winter, one cold and windy night.

When she wept again, the tears were salty human tears of relief.

Years passed, and people came back to the river, and fished, and gigged frogs, and sailed boats, and washed clothes. Some of those people were so grateful for their new lives that they took a new name to go along with them, a name that means "those who dwell on the banks of the great river" in a fine old language. That's what our name means, and where it comes from, little one.

Some say that old woman made a raft and sailed up and down the length of her son the river, singing to him and hearing songs in return, as proud of him as any mother could ever be of her son, as proud as I will be of you someday, I think. Some say that old woman still sails to this day, and when the water birds and frogs make music, it is the river, singing his mother a lullaby he learned long ago at her breast.

Close your eyes, little one. Listen to the river. Listen to him sing.

—*For my son*

ACID AND STONED REINDEER

Rebecca Ore

The reindeer were stoned. Flat Nan, Ken, Ro, some other girls and boy who'd just discovered sex and I were chasing mammoths off the summer range so the horses could eat in peace and so we'd have some hazel nuts left for the winter. We didn't hunt mammoths until snow fell which made tracking them like following a herd of Buicks. Mammoths always looked surprised when we found them so I don't think they were that smart.

Centuries later, I was at a loft party in New York City, having gone back to see how some people I'd met in 2001 had gotten that way. It was easy to wrangle invitations to parties in the early 1970s if you were a presentable boy, and I've always been a presentable boy. The loft was full of painters with real gallery shows, of famous painters' future, present, and ex-wives and boyfriends, of the kinds of people who showed up to be at a party with famous painters, poets, and the various entertainments people who threw loft parties had to offer. Dancers danced. Painters chatted up art critics. Poetry professors chatted up graduate students past, present, and future. And I felt both in place and out of place, remembering parties in places that must have been Rome that felt like this, or which could have been provincial capitals pretending to be as vicious as Rome. Clothes change; bodies and poses don't. I was maneuvering for the drinks table when someone said, "If you want to try acid, the punch is spiked."

If I was going to get drunk, I was going to be pinned down in time for the duration anyway, just like being sleep, so I might as well try something new. To lock me to the party time, I drank two big glasses of white wine, which was the screw-neck bottled cheap Chablis available at all bohemian party those years. Then I took a drink of the punch. I'd heard about acid, like rye fungus without the fingers dropping off, and I was feeling reckless, which happens when you spend a couple of centuries being really cautious after seeing a lover hanged, and your caution starts to recoil. Stonewall marked the change; New York was full of possibilities those days. The revolution hadn't quite faded.

Even before the acid hit, I'd spotted a couple of guys who liked what they saw. And saw one man who'd lost his old lover and who would lose his young lover to AIDS, but this isn't that kind of story, so we've got to move on.

I knew not to spend too much time with the people who'd wonder why I didn't recognize them in 2001, so I found a couple of people who I knew would have moved away by then, two women, one also tripping and sitting in a chair while people worried about her which amused her, another one curled up on a sofa talking to someone who wasn't ever going to be famous. Just when I was wondering if the punch had really been spiked, I remembered . . .

The reindeer were stoned. I had a vivid dream while awake, of reindeer eating mushrooms, the ones we'd been told were poisonous to average people, and wandering around, bumping into trees, goosing each other with their antlers, eating the mushrooms, and jumping into the air.

I was carrying a small pack with flint, fire stone, tinder mushrooms, and some dried meat, and I had a spear and throwing stick with me, but these reindeer were acting so silly, I didn't have the heart to kill one. The boy we'd traded a sister for said, "They get drunk eating the mushrooms. If you drink their piss, you'll see visions and can fly and talk to them."

"How do you get their piss?" asked Flat Nan, ever practical except when she was trying to get someone to sleep with her despite not having much in the way of breasts.

"Walk right up to them and ask," the boy said. He walked right up to one of the reindeer and blew it.

I had Ro for that. Ro looked back at me, obviously thinking the same thing. Neither of us wanted to eat the mushrooms or the yellow snow.

Al, who was always his alpha daddy's son, stabbed one of the reindeer and cut out the bladder and began chasing the girls and squirting the piss into them. I walked over to one of the reindeer and asked it to piss in my lamp. Oddly enough it did. The piss tasted nasty, but I gulped it down and stood there. The reindeer looked at me. I looked at the reindeer.

And back in New York, I was telling someone, "Mushrooms, man, they will get you fucked up almost as good as acid."

"Mushrooms will make you sick," the girl said.

"Not if you filter them through reindeers," I said.

"And you're going to get reindeers where in New York?" she replied.

And after the drugs took hold, the reindeer and I started chatting, and I started telling someone the story, but in the old language, so he led me into a back bedroom and asked, "Do you have any friends here?"

"The girl in the swing," I managed to get out in English. "The chair swing."

He led me back out and put me at her feet. I kept telling the story as I saw it unfolding in my awake dream, but I don't remember if I managed to get the story all the way up to English or not and I was careful to whisper so I didn't bother anyone. One girl started crying over in another time, um, place in the party and someone pushed her out in the hall. These were a tough drug people, not as friendly as the reindeer. It was important not to bother anyone.

I put my arm on the reindeer's shoulder and said, "Why do you want to get stoned? I'm never going to do this again." Back in New York, I laughed.

The reindeer said, "Look, we're prey animals. We're too smart to forget that we're prey animals, but it's a pain to be always knowing that you're a prey animal and that everything from lions to dogs to you to eagles wants to kill and eat you or your children. So, since we can't dumbly forget like the horses who hang around you despite you eating one or two of them every so often, we pig out on mushrooms from time to time. So, kill me already."

"I can't kill you. I'm talking to you."

"That's the drug talking," the reindeer said.

I started crying and checked back with my body in New York to make sure I wasn't crying there. Nope, so back to the reindeer. "So what I'm imagining you saying is just the drug making me think what you're telling me isn't what you'd really be thinking?"

"I'm sorry," the reindeer said. "I'm just not used to sentences that twist and curl back on themselves like that."

"That's okay," I said. "What I meant to ask was isn't the drug giving me special insights, like magic, into your thinking?"

"Hey, man, don't try to make my trip your trip," the reindeer said. "I'm sure your elders and all those kids over there are going to have some magical explanation for all of this, but I'm a reindeer and we don't do metaphysics. We just fly around after we eat mushrooms and we giggle."

"You're saying just enjoy it?"

The reindeer sighed and tried to shrug his arm off his shoulder. I didn't shrug off. "Look at you. You've killed off the giant deer. You're killing off the mammoths. We're not doing real well, either, despite being able to sneak a whole lot better than mammoths. You'll probably eat us out of here. And you want to have me prep your drugs for you."

"But we love you. We eat you to assimilate your virtues."

"You know that most of what you people painted in your caves is extinct now."

This jolted me back to the loft party. I remembered the reindeer being stoned, but the acid was probably giving me a mental remix of what really happened. But then my life is often like that, first the ending, then the beginning, and then the parallel that happened earlier than the incident it was paralleling.

———

Vel paused, holding an old stone oil lamp in his hands. He sniffed it as though something should have remained of the urine. "Nothing but dust now," he said to Quince. "Should I go into details about the sex or not?"

"More just the blow by blow," Quince said. "You can skip some of the details when you describe your encounters."

I felt confused about what I was doing at this party and remembered the first time I'd stepped into a Seeing. I'd been around 16 or 17. What I'd seen was a bunch of guys wearing towels and having sex. Looked like loincloths to me, so I jumped right in, totally unable to speak any language in the scene, unaware that this was centuries in my future, thinking it was somewhere else in the Paleolithic. I laughed in the loft, thinking that I was probably now close to the time when I'd first jumped. I just thought they had really better lamps somewhere else in the Paleolithic. So, I turned to the hallucinating and hallucinated reindeer in that vivid half dream and said, "I remember you. I haven't remembered you in thousands of years, but I must have dreamed about you to remember this now."

The reindeer looked at me and said, "I'm long since dead. My descendents are now working for the Sami in Norway and dragging children around on sleds in upstate New York."

I tried to fish though my memories for the real story, the original drinking of reindeer piss. The reindeer said, "You know you're not going to find all of it. You haven't remembered all of it in so long those brain cells have been recycled and recycled again. You remember better the things you understood at the time, but only if they were really different from day to day life. Big pains. But big joys, too."

"That's not fair," I said. "What's the point in living a very long time if you can't remember everything."

"Even I, who you're going to eat when you catch me next, don't remember everything. I suspect I won't remember anything of this conversation," the reindeer said. "Now will you shut up and let me enjoy my mushrooms."

"Sorry," I said. I turned my attention to the party and found someone really cute to go chase. We went into the bathroom that wasn't full of people doing lines of coke.

Under the light, he saw just how drugged I was and how young I looked. "You're balls out tripping. I can't take advantage of you like this."

My frustration levels were about to pop my zipper. "I want you to take advantage of me," I said in the voice of the reindeer.

He said, "I'll blow you. Just don't follow me home like a puppy, okay." He wasn't the best of lovers, but I didn't need the best of lovers with my imagination burning acid. The reindeer stuck his nose against my asshole and licked my taint from asshole to balls, and I just exploded.

The guy looked at me and took a warm towel and began cleaning up and the reindeer was giving me head and I came again. "Oh, to be young again and be able to endlessly come. I think that should enough," the man said. "And other people need to use this bathroom."

I hopped up on the sink and waved my legs at him. "Come on, already," he said. He zipped up my jeans as I was starting to shrug myself out of them.

"Listen to him," the reindeer said from the scene inside my mind. "You'll be embarrassed later."

"I can give you a blow job you'll never forget," I said.

"My dear, I don't stick my cock in the mouths of people who are tripping their heads off."

Ouch, that hurt. I curled up like a snail, and the man pulled me off the counter and sat me down by the woman in the swing chair who was grinning wickedly at someone who'd come by to make sure she was okay.

Back in the half imaginary, half real past, the reindeer and I were sobering up. We hadn't been talking for a couple of hours, just wandering about with my arm resting on his back, him being about waist high to me. He rolled his eyes back at me as though he'd just realized he'd been walking around with a human hanging on to him for hours.

Most of the dogs had gone off once they realized we weren't going to help them and we were acting as crazy as the deer. One came back and sat down, looking eager. My reindeer friend thrashed his rack against my hand and took off running, the dog chasing him. I washed out my lamp and pissed. A reindeer crept up, weirdly cringing like a dog, and lapped up my piss. The other humans looked wrecked. I supposed that I looked wrecked, too.

I got a cab home from the party, with two other people, including the woman from the wicker chair, and went back to the Chelsea, different room this time, and lay down on the bed, not quite coming down yet, but aware, as I had been aware 14,000 years ago, that what I'd done was take a neurotoxin and semi-poison myself, and that if this worked like alcohol, I couldn't step out of this time until I was completely sober. But then I remembered I'd had two glasses of white wine before all this started. And I had wanted to follow home the guy who'd blown me, just like a puppy, but knew that was the acid, too.

We built a fire back by the reindeer the foreign boy had killed and sat around eating it for a couple of days, fucking, the way kids did when they made a kill off away from the grown-ups. Flat Nan and one of the other girls skived the deer hide and we all stomped brains into it and folded it. I wondered if eating a stoned deer would make us stoned again, so went off to find another one and killed a fawn of the season, so we had two deer and lots of time to hang around being young humans with each other until the girls got pregnant again from all the good eating. Better with mammoths because you could slide and slip on all that flesh as you were dressing it out, but two deer in the fall before it got cold and snowy and mammoth season were nice.

Hard to hide what Ro and I were up to, and the het boys and girls were curious and we were all just still stoned enough to talk and demonstrate. I don't know what the half-life of the mushroom drug is in reindeer flesh. The deer had bleed out and the liver and innards were foul from being left in the body after the foreign boy had cut the bladder out, so we probably weren't getting the most psychoactive parts.

"So, why don't you use females to put your cock in?" Ken asked.

Ro said, "Just don't. Females can't know what it's like to touch the pleasure thing inside."

"You have a pleasure thing inside your ass?"

"Probably you do, too," I said. "There's one you can feel up the asshole."

Ken looked like he didn't believe us at all. He asked Ann, "Put your finger up there and see what you feel."

Ro and I leaned into each other and watched while Ann put her finger up Ken's butt. She wiggled around and Ken breathed out, "Okay, but she can do this for me." Ann looked like she'd figured out a new way to wrap boys around her fingers.

The foreign boy said, "You can cut her a stick and make her a harness so she can fuck you."

"No," Ken said. Ann was busy cleaning her finger with leaves. She went down to a branch and cleaned it more. "Okay, so it's not just the one pushing his dick in who gets something from this."

"No, and we have hands," I said. "We trade off being the girl."

Ann looked at us as though we'd said something impossible. "What about this sucking thing?"

Ro said, "You should be able to do this just as well as we can, but you need to look at it carefully and find the little raised ridge behind the cock skin."

I said, "Helps to wash good."

The foreign boy said, "The guys who go for guy are good with their sister's children."

"We know that," Ken said. "That's why we like having a few in the group."

Ro and I looked at each other and smiled slightly. Ken was going to challenge his father's uncle sometime really soon now.

Flat Nan said, "Since I don't have good breasts, could you find me sexy?"

Ro looked at her. "Possibly, Nan. I don't think people should be frustrated. And women get smarter if they have children, I've heard."

I looked at Ro with some concern. "She's got a slit, not a dick."

"I could try pretending I was with you."

Nan started to cry. I wish I could give her tits or something so she could get laid without having to get my tenderhearted boyfriend to have to try to satisfy her.

First love. For all of us. Nan got someone to get her with child not long after that and grew a pair for nursing the child, so she wasn't Flat Nan anymore. I suspected it was Ro, since he was capable of being really generous, especially when he could use his dick to make someone smile. We didn't invent man-man sex, but I think he did invent penis puppetry.

The dogs got the hides away from us and ate them, and the deer's guts and then ran home and hid in their own cave for a few days. Dogs hate drugs and scary things.

The grownups had taken a mammoth that refused to stop pestering the horses so nobody was really impressed with what was left of our two little reindeer. We all made some lamps and went hunting for tinder conk, those big fungus that grow on trees, so we could start getting things together for Bringing back the Sun, Winter Solstice.

I love Winter Solstice, still, having the family around. Never get tired of it.

Back in New York, I remembered all that, some of it again, some of it messed by the acid which framed understand what the first time was, even if the details were totally confused by what I knew about drugs in the late 1960s and early 70s. And I slept in and went running in Central Park and we were still before AIDS and after Stonewall. I called one of the poets who'd told me we'd met (in that one's case, I had read enough about him so that I could fake it) and met him again for the first time at his reading at St. Marks Church.

But that's another story.

We want to get back to the Paleolithic, at least some of us, and the last part of the Paleolithic wanted to get to our time. 30,000 years of chasing big game, less than that to get to atomic fission and high-speed computers. As long as the ice doesn't come and scrape us off this island, we'll be fine.

Quince remembered playing with some of the things in the storeroom when she was a child and being scolded when her mother finally caught me wearing a 13,000-year-old necklace made of amber carved into wolf heads, restrung every couple of centuries.

Even the time-bound can't remember all the time.

WORM WITHIN

———

Cat Rambo

The LED bug kicks feebly, trying to push itself away from the wall. Its wings are rounds of mica, and the hole in its carapace where someone has tacked it to the graying boards reveals cogs and gears, almost microscopic in their dimension. The light from its underside is the cobalt of distress.

It flutters there, sputtering out blue luminescence, caught between earth and air, between creature life and robot existence. Does it believe itself insect or mechanism? How can it be both at once?

I glide past, skirting the edge of the light it casts, keeping my hood up, watching fog tendrils curl and dissipate. A large street, then a smaller one, then smaller yet, in a deserted quarter that few, if any, occupy. Alleys curling into alleys, cursive scrawls of crumbling bricks and high wooden fences. My head down, I practice walking methodically, mechanically until I find a tiny house in the center of the maze. Mine. Another LED bug is tacked beside the entrance, but this one is long dead, legs dangling.

Once inside, I linger in the foyer, taking off my cloak, the clothes that drape my form as though I were some eccentric, an insistent Clothist, or anxious to preserve my limbs from rust or tarnish. Nude, I revel in my flesh, dancing in the hallway to feel the body's sway and bend. Curved shadows slide like knives over the crossworded tiles on the floor, perfect black and white squares. If there were a mirror I could see myself.

But after only a single pirouette, my inner tenant stirs. He plucks pizzicato at my spine, each painful twang reminding me of his presence, somewhere inside.

He says, They'll find you soon enough TICK they'll hunt you down. They'll realize TICK what you are, a meat-puppet in a TICK robot world, all the shiny men and women and TICK in-betweens will cry out, knowing what you are. They'll find TICK you. They'll find you.

I don't know where he lives in my body. Surely what feels like him winding, wormlike, many-footed and long-antennaed through the hallways of my lungs, the chambers of my heart, the slick sluiceway of my intestines—surely the sensation is him using his telekinetic palps to engage my nervous system. I think he must be curled, encysted, an ovoid somewhere between my shoulder blades, a lump below my left rib, a third ovary glimmering deep in my belly.

He says, You could go out with TICK a bang, you could leap into TICK the heart of a furnace or dive TICK from a building's precipice, before they put you TICK in a zoo with a sign on the wall TICK, "Last Homo Sapiens." Last Fleshbag. Last Body.

I do not reply. I gather my clothing back to myself and shrug my shoulders underneath the layers, hiding. He flows back and forth, like a scissoring centipede, driving himself along my veins.

In the kitchen, I stuff food in my mouth without thinking about it, wash it down with gulps of murky fluid from the decanter I fill each night from the river. The liquid glistens with oily putrefaction as it pours through my system.

He says, You disgust me. There are TICK hairs growing inside your body, there TICK are lumps of yellow fat, there are TICK snot and blood clots and bits of refuse TICK. Why won't you die and set me free?

If only I could wash him away, I'd wallow by the riverside, mouth agape in the shallows, swallowing, swallowing bits of gravel and rusted bolts and the tinny taste of antique tadpoles.

I can't, but even so he doesn't like the thought. He saws at the back of my skull with fingers like grimy glass, until the bare bulb shining above the kitchen table shatters, rains down in shards of migraine light, my vision splintering into headache.

When I sleep, I lie down on a shelf beneath the window on the upper floor. I don't know who used to live in this house—when I found it, the only closet was full of desiccated beetles and rows of blue jars. I fold the spectacles I wear—two circles of glass and brass that I found in a drawer. I set them on the windowsill with the drawing of a clock face I have made. I slide my eyelids closed.

Even asleep, I can feel my parasite whispering to himself, thoughts clicking and ticking away. Turning the circuitry and gears of my brain for his own use.

I dream that I am dreaming I'm not dreaming.

The morning sky unfolds in the window, mottled crimson and purple, like marbled bacon, speckled sausage. Brown clouds devour it to the sound of morning shuffling. I get up. I take the mass transit, I go to the store and buy replicas of food, the same pretense everyone else makes, mourning the regularities of a lost life. I stand on a street corner with a pack of robots, looking at a wall screen. A few are clothed, but most are bare, moisture beading on their chrome and brass forms. Some are sleek, some are retro. No one is like me.

I walk in the park. Where did all these robots come from? What do they want? They look like the people that built them, and they walk along the sidewalk, scuffed and marred by their heavy footsteps. They pretend. That's the only thing that saves me, the only thing that lets me walk among them pretending to be something that is pretending to be me.

I sit on a bench by the plaza's edge, a bend of concrete, splotched with lichen. Little sparrows hop along the back, nervous hops, turning their heads to look at me, one beady eye, then the other. I hold my hand out, palm upward. One hops closer.

Inside my ears, inside my lungs, vibrating inside my bones, I hear him whispering. He tells me where I could throw my body in front of a tram, where I could undermine a bridge, where I could leap in a shower of glass, where I could embrace a generator.

The sparrow lands popcorn-light on my palm. My fingers close over it. The other sparrows panic and fly away as my hand clenches tighter and tighter, latching my thumb over the cage my hand has become, feeling the crunch beneath the fluff.

My fingers spasm before my thumb swings away to let them open. Tiny gears fall and bounce on the concrete, and fans of broken plastic feathers flutter down. I stand and try to walk away, but he keeps talking and talking in my head.

You disgust me, he says, and then for once he is silent, as another presence intrudes, as something touches my arm. It is the creature that raised me, it is my mother robot, made of lengths of copper tubing and a tank swelling for a bosom. Carpet scraps are wrapped around its wrists and ankles. It says through the grillework, its beetle-like mouth hissing and crackling with static. You are not well, you must come home with me, won't you come home with me? I worry about you.

How can robots worry? I shake my skull, I turn away so it won't see the meat, the flesh, the body.

You don't know what you're doing, who you are, what you are, it says. The voice is flat, emotionless. It stops, then begins again. You are *wrong*, it says. Something inside of you is *wrong*.

It pulls at me again, but I brace myself and it cannot budge me. It walks away and does not look back. It will come tomorrow and say the same words.

He begins in my head again and I make it only a few steps before crouching down in the middle of the plaza, feeling the passing robots stare at me. I must master this, must master him before the Proctors come and discover me.

I say to the insides of my wrists, the delicate organic bones of my wrists, clothed in blood and sinew, Listen to me, listen to me. Let me get home, home to safety and I'll give you what you want, whatever you want.

He releases his grip on my sanity and we walk home quietly. I eat and drink and say What do you want?

Sleep, he says, and for once the voice is gentle. That's all. Go to sleep. Things will be better in the morning.

At half past midnight, I open my eyes. On the floor are legs torn from an LED bug, dried shells, silver scraps. I watch and he lifts one, then another, drifts and clicks so quiet I cannot hear them. One, then another, and then both. As though he was practicing. As though he was getting better. Stronger.

I didn't know he could use his telekinesis outside my body. As the last shell falls, I feel him lapse, exhausted, into his own simulacrum of sleep.

Downstairs there are no knives in the kitchen, but there is a piece of metal molding that I can peel away from the counter's edge. Slipping and sliding across the floor and the fungus growing on the ancient bits of food scattered there, I go into the living room, an empty box like every other room here, but here the walls are red, red as blood. The blood I imagine, over and over, in my veins.

I poise the knife before my belly and I say goodbye to my body, to the burps and the shit, to the unexpected moles and the cramps and the itches, and flakes of skin and hot sore pimples. To my good, hallucinatory-rich flesh. To my bones that have pretended to carry me for so long. To my delusive blood.

He wakes and says What are you doing? And No. Even as the length of metal slides into me, and I look down to see my foil skin sliding away, to reveal my secret's secret to the world, to show my gears and cogs and shining steaming lunatic wires, and in the midst of it, the clockwork centipede uncoiling, he is my brain seeing itself uncoiling and recoiling and discoiling, my mechanical, irrational brain saying No and No and No again.

CAN YOU SEE ME NOW?

———

Eric M. Witchey

Two miles of sea water overhead pretty well filtered out the ill effects of sunlight and mankind. Alone in her hard suit, *lights on for safety*, Lori's boots settled and held in the pale, diatomaceous silt cover over the San Bernardino Highway. Helmet speakers trickled distant Vivaldi into her ears, and her feeder tube pumped nutrients in accordance with strict protocols for preservation of cultural authenticity. She'd gotten the job because she fit the restored hard suit and because her body was a perfect museum piece, a monument to the ancient submerged civilization of Los Angeles.

She was forty minutes out on her commute after leaving suburb dome one. She knew the route well enough. She walked it every day of the week except Sixth and Seventh. Evenings, Sixth, and Seventh she did H&H, Home-and-Hearth duty, in her Hollywood bungalow diorama.

First through Fifth, she did commute and hard-shell welding on oil pumps.

Her equipment was archaic. The cumbersome hard shell suit with its jutting bumpers and lights made for a slow commute, and sometimes she'd let herself keel over just to demonstrate how hard it must have been for ancient Angelinos to go to work every day—millions of them. No wonder traffic had often halted for hours at a time.

No matter how many times she read the old texts, data from laser-etched, polymer, digital disc fragments discovered in the silt, she couldn't really imagine millions of people. Nobody could really imagine millions of people on the highway in hard suits, bumper-to-bumper, stretched up and down the highway heading off to serve in the major industries of the time: making films, drilling wells, making wars, and selling drugs. It was her job to represent all of them.

Sometimes, on special occasions—translate, when people who influenced funding came to inspect the cultural preserve—there would be five or six other hard suits on the highway.

Once, because of her careful and realistic stumbles, she'd been chosen to work with the famous decryptologist, Doctor Argos Chew. For six months, she worked side-by-side with the man who had first figured out how to read the ancient texts. They actually simulated a fender bender, including the road rage firefight and celebratory goat barbeque.

Not today, though. Today, she was on her own like most days; and she was, like most days, going to weld a support spar on a pipe fitting for upstream production of fossil fuels.

She flipped on her brights. The expected circle of white light appeared. An oarfish undulated slowly through her field of vision. Several tube worms retracted into the smooth, pale silt. The rocking, seahorse shape of an oil well pump, her destination, loomed ahead of her. By the numbers, she hit her turn signal, lit up her tail lights, and plodded along the restored off ramp.

"Lori." The word appeared on the cell phone view of her faceplate display. She held her hand to her head like the texts said she would have.

The words scrolled across her faceplate. "Solo?"

"Yes," she said. The words appeared in a separate response line. "Who?"

"Aaron here."

"What?"

"GTTP?"

"Got Time To Play, *NOT*." She moved up to her favorite pipe fitting, one that would allow full view of her work if there were any visitors to the observation domes or remote library viewing centers.

While appearing to clean the pipe fitting, she looked over the fusion splitter box at the base of the rocker pump. It provided the power to keep the pump rocking up and down like a steel seahorse bobbing for plankton. Tiny bubbles streamed up from the box, the oxygen by-product of sucking in sea water and separating hydrogen from oxygen.

The pump would rust and turn to silt before that little box gave up trying to convert the ocean into hydrogen fuel. It would run forever if nobody recycled it.

She ignited her torch finger. Her face plate darkened to filter out the blinding glare of her torch, and she set her finger to the pipes.

"Don't be like that, babe."

"Your babe, *NOT*," she answered. Aaron was not part of the preserve. He was illegal, and he broke in on her channel while she worked. He tried to pretend he was part of the time/place illusion.

"Mall noon Starbucks?"

She almost broke character to laugh. Like he could get into the preserve. Still, he was on channel now, and she was working, and somebody might be watching today.

"Venice Beach noon. Skating. Sorry."

"Meet sweet. Skate 4 2?"

"Natch."

"Sweat and wrestle steady?"

"Your business, NOT," she said. "WORK-ing."

"Suit hot?" he asked.

She knew where he was going. Phone sex was not part of her work script. No matter that Doctor Argos said all California Girls loved to have phone sex and got paid for it. No matter that she was considered an expert because she had practiced with Argos.

Today, she wanted to be alone. She had hoped for the quiet place she only found in her hard suit while welding.

"Gawd, Aaron," she said. "1 track mind."

"Luvly Lori. 1 track. Repeat play 4ever."

"Buh-bye." She hung up. Vivaldi ended. Cold, green silence filled her helmet. She switched off her welder and lights and let the darkness of the deeps embrace her. Heartbeats echoed in her ears, and the cold outside her suit made tiny inroads into her flesh.

In the silence, she wondered what Aaron's life must be like. She wondered why he wanted to talk to a historian like her at all. He went to some trouble to make his illegal calls.

She pretended to adjust her welding finger, as if her reproduction could actually break.

He must have one of those high-stress jobs—likely a Progeny Projection Consultant or a Future Futures Trader—one of those guys who sold his brain early on and lived in the ether full-time. Maybe he had no body at all.

Phone sex wasn't so bad, really. Sometimes on Bungalow duty she performed with her polymates. Terry, their norm geek-hubby, was pretty good at it. Anella, their bisubmissive accountant, was a true artist, though she wasn't recognized for her work because she didn't have Lori's credentials.

She finished yaddaing her welder, checked her time out heads-up, and turned back toward the preserve dome complex. Twenty minutes of actual work was all the people of LA were allowed before they had to commute again.

Sometimes, she wished she could stay out forever, and sometimes she thought she might. She had a theory that the Angelinos would have too, and that was why they were only allowed to work for twenty minutes a day.

Going back to the noise and crowds of the domes and towers wasn't the part of historical research that she liked. Still, she turned. She walked, trudged, and even threw in a potentially traffic snarling fall just in case somebody was watching her. She had to keep her rep as an obsessive for authentic detail.

H&H duty on Sixth: script said she was alone all day. Three-way phone sex at lunch. Waiting for Cableguy. Computer crashing. Neighborhood watch gunfight. Sixth was a no-brainer. Normal Angelino day. Mostly, she got to spend it eating, pacing, and cursing Cableguy—well, at least after ten she got to curse Cableguy.

By ten, she was up, caffeinating, and pacing in her terrycloth robe. She'd brushed her blond hair out so it feathered over her shoulder blades the way it was supposed to. Her sun bleaching was in. She was in the groove, and she hoped somebody was watching today, somebody to make all her research, training, and hard work worth it.

The doorbell rang.

The doorbell wasn't supposed to ring. Cableguy wasn't supposed to show up.

She went to the door, stood on bare tiptoes, and peered through the peephole. It might, after all, have been a random attacker. Sometimes, especially if dignitaries were on-site, Admin might budget in a little extra realism.

It was Cableguy. He had the truck. He had the uniform. She didn't recognize the researcher playing him—a newbie.

Last thing she needed was a newbie to mess up the historical accuracy of her H&H shift. At least he had the hat and toolbox. He was, all-in-all, a great Cableguy: tall and lean; dark, short hair. His sharp jaw-line worked on chewing gum, and practiced glances at his watch and side-to-side made him look impatient.

He rang the doorbell again.

She opened the door.

"Sweet meet," he said. "Cableguy."

She caught the name on his uniform tag. "Aaron." She almost broke character. She almost told him to go away, to get out of the dome and the preserve before he got arrested. Almost, but not quite. Breaking character would only draw criticism no matter how screwy things got. Criticism meant more training, less research, less time alone in her hard suit, less time pacing—less time to herself. *Someone* might be watching. No matter what, she had to look good, look her period LA part.

She flipped her hair, giggled, and said, "Come in. The sets are over there." She gestured to her requisite five TV sets—one for each room of the house. They sat in a row on an altar at the far end of her tile-and-plush living room. At the end of the row, they even had a palm-sized, waterproof watchman for the bathroom. In addition to room support, each set represented one of the five major uses: gaming, webbing, dissemination of dissatisfaction, news obsession, and babysitting.

The watchman ran a constant loop of Mouse illusions.

"What's the problem, ma'am?" he asked.

"Two hundred and fifty-six channels and nothing on." At least he knew the Cableguy script. He might even make her look good.

"I'll see what I can do." He headed to the sets. Tools settled on the carpet, he pulled his pants down far enough to show his butt crack, then he bent and fiddled with the sets.

She began to think maybe Aaron was a professional, an actual historian. He seemed to know what he was doing.

"Can I get you something to drink?" she asked.

"Bottled water would be nice." He stayed focused on the sets. "Universal remote?"

"Yeah-huh." She went to the kitchen for a bottle of water. When she came back, he acted like he had fixed the cable feeds. The sets flickered, each with their own representation of life in LA.

She handed him the water.

He smiled.

Fingers touched. He was definitely on script.

During their sex scene, she got her lips up to his ear. "What the hell do you think you're doing? You can get recycled for this."

"Research," he said. "Grad school."

She gasped and moaned slightly out of time, doing her breathless best to stay in character.

Afterward, nestled up against him, waiting for the five minutes before he would play out the "Got more homes to service" end to their scene, she whispered, "You aren't authorized, are you?"

"Not." He pulled her closer to him, tighter and warmer.

Two days later, on First, Argos told Lori she had a special assignment, but she hadn't been given a script. She'd been told authenticity would depend on surprise. She was coming off shift and stripping out of her hard suit when a camera crew arrived. It was a full-on truck and uplink unit with roving cameramen and a blue-suited Talentbimbo replica. Lori was surprised. A Warhol Moment with a full-unit vid crew meant serious funding. Somebody had pulled strings.

Talentbimbo, a Sino-Hispanic homogenized, accent-free woman with silky, shiny, bouncy-flow hair stepped up and said, "Action." Talentbimbo pushed a long-handled mike between them. "Lori Welder," she said, "Do you have any comment on the capture of the Cableguy Rapist?"

She finished racking her suit. She hoped someone was watching, someone could see how cool she was, how authentic, how well she played for the crew.

This wasn't planned history, but it was sure as hell funded. Good work could mean bigger things for her. More solitude. "No comment," she said.

"Our sources suggest you had secret communications with him."

She froze, suppressing a grin. Somebody *had* been watching.

"Who are your sources?" Lori asked.

"We have transcripts of your cell phone sex addiction extra-polyamorous affair." Talentbimbo twisted her perfect, plastic face into a smirk. "Lori Welder, do you care to comment now?"

She squared off with Talentbimbo. "He isn't a rapist."

"He used a scanner to listen to dispatch calls, wore the Cableguy uniform, made a replica of a Cableguy truck, and used the public trust in Cableguy to gain access to the homes of young women like yourself."

"Aaron would never rape anyone," she said. "He's a good man and a great Cableguy."

"Now you admit that you knew him?"

She remembered a political axiom from her period polisci class. *Denial causes downfall. If caught, become the victim to gain public sympathy.* "Of course," she said. "I knew him. I love him."

"Well." Talentbimbo pulled the mike back. "There it is. Another victim of this monster, but this one claims she loved him."

Lori grabbed the mike. "Aaron!" she exclaimed. "Baby, if you can hear me, I'll wait for you. I swear it. I'll write. I'll visit! I love you, Baby."

Talentbimbo made a show of wrestling for the mike. She made the cut sign several times, then the lights went dim. Talentbimbo gave Lori a very real dirty look.

Lori realized she had adlibbed right off the map of her colleague's education and experience. She squared her shoulders, made a show of standing up straight, then strode past the news crew. Passing Talentbimbo, she whispered, "Good girls who love bad boys."

The news lady lit up. She had a new line of research, and she knew it. Lori had a new stage and likely some better diorama work coming up. No doubt, Aaron would get his degrees, and if she played things right they'd pull a grant for conjugal visits, letter reproduction, and maybe even an escape and helicopter chase.

She hoped someone was watching. History didn't get more real than this.

THE SKY THAT WRAPS THE WORLD ROUND, PAST THE BLUE AND INTO THE BLACK

Jay Lake

I believe that all things eventually come to rest. Even light, though that's not what they tell you in school. How do scientists know? A billion billion years from now, even General Relativity might have been demoted to a mere Captain. Photons will sit around in little clusters of massless charge, bumping against one another like boats in the harbor at Kowloon.

The universe will be blue then, everything from one cosmic event horizon to the other the color of a summer sky.

This is what I tell myself as I paint the tiny shards spread before me. Huang's men bring them to me to work with. We are creating value, that gangster and me. I make him even more immensely wealthy. Every morning that I wake up still alive is his gratuity to me in return.

It is a fair trade.

My life is comfortable in the old house along the alley with its central court crowded with bayberry trees. A gutter trickles down the center of the narrow roadway, slimed a greenish black with waste slopped out morning and evening from the porch steps alongside. The roofs are traditional, with sloping ridges and ornamented tile caps. I have studied the ones in my own courtyard. They are worn by the years, but I believe I can see a chicken stamped into each one. "Cock," my cook says with his thick Cantonese accent, never seeing the vulgar humor.

Even these tired old houses are topped with broadband antennae and tracking dishes which follow entertainment, intelligence or high finance beamed down from orbit and beyond. Sometimes the three are indistinguishable. Private data lines sling on pirated staples and cable ties from the doddering concrete utility poles. The poles themselves are festooned with faded prayer flags, charred firecracker strings, and remnants of at least half a dozen generations of technology dedicated to transmission of *something*.

Tesla was right. Power is nothing more than another form of signal, after all. If the lights come on at a touch of your hand, civilization's carrier wave is intact.

Despite the technology dangling overhead in rotting layers, the pavement itself holds life as old as China. Toddlers wearing only faded shirts toss stones in the shadows. A mangy chow dog lives beneath a vine-grown cart trapped against someone's garden wall. Amahs air their families' bedding over wooden railings worn shiny with generations of elbows. Tiny, wrinkled men on bicycles with huge trays balanced behind their seats bring vegetables, newspapers, meat and memory sticks to the back doors of houses. Everything smells of ginger and night soil and the ubiquitous mold.

I wake each day with the dawn. Once I overcome my surprise at remaining alive through another sunrise, I tug on a cheaply printed yukata and go hunting for coffee. My cook, as tiny and wrinkled as the vendors outside but decorated with *tong* tattoos that recall another era long since lost save for a few choppy-sockie movies, does not believe in the beverage. Instead he is unfailing in politely pressing a bitter-smelling black tea on me at every opportunity. I am equally unfailing in politely refusing it. The pot is a delicate work of porcelain which owes a great deal to a China before electricity and satellite warfare. It is painted a blue almost the shade of cornflowers, with a design of a round-walled temple rising in a stepped series of roofs over some Oriental pleasaunce.

I've seen that building on postage stamps, so it must be real somewhere. Or had once been real, at least.

After the quiet combat of caffeine has concluded its initial skirmish, I shuffle to my workroom where my brushes await me. Huang has that strange combination of stony patience and sudden violence which I have observed among the powerful in China. When my employer decides I have failed in my bargain, I am certain it is the cook who will kill me. I like to imagine his last act as the light fades from my eyes will be to pour tea down my throat as a libation to see my spirit into the next world.

There is a very special color that most people will never see. You have to be out in the Deep Dark, wrapped in a skinsuit amid the hard vacuum where the solar wind sleets in an invisible radioactive rain. You can close your eyes there and let yourself float in a sensory deprivation tank the size of the universe. After a while, the little mosaics that swirl behind your eyelids are interrupted by tiny, random streaks of the palest, softest, sharpest electric blue.

I've been told the specks of light are the excitation trails of neutrinos passing through the aqueous humor of the human eye. They used to bury water tanks in Antarctic caves to see those things, back before orbit got cheap enough to push astronomy and physics into space where those sciences belong. These days, all you have to do is go for a walk outside the planet's magnetosphere and be patient.

That blue is what I capture for Huang. That blue is what I paint on the tiny shards he sends me wrapped in day-old copies of the high orbital edition of *Asahi Shimbun*. That blue is what I see in my dreams.

That blue is the color of the end of the universe, when even the light is dying.

Out in the Deep Dark we called them caltrops. They resemble jacks, that old children's toy, except with four equally-spaced arms instead of six, and slightly larger, a bit less than six centimeters tip to tip. Many are found broken, some aren't, but even the broken ones fit the pattern. They're distributed in a number of places around the belt, almost entirely in rocks derived from crustal material. The consensus had long been that they were mineral crystals endemic to Marduk's surface, back before the planet popped its cork 250 megayears ago.

Certainly their microscopic structure supported the theory—carbon lattices with various impurities woven throughout.

I couldn't say how many of the caltrops were discarded, damaged, or simply destroyed by being slagged in the guts of some ore processor along with their enclosing rock. Millions, maybe.

One day someone discovered that the caltrops had been manufactured. They were technology remnants so old that our ancestors hadn't even gotten around to falling out of trees when the damned things were fabricated. The human race was genetic potential lurking in the germline of some cynodont therapsid when those caltrops had been made.

It had not occurred to anyone before that discovery to consider this hypothesis. The fact that the question came up at all was a result of a serious misunderstanding of which I was the root cause. In my greed and misjudgment I forced the loss of a device one of my crewmates discovered, an ancient piece of tech that could have allowed us to do *something* with those caltrops. My contribution to history, in truth, aside from some miniscule role in creating a portion of Huang's ever-growing millions. That the discovery of the caltrops' nature arose from human error is a mildly humorous grace note to the confirmation that we are indeed not alone in the universe.

Or at least weren't at one point.

The artificial origin of the caltrops has been generally accepted. *What* these things are remains a question that may never be answered, thanks to me. Most people prefer not to discuss the millions of caltrops lost to Belt mining operations over the decades that Ceres Mineral Resources has been in business.

Despite their carbon content, caltrops viewed under Earth-normal lighting conditions are actually a dull grayish-blue. This fact is not widely known on Earth. Not for the sake of being a secret—it's not—but because of *Deep Dark Blues*, the Academy Award-winning virteo about Lappet Ugarte. She's the woman who figured so prominently in the discovery of the artificial origin of the caltrops. The woman I tried to kill, and steal from. In their wisdom, the producers of that epic Bollywood docudrama saw fit to render the caltrops about twice as large as they are in real life, glowing an eerie Cherenkov blue. I suppose the real thing didn't look like much on camera.

So most of the citizens of planet Earth don't believe that they're seeing actual outer space caltrops unless they're seeing end-of-the-universe blue.

Huang sends me paint in very small jars. They're each cladded with lead foil, which makes them strangely heavy. When I take the little lead-lined caps off, the paint within is a sullen, radioactive copy of the color I used to see behind my eyelids out there in the Deep Dark.

Every time I dip my brush, I'm drawing out another little spray of radiation. Every time I lick the bristles, I'm swallowing down a few drops of cosmic sleet. I'm the last of the latter day Radium Girls.

Huang doesn't have to order the old cook to kill me. I'm doing it myself, every day.

I don't spend much time thinking about where my little radioactive shards go when they leave my house off the alleyway here in Heung Kong Tsai. People buy them for hope, for love, to have a piece of the unspeakably ancient past. There's a quiet revolution in human society as we come to terms with that history. For some, like a St. Christopher medal, touching it is important. Cancer will be important as well, if they touch them too often.

The truly odd thing is that the shards I sit here and paint with the electric blue of a dying heaven are actual caltrop shards. We're making fakes out of the real thing, Huang and I.

A truth as old as time, and I'm dressing it in special effects.

I swear, sometimes I kill myself.

This day for lunch the cook brings me a stir fry of bok choi and those strange, slimy mushrooms. He is as secretive as one of the Japanese soldiers of the last century who spent decades defending a lava tube on some Pacific island. There is tea, of course, which I of course ignore. We could play that ritual with an empty pot just as easily, but the cook executes his culinary warfare properly.

The vegetables are oddly ragged for having recently spent time in a searing hot wok. They are adorned with a pungent tan sauce the likes of which I had never tasted before entering this place. The whole mess sits atop a wad of sticky rice straight from the little mauve Panasonic cooker in the kitchen.

Food is the barometer of this household. When the cook is happy, I eat like a potentate on a diplomatic mission. When the cook is vexed by life or miffed about some slight on my part, I eat wretchedly.

I wonder what I have done this day to anger him. Our morning ritual was nothing more than ritual, after all.

When I meet the cook's eyes, I see something else there. A new distress lurks in the lines drawn tight across his forehead. I know what I gave up when I came here. It was no more than what I'd given up long ago, really, when the fates of people and planets were playing out somewhere in the Deep Dark and I went chasing the fortune of a dozen lifetimes. Still, I am not prepared for this new tension on the part of my daily adversary.

"Have you to come to kill me?" I ask him in English. I have no Cantonese, and only the usual fractured, toneless pidgin Mandarin spoken by non-Chinese in the rock ports of the asteroid belt. I've never been certain he understands me, but surely the intent of my question is clear enough.

"Huang." There is a creaky whine in his voice. This man and I can go a week at a time without exchanging a single word. I don't think he speaks more than that to anyone else.

"He is coming here?"

The cook nods. His unhappiness is quite clear.

I poke the bok choi around in my bowl and breathe in the burnt ginger-and-fish oil scent of the sauce. That Huang is coming is a surprise. I have sat quietly with my incipient tumors and withering soul and made the caltrop shards ready for market. They are being handled by a True Hero of the Belt, just as his advertising claims. Our bargain remains intact.

What can he want of me? He already holds the chitty on my life. All my labors are his. I have no reputation left, not under my real name. I bear only the memory of the heavens, and a tiny speck of certain knowledge about what once was.

It should be enough.

After a while, by way of apology, the cook removes my cooling lunch bowl and replaces it with a delicate porcelain plate bearing a honey-laden moon cake. I suspect him of humor, though the timing is hideously inappropriate.

"*Xie xie*," I tell him in my Mandarin pidgin. He does not smile, but the lines around his eyes relax.

Still, I will not stoop to the tea.

Huang arrives to the sound of barking dogs. I stand behind a latticed window in my garden wall and look out into the alley. The gangster's hydrogen-powered Mercedes is a familiar shade of Cherenkov blue. I doubt the aircraft paint his customizers use is hot, though.

There is a small pack of curs trailing his automobile. The driver steps out in a whirr of door motors which is as much noise as that car ever makes. He is a large man for a Chinese, tall and rugged, wearing the ubiquitous leather jacket and track pants of big money thugs from Berlin to Djakarta. His mirror shades have oddly thick frames, betraying a wealth of sensor data and computing power. I wonder if he ever removes them, or if they are implants. Life in this century has become a cheap 1980s science fiction novel.

The driver gives the dogs a long look which quiets them, then opens Huang's door. The man himself steps out without any ceremony or further security. If there is air cover, or rooftop snipers, they are invisible to me.

Huang is small, with the compact strength of a wrestler. His face is a collapsed mass of wrinkles that makes his age impossible to guess. There are enough environmental poisons which can do that to a man without the help of time's relentless decay. Today he wears a sharkskin jacket over a pale blue cheongsam. His eyes when he glances up to my lattice are the watery shade of light in rain.

I walk slowly through the courtyard. That is where Huang will meet me, beneath a bayberry tree on a stone bench with legs carved like lions.

He is not there when I take my seat. Giving instructions to the cook, no doubt. The pond occupies my attention while I wait. It is small, not more than two meters across at its longest axis. The rim is walled with rugged rocks that might have just been ejected from the Earth moments before the mason laid them. Nothing is that sharp-edged out in the Belt, not after a quarter billion years of collision, of dust, of rubbing against each other. The water is scummed over with a brilliant shade of green that strikes fear in the heart of anyone who ever has had responsibility for a biotic air recycling plant.

They say water is blue, but water is really nothing at all but light trapped before the eyes. It's like glass, taking the color of whatever it is laced with, whatever stands behind it, whatever shade is bent through its substance. Most people out in the Deep Dark have a mystical relationship with water. The very idea of oceans seems a divine improbability to them. As for me, my parents came from Samoa. I was born in Tacoma, and grew up on Puget Sound before finding my way Up. To me, it's just water.

Still, this little pond choked with the wrong kind of life seems to say so much about everything that is wrong with Earth, with the Deep Dark, with the little damp sparks of colonies on Ceres and Mars and elsewhere. I wondered what would happen to the pond if I poured my blue paint out of its lead-lined bottles into the water.

"Your work holds fair," says Huang. I did not hear him approach. Glancing down, I see his crepe-soled boat shoes, that could have come straight off some streetcorner vendor's rack to cover his million dollar feet.

I meet his water-blue eyes. Pale, so pale, reflecting the color of his golf shirt. "Thank you, sir."

He looks at me a while. It is precisely the look an amah gives a slab of fish in the market. Finally he speaks again: "There have been inquiries."

I reply without thinking. "About the radioactives?"

One eyebrow inches up. "Mmm?"

I am quiet now. I have abandoned our shared fiction for a moment, that pretense that I do not know he is poisoning thousands of homes worldwide through his artifact trade. Mistakes such as that can be fatal. That the entire present course of my life is fatal is not sufficient excuse for thoughtless stupidity.

Huang takes my silence as an answer. "Certain persons have come to me seeking a man of your description."

With a shrug, I tell him, "I was famous once, for a little while." One of history's villains, in fact, in my moment of media glory.

"What you paid me to keep you . . . they have made an offer far more generous."

I'd sold him my life, that strange, cold morning in a reeking teahouse in Sendai the previous year. Paid him in a substantial amount cash, labor and the last bare threads of my reputation in exchange for a quiet, peaceful penance and the release of obligation. Unfortunately, I could imagine why someone else would trouble to buy Huang out.

He was waiting for me to ask. I would not do that. What I would do was give him a reason not to send me away. "My handiwork meets your requirements, yes?" Reminding him of the hot paint, and the trail of liability which could eventually follow that blue glow back to its source.

Even gangsters who'd left any fear of law enforcement far behind could be sued in civil court.

"You might wish me to take this offer," he says slowly.

"When has the dog ever had its choice of chains?"

A smile flits across Huang's face before losing itself in the nest of wrinkles. "You have no desires in the matter?"

"Only to remain quietly in this house until our bargain is complete."

Huang is silent a long, thoughtful moment. Then: "Money completes everything, spaceman." He nods once before walking away,

It is difficult to threaten a man such as myself with no family, no friends, and no future. That must be a strange lesson for Huang.

I drift back to the latticed window. He is in the alley speaking to the empty air—an otic cell bead. A man like Huang wouldn't have an implant. The dogs are quiet until he steps back into the blue Mercedes. They begin barking and wailing as the car slides away silent as dustfall.

It is then that I realize that the dog pack are holograms, an extension of the car itself.

Until humans went into the Deep Dark, we never knew how kindly Earth truly was. A man standing on earthquake-raddled ground in the midst of the most violent hurricane is as safe as babe-in-arms compared to any moment of life in hard vacuum. The smallest five-jiǎo pressure seal, procured low bid and installed by a bored maintech with a hangover, could fail and bring with it rapid, painful death.

The risk changes people, in ways most of them never realize. Friendships and hatreds are held equally close. Total strangers will share their last half-liter of air to keep one another alive just a little longer, in case rescue should show. Premeditated murder is almost unknown in the Deep Dark, though manslaughter is sadly common. Any fight can kill, even if just by diverting someone's attention away from the environmentals at a critical moment.

So people find value in one another that was never been foreseen back on Earth. Only the managers and executives who work in the rock ports and colonies have kept the old, human habits of us-and-them, scheming, assassination of both character and body.

The question on my mind was whether it was an old enemy come for me, or someone from the Ceres Minerals Resources corporate hierarchy. Even setting aside the incalculable damage to our understanding of history, in ensuring the loss of the first verifiable nonhuman artifact, I'd also been the proximate cause of what many people chose to view as the loss of a billion tai kong yuan. Certain managers who would have preferred to exchange their white collars for bank accounts deeper than generations had taken my actions very badly.

Another Belt miner might have yanked my oxygen valve out of

sheer, maddened frustration, but it took an angry salaryman to truly plot my ruin in a spreadsheet while smiling slowly. Here in Huang's steel embrace I thought I'd managed my own ruin quite nicely. Yet someone was offering good money for me.

Oddly, Huang had made it all but my choice. Or seemed to, at any rate. Which implied he saw this inquiry as a matter of honor. Huang, like all his kind, was quite elastic in his reasoning about money, at least so long as it kept flowing, but implacable when it came to his notions of honor.

Even my honor, it would seem.

All of this was a very thin thread of logic from which to dangle. I could just keep painting shards until any one of several things killed me—radiation sickness, cancer, the old cook. Or I could tell Huang to break the deal he and I had made, and pass me back out of this house alive.

Given how much trouble I'd taken in order to surrender all control, there was something strangely alluring about being offered back the chitty on my life.

That night when the cook brought me the tea, I poured some into the tiny cup with no handles. He gave me a long, slow stare. "You go out?"

"With Mr. Huang, yes," I told him.

The cook grunted, then withdrew to the kitchen.

The tea was so bitter that for a moment I wondered if he'd brewed it with rat poison. Even as this thought faded, the cook came back with a second cup and poured it out for himself. He sat down opposite me, something else he'd never done. Then he drew a small mesh bag on a chain out from inside his grubby white t-shirt.

"See this, ah." He tugged open the top of the bag. Out tumbled one of my little blue caltrop fragments. I could almost see it spark in his hand.

"You shouldn't be holding that."

The cook hefted the mesh bag. "Lead. No sick."

I reached out and took the caltrop arm. It was just that, a single arm broken off below the body. I fancied it was warm to my touch. It was certainly very, very blue.

"Why?" I asked him.

He looked up at the ceiling and spread one hand in a slow wave, as if to indicate the limitless stars in the Deep Dark far above our heads. "We too small. World too big. This—" He shook his bag "—this time price."

I tried to unravel the fractured English. "Time price?"

The cook nodded vigorously. "You buy time for everyone, everything."

I sipped my tea and thought about what he'd told me. I'd *been* out in the Deep Dark. I'd touched the sky that wraps the world round, past the blue and into the black.

"Blue," he said, interrupting my chain of thought. "We come from sea, we go to sky. Blue to blue, ah?"

Blue to blue. Life had crawled from the ocean's blue waters to eventually climb past the wide blue sky. With luck, we'd carry forward to the dying blue at the end of time.

"Time," I said, trying the word in my mouth. "Do you mean the future?"

The cook nodded vigorously. "Future, ah."

Once I'd finished eating the magnificent duck he'd prepared, I trudged back to my workroom. I'd already bargained away almost all of my time, but I could create time for others, in glowing blue fragments. It didn't matter who was looking for me. Huang would do as he pleased. My sins were so great they could never be washed away, not even in a radioactive rain.

I could spend what time was left to me bringing people like the old cook a little closer to heaven, one shard after another.

BIOGRAPHIES

KEN SCHOLES's quirky, speculative short fiction has been showing up over the last eight years in publications like *Clarkesworld, Realms of Fantasy, Weird Tales* and *Writers of the Future*. Ken's first novel, *Lamentation*, debuted from Tor in February 2009. It is the first of five volumes in the Psalms of Isaak series. Ken's first short story collection, *Long Walks, Last Flights and Other Strange Journeys*, is available from Fairwood Press.

Ken lives near Portland, Oregon, with his amazing wonder-wife Jen West Scholes. He invites folks to look him up through his website at www.kenscholes.com

MEGHAN MCCARRON's work has appeared in *Lady Churchill's Rosebud Wristlet, Strange Horizons,* and *Best American Fantasy*. She has been a rare book wrangler, a Hollywood assistant, and a boarding school English teacher. She has just moved to Brooklyn, where she will be something else completely.

YOON HA LEE's fiction has appeared in *The Magazine of Fantasy and Science Fiction* and *Sybil's Garage*. She is one of the section editors at the *Internet Review of Science Fiction*. Currently she lives in Pasadena, CA with her husband and daughter. Visit her at yhlee.livejournal.com

SAMANTHA HENDERSON lives in Southern California. Her fiction and poetry have been published in *Strange Horizons, Chizine, Realms of Fantasy, Fantasy Magazine, Helix, Lone Star Stories,* and *Weird Tales,* and her first book was published in 2008 by Wizards of the Coast.

MARY ROBINETTE KOWAL is a professional puppeteer who moonlights as a writer. She has performed for LazyTown (CBS), the Center for Puppetry Arts, Jim Henson Pictures and founded Other Hand Productions. Her design work has garnered two UNIMA-USA Citations of Excellence, the highest award an American puppeteer can achieve.

Mrs. Kowal's short fiction appears in *Strange Horizons, Cosmos* and *Cicada*. She is the art director of *Weird Tales* and a graduate of Orson Scott Card's Literary BootCamp.

JEREMIAH STURGILL lives and writes in Fredericksburg, Virginia. "Flight" is his second published story. The first, "Songbird," was published by *Baen's Universe* in late 2006. In 2005, he graduated from Mary Washington University and started *Son and Foe*, a fiction e-zine that crashed and burned a year later with spectacular predictability (but not before publishing a number of really great stories). In late 2007, he stopped talking at parties about this novel he planned on writing, and he began talking about this novel he'd finished. Sometime in the next twenty years, he hopes to actually sell the damn thing.

STEPHEN GRAHAM JONES' latest novel is *Ledfeather*. His short fiction is in textbooks and anthologies and annuals and everywhere else, times two.

GARTH UPSHAW lives in Portland, Oregon with his brilliant, gorgeous wife, Katrina, and his three super-genius children: Chris, Kami, and Luken. He's had jobs ranging from foundry drudge, bell packer, and tarantula minder to .com CEO, and has recently embarked on a guinea pig breeding project. Garth is an avid biker, refusing to remove his feet from the pedals even in the icy rain that mars the Mediterranean climate of the Pacific Northwest only six to nine months a year.

LOREEN HENEGAN lives in Oregon with her husband and infant daughter. They have a very small house in the shadow of an enormous sweetgum tree. She began writing stories at the age of three, but took a couple of decades off to gain life experience before trying to make a name for herself. This is Loreen's second published work. Her first can be heard at the podcast magazine Pseudopod. She no longer illustrates her stories in crayon.

SERGEY GERASIMOV lives in Kharkiv, Ukraine with his wife and daughter. He has a degree in theoretical physics from Kharkiv University and has sold twelve novels and nearly a hundred stories in Russia and Ukraine. This is his fifth story published in English.

STEPHEN DEDMAN was exposed to the works of Ray Bradbury and Edgar Allan Poe at an early age, and has never quite recovered. The author of four novels and more than 100 short stories published in an eclectic range of magazines and anthologies, he has won the Aurealis and Ditmar awards for short fiction and been nominated for the Bram Stoker Award, the BSFA Award, the Seiun Award, the Spectrum Award, the Sidewise Award and a Sainthood.

Born in the Pacific Northwest in 1979, CATHERYNNE M. VALENTE is the author of *Palimpsest* and the Orphan's Tales series, as well as *The Labyrinth, Yume no Hon: The Book of Dreams, The Grass-Cutting Sword*, and several books of poetry. She is the winner of the Tiptree Award, the Mythopoeic Award, the Rhysling Award, and the Million Writers Award. She has been nominated nine times for the Pushcart Prize, shortlisted for the Spectrum Award, and was a World Fantasy Award finalist in 2009. She currently lives on an island off the coast of Maine with her partner and two dogs. Her crowdfunded novel, *The Girl Who Circumnavigated Fairyland in a Ship of Her Own Making*, can be found at http://catherynnemvalente.com/fairyland

JEFFREY FORD's most recent novels are *The Portrait of Mrs. Charbuque*, *The Girl in the Glass*, and *The Shadow Year*. His short stories have been collected into three books, *The Fantasy Writer's Assistant*, *The Empire of Ice Cream*, and *The Drowned Life*. Ford's stories have appeared in a variety of magazines and anthologies, and his work has been awarded The World Fantasy Award, The Nebula, The Edgar Allan Poe Award, The Fountain Award, and Le Grand Prix de l'imaginaire. He lives in South Jersey with his wife and two sons and works as a professor of Writing and Literature at Brookdale Community College.

BRIAN AMES writes from St. Charles County, Missouri. He is the author of the novel *Salt Lick* (Pocol Press, 2007) and four short-fiction collections: *Smoke Follows Beauty* (Pocol Press, 2002), *Head Full of Traffic* (Pocol Press, 2004), *Eighty-Sixed* (Word Riot Press, 2004), and *As Many Hands as God* (Pocol Press, 2008).

MARGARET RONALD's fiction has appeared in such venues as *Fantasy Magazine*, *Strange Horizons*, *Realms of Fantasy*, *Baen's Universe*, and *Helix*. Her first novel, *Spiral Hunt*, came out from Eos Books in 2009. She is an alum of the Viable Paradise workshop and a member of BRAWL. Originally from rural Indiana, she now lives outside Boston.

ALEXANDER LUMANS is originally from Aiken, South Carolina. He has fiction forthcoming from *StoryQuarterly*. He has also been nominated for the anthology *Best New American Voices 2009* as well as for a 2008 AWP Intro Award. Currently, he is enrolled in the MFA Program at Southern Illinois University of Carbondale.

PAUL JESSUP has been published in many magazines, including *Post Script*, *Fantasy Magazine*, *Apex Digest*, *Farrago's Wainscoat*, *Electric Velocipede*, *Psuedopod* and the *Journals of Experimental Fiction* as well as many others. In 2009 a short story collection came out, *Glass Coffin Girls*, as part of their PS Showcase series, and Apex Publishing released his surrealistic space opera, *Open Your Eyes*.

When not scribbling, LISA MANTCHEV can be found on the beach, up a tree, making jam or repairing things with her trusty glue gun. Her stories have appeared in *Strange Horizons, Weird Tales, Fantasy Magazine, Aeon*, and *Abyss & Apex*. More will be appearing soon in *Japanese Dreams* and *Electric Velocipede*. She is currently at work on the third novel in the Théâtre Illuminata trilogy. You can Taste the Bad Candy at her website, www.lisamantchev.com

KRISTIN MANDIGMA lives in Manila, Philippines where she works as a research analyst. She also helps out with a small non-profit called Read Or Die (also known as First World Imperialists Please Send Books), which promotes literacy and literary awareness in the Philippines, and maintains a website on Filipino literature at http://libro.ph.

TIM PRATT lives in Oakland California with his wife Heather Shaw and their son River. His short fiction has appeared in *The Best American Short Stories, The Year's Best Fantasy and Horror*, and other nice places, and last year his story "Impossible Dreams" won a Hugo Award. Just lately he's been publishing a series of urban fantasy novels under the name T.A. Pratt, which include *Blood Engines, Poison Sleep, Dead Reign*, and *Spell Games*.

REBECCA ORE is a native of Louisville, KY, who has spent considerable time in New York City, Charlotte, NC, Philadelphia, and various part of Virginia, my father's home state. She should be a resident of Northern Virginia by the time this is out. Rebecca has published under the name Rebecca Brown as a poet (Siamese Banana Press, Telephone Books, and Adventures in Poetry Press) and under the name Rebecca Ore as a science fiction writer. Her next book was published by Aqueduct Press, titled *Centuries Ago and Very Fast*. "Acid and Stoned Reindeer" will be included in the collection.

Rebecca also collects film cameras and Chinese painting brushes and tea sets.

CAT RAMBO lives and writes beside eagle-haunted Lake Sammammish in the Pacific Northwest. She has had over two dozen stories published in venues that include *Strange Horizons, Fantasy Magazine,* and *Chiaroscuro.* Her second collection, *Eyes Like Smoke and Coal and Moonlight,* was published last year by Paper Golem Press. She is a member of the writers' groups Horrific Miscue and Codex. She holds an MA in fiction from the Johns Hopkins Writing Seminars and was a member of the Clarion West class of 2005.

ERIC WITCHEY's fiction has appeared nationally and internationally in magazines and anthologies. He has published in multiple genres under several names. His how-to articles have appeared in *The Writer Magazine, Writer's Digest Magazine, Writer's Northwest Magazine, Northwest Ink,* and in a number of on-line publications. His fiction has won recognition from *Writers of The Future, New Century Writers, Writer's Digest,* and www.ralan.com. When not teaching or writing, he restores antique HO locomotives or tosses bits of feather and pointy wire at laughing trout.

JAY LAKE lives and works in Portland, Oregon, within sight of an 11,000 foot volcano. He is the author of over two hundred short stories, four collections, and a chapbook, along with novels from Tor Books, Night Shade Books and Fairwood Press. Jay is also the co-editor with Deborah Layne of the critically-acclaimed *Polyphony* anthology series from Wheatland Press. His next few projects for 2010 include *Pinion, Reign of Flowers, The Sky That Wraps,* and two novellas, *The Baby Killers,* and *The Specific Gravity of Grief.* In 2004, Jay won the John W. Campbell Award for Best New Writer. He has also been a Hugo nominee for his short fiction and a three-time World Fantasy Award nominee for his editing.

THE CLARKESWORLD CENSUS

Clarkesworld welcomes and thanks the following citizens:

Z.S. Adani *

Kathryn Baker

Jenny Barber

Johanne Barron

Jennifer Bartolowits *

Heidi Berthiaume ***

Michael Blackmore ***

Samuel Blinn *

Adam Blomquist

Nathan Blumenfeld **

Jennifer Brissett

Michelle Broadribb **

Jennifer Brozek ***

Patricia Buehler *

Karen Burnham ***

Evan Cassity *

Catherine Cheek

Elizabeth Coleman

Brenda Cooper *

Carolyn E. Cooper **

Lisa Costello

Danieldeskbrain—Watercress
Munster

Maria-Isabel Deira

Daniel DeLano

Paul DesCombaz

John Devenny *

Brian Dolton **

Aidan Doyle

Jesse Eisenhower

Fabio Fernandes

Eric Francis

Fran Friel

Michael Frighetto

Eleanor Gausden

Mark Gerrits *

Inga Gorslar *

Jaq Greenspon *

Eric Gregory *

Geoffrey Guthrie

Jordan Hanie *

James Hartley **

Andrew Hatchell ***

Dave Hendrickson

John Higham

Andrea Horbinski

Clarence Horne III

Richard Horton

Justin Howe *

Chris Hurst *

Marc Jacobs *

Toni Jerrman *

Audra Johnson *

Dr. Philip Edward Kaldon

Robert Keller
Joshua Kidd *
Krista Hoeppner Leahy *
Darren Ledgerwood
Susan H Loyal *
Thomas Loyal
Dominique Martel
Peter McClean *
Tony McFee *
Mark McGarry *
Brent Mendelsohn
Seth Merlo
Terry Miller
Sharon Mock *
Cheryl Morgan ***
Anne Murphy **
Patricia Murphy
Charles Norton **
Vincent O'Connor **
Lydia Ondrusek
Thomas H Pace Jr.
Richard Parks *
Beth Plutchak
Adam Rakunas
Robert Redick
Jo Rhett ***
Tansy Roberts
Abigail Rustad
Steven Saus
Espana Sheriff
Chugwangle Sparklepants III **
Sally Squire
Kevin Standlee **
Jerome Stueart *

Robert Stutts *
Terhi Tormanen **
Damien Walter *
Diane Walton
Tom Waters *
Tehani Wessely *
Peter Wetherall
Jeff Williamson
Neil Williamson
Eric Witchey
Chalmer Wren III
Tero Ykspetäjä *
Anonymous

*Bürgermeister
**Royalty
***Overlord